DOOMSDAY: Civil War

The Doomsday Series
Book Five

A novel by

Bobby Akart

Copyright Information

Other Works by Amazon Top 50 Author, Bobby Akart

The Doomsday Series

Apocalypse

Haven

Anarchy

Minutemen

Civil War

The Yellowstone Series

Hellfire

Inferno

Fallout

Survival

The Lone Star Series

Axis of Evil

Beyond Borders

Lines in the Sand

Texas Strong

Fifth Column

Suicide Six

The Pandemic Series

Beginnings

The Innocents

Level 6

Quietus

The Blackout Series

36 Hours

Zero Hour

Turning Point

Shiloh Ranch

Hornet's Nest

Devil's Homecoming

The Boston Brahmin Series

The Loyal Nine

Cyber Attack

Martial Law

False Flag

The Mechanics

Choose Freedom

Patriot's Farewell

Seeds of Liberty (Companion Guide)

The Prepping for Tomorrow Series

Cyber Warfare

EMP: Electromagnetic Pulse

Economic Collapse

DEDICATIONS

For many years, I have lived by the following premise:

Because you never know when the day before is the day before, prepare for tomorrow.

My friends, I study and write about the threats we face, not only to both entertain and inform you, but because I am constantly learning how to prepare for the benefit of my family as well. There is nothing more important on this planet than my darling wife, Dani, and our two girls, Bullie and Boom. One day, doomsday will come, and I'll be damned if I'm gonna let it stand in the way of our life together.

The Doomsday series is dedicated to the love and support of my family. I will always protect you from anything that threatens us.

ACKNOWLEDGEMENTS

Writing a book that is both informative and entertaining requires a tremendous team effort. Writing is the easy part. For their efforts in making the Doomsday series a reality, I would like to thank Hristo Argirov Kovatliev for his incredible cover art, Pauline Nolet for her editorial prowess, Stef Mcdaid for making this manuscript decipherable in so many formats, Chris Abernathy for his memorable performance in narrating this novel, and the Team—Denise, Joe, Jim, and Shirley—whose advice, friendship and attention to detail is priceless.

In addition, my loyal readers who interact with me on social media know that Dani and I have been fans of the television reality show *Big Brother* since it began broadcasting on CBS in the summer of 2000. The program was one of the greatest social experiments ever imagined. Each season, more than a dozen contestants compete for a half-million-dollar cash prize.

During the months-long airing of the program, the houseguests are isolated from the outside world, but we, the viewers, get to watch their every move via more than a hundred cameras and microphones. The opportunity to study how people interact under these unusual stressful circumstances has allowed me to create diverse and interesting characters for you, dear readers.

Over the years, we've been fortunate to meet several of the past *Big Brother* contestants, and this year, for the second time (the first being our friend Judd Daugherty, who was a doctor in the Boston Brahmin series), I've actually written four of them into the characters through the use of their first name and unique character attributes.

During the airing of season twenty during the summer of 2018, early on in the show, an alliance formed between a group of six who controlled the game from start to finish. You can imagine the high fives Dani and I exchanged when they named their alliance *Level 6*, the title of book three in my Pandemic series released in the summer of 2017.

To season twenty winner, Kaycee Clark; our favorite *showmance* of all time, Angela Rummans and Tyler Crispen; and to one of the funniest, most real people I've ever seen on television, "JC" Mounduix—thank you for inspiring the Rankin family in the Doomsday series!

Thank you all!
Choose Freedom and Godspeed, Patriots!

About the Author

Bobby Akart

Author Bobby Akart has been ranked by Amazon as #55 in its Top 100 list of most popular, bestselling authors. He has achieved recognition as the #1 bestselling Horror Author, #2 bestselling Science Fiction Author, #3 bestselling Religion & Spirituality Author, #6 bestselling Action & Adventure Author, and #7 bestselling Historical Author.

He has written over twenty-six international bestsellers, in nearly fifty fiction and nonfiction genres, including the chart-busting Yellowstone series, the reader-favorite Lone Star series, the critically acclaimed Boston Brahmin series, the bestselling Blackout series, the frighteningly realistic Pandemic series, his highly cited nonfiction Prepping for Tomorrow series, and his latest project—the Doomsday series, seen by many as the horrifying future of our nation if we can't find a way to come together.

His novel *Yellowstone: Fallout* reached the Top 50 on the Amazon bestsellers list and earned him two Kindle All-Star awards for most pages read in a month and most pages read as an author. The Yellowstone series vaulted him to the #1 best selling horror author on Amazon, and the #2 best selling science fiction author.

Bobby has provided his readers a diverse range of topics that are both informative and entertaining. His attention to detail and impeccable research have allowed him to capture the imaginations of his readers through his fictional works and bring them valuable knowledge through his nonfiction books.

SIGN UP for Bobby Akart's mailing list to receive special offers, bonus content, and you'll be the first to receive news about new releases in the Doomsday series:

eepurl.com/bYqq3L

VISIT Amazon.com/BobbyAkart, a dedicated feature page created by Amazon for his work, to view more information on his thriller fiction novels and post-apocalyptic book series, as well as his nonfiction Prepping for Tomorrow series.

Visit Bobby Akart's website for informative blog entries on preparedness, writing, and a behind-the-scenes look into his novels.

BobbyAkart.com

AUTHOR'S INTRODUCTION TO THE DOOMSDAY SERIES

November 8, 2018
Are we on the brink of destroying ourselves?

Some argue that our nation is deeply divided, with each side condemning the other as the enemy of America. By way of example, one can point to the events leading up to the Civil War in the latter part of the 1850s, right up until the first cannon fire rained upon Fort Sumter in Charleston, South Carolina. It's happened before, and it could happen again.

The war of words has intensified over the last several decades, and now deranged people on the fringe of society have taken matters into their own hands. Ranging from pipe-bomb packages mailed to political leaders and supporters, to a gunman shooting congressmen at a softball practice, words are being replaced with deadly, violent acts.

To be sure, we've experienced violence and intense social strife in this country as a result of political differences. The Civil War was one example. The assassination of Martin Luther King Jr., followed by the raging street battles over civil rights and the Vietnam War, is another.

This moment in America's history feels worse because we are growing much more divisive. Our shared values are being forgotten, and a breakdown is occurring between us and our government, and between us and the office of the presidency.

Our ability to find common ground is gradually disappearing. We shout at the television or quit watching altogether. Social media has become anything but *social*. We unfollow friends or write things in a post that we'd never dream of saying to someone's face.

Friends and family avoid one another at gatherings because they fear political discussions will result in an uncomfortable, even hostile exchange. Many in our nation no longer look at their fellow Americans as being from a different race or religion but, rather, as supporting one political party or another.

This is where America is today, and it is far different from the months leading up to the Civil War. Liberal historians label the conflict as a battle over slavery, while conservative historians tend to argue the issue was over states' rights. At the time, the only thing agreed upon was the field of battle—farms and open country from Pennsylvania to Georgia.

Today, there are many battlefronts. Media—news, entertainment, and social—is a major battlefield. The halls of Congress and within the inner workings of governments at all levels is another. Between everyday Americans—based upon class warfare, cultural distinctions, and race-religion-gender—highlighting our differences pervades every aspect of our lives.

Make no mistake, on both sides of the political spectrum, a new generation of leaders has emerged who've made fueling our divisions their political modus operandi. I remember the bipartisan efforts of Ronald Reagan and Tip O'Neill in the eighties. Also, Bill Clinton and Newt Gingrich in the mid-nineties. The turn of the century hasn't provided us the types of bipartisan working relationships that those leaders of the recent past have generated.

So, here we are at each other's throats. What stops the political rancor and division? The answer to this question results in even more partisan arguments and finger-pointing.

Which leads me to the purpose of the Doomsday series. The term *doomsday* evokes images of the end of times, the day the world ends, or a time when something terrible or dangerous will happen. Sounds dramatic, but everything is relative.

I've repeated this often, and I will again for those who haven't heard it.

All empires collapse eventually. Their reign ends when they are either defeated by a larger and more powerful enemy, or when their financing runs out. America will be no exception.

Now, couple this theory with the words often attributed to President Abraham Lincoln in an 1838 speech interpreted as follows:

America will never be destroyed from the outside. If we falter and lose our freedoms, it will be because we destroyed ourselves.

The Doomsday series depicts an America hell-bent upon destroying itself. It is a dystopian look at what will happen if we don't find a way to deescalate the attacks upon one another. Both sides will shoulder the blame for what will happen when the war of words becomes increasingly more violent to the point where one side brings out the *big guns.*

That's when an ideological battle will result in the bloodshed of innocent Americans caught in the crossfire. Truly, for the future of our nation, doomsday would be upon us.

Thank you for reading with an open mind and not through the lens of political glasses. I hope we can come together for the sake of our families and our nation. God bless America.

EPIGRAPH

"What country can preserve its liberties if their rulers are not warned from time to time that their people preserve the spirit of resistance. Let them take arms ..."
~ Thomas Jefferson, Founding Father, calling for armed resistance
*****

"We are not enemies, but friends. We must not be enemies. Though passion may have strained, it must not break our bonds of affection. The mystic chords of memory, stretching from every battlefield and patriot grave to every living heart and hearthstone all over this broad land, will yet swell the chorus of the Union, when again touched, as surely they will be, by the better angels of our nature."
~ President Abraham Lincoln, at his inauguration before Civil War ensued
*****

"The Civil War has not ended. I question whether any serious civil war ever does end."
~ T. S. Eliot, author and poet
*****

"Before you embark on a journey of revenge, dig two graves."
~ Confucius
*****

"A nation cannot be civil without civility.
To some, civility cannot be restored until power is regained.
A Civil War was a necessary evil, but make no mistake, it was evil."
~ Author Bobby Akart

PREVIOUSLY IN THE DOOMSDAY SERIES

Dramatis Personae

PRIMARY CHARACTERS

George Trowbridge — A wealthy, powerful Washington insider. Lives on his estate in East Haven, Connecticut. Yale graduate. Suffers from kidney failure. Father of Meredith Cortland.

The Sheltons — Tom is retired from the United States Navy and is a former commander at Joint Base Charleston. Married to his wife of forty years, Donna. They have two daughters. Tommie, single, is with Naval Intelligence and stationed on a spy ship in the Persian Gulf. Their oldest daughter, Willa, is married with two young children. The family lives north of Las Vegas. Willa is a captain at Creech Air Force Base, where she serves as a drone pilot. Tom and Donna reside in downtown Charleston.

The Rankin Family — Formerly of Hilton Head, South Carolina, now residing in Richmond, Virginia. Dr. Angela Rankin is a critical care physician at Virginia Commonwealth Medical Center in Richmond. Her husband, Tyler, is a firefighter and a trained emergency medical technician. He was formerly a lifeguard. They have two children. Their daughter, Kaycee, age eleven, nearly died in a helicopter crash as a child. Their youngest child, J.C., age eight, loves history and is a devoted student of America's founding.

The Cortland Family — Michael *Cort* Cortland is chief of staff to a prominent United States Senator from Alabama. His wife, Meredith, is a teacher and the daughter of George Trowbridge. The couple met while they attended Yale University. They have one child, twelve-year-old daughter Hannah. They live in Cort's hometown of Mobile, Alabama. They have an English bulldog named after Yale's mascot, Handsome Dan.

The Hightower Family — Will Hightower is retired from the Philadelphia Police Department and in his mid-forties. After he left Philly SWAT, he got divorced from his wife, Karen. He moved to Atlanta to work for Mercedes-Benz security, only seeing his children—Ethan, age fifteen, and daughter Skylar, age eleven—periodically. Will also has a second job as *Delta.*

Hayden Blount — Born in North Carolina, but now resides in the Washington, DC, area. She is an attorney with a powerful law firm that represents the president in front of the Supreme Court. She formerly clerked for Justice Samuel Alito, a Yale graduate. Single, she lives alone with her Maine coon cat, Prowler.

Ryan and Blair Smart, Chubby and the Roo — Former residents of Florida, and now founders of the Haven, a prepper community built on the former location of the Hunger Games movie set in Henry River Mill Village, North Carolina, just west of Charlotte. The Smarts, together with their two English Bulldog sisters, Chubby and the Roo, now reside at Haven House within the community and have surrounded them with like minded thinkers as they prepare for the coming collapse.

György Schwartz and his son, Jonathan — The Schwartz family name was synonymous with high-flying financial deals, currency manipulations, and wealth. One of the thirty richest and most powerful men in the world hadn't come easy, but once attained, it allowed him to engage in shrewd financial arrangements and political machinations. They live on the Schwartz Estate in Katonah, New York, just across the Connecticut state line.

SECONDARY CHARACTERS

Alpha, Bravo, Charlie — The Haven needed a security team, but these individuals needed to have other skills that contributed to the daily operations and development of the community. The Smart's first hire was Alpha. Ex-military with an expertise in building primitive, log structures, he was a perfect fit and became the head of the security detail which included recruits Bravo and Charlie. Will Hightower, who was referred to as Delta at the Haven, was also a member of the team.

Echo — real name, Justin Echols, and his wife, Charlotte, were the oldest members of the Haven until the Sheltons arrived. Although not a member of the security team, Echo was part of the Haven's hierarchy. He and Charlotte were former farmers who had an expertise in sustainable living and caring for livestock. Their role as providers to the Haven community was invaluable.

X-Ray — real name, Eugene O'Reilly, was the newest member of the Haven community, having arrived on the afternoon of New Year's Eve. Bearing the same name as the famous character on the *M*A*S*H* television show, his grandfather provided him the nickname X-Ray, and it fit his perfectly. A science nerd growing up, X-Ray was especially adept at all things electronic or associated with the internet. His elaborate Faraday Cages and computer setups seemed to be a perfect fit for the Haven.

Book One: *Doomsday: Apocalypse*

It was the beginning of great internal strife, neighbor versus neighbor, warrior versus warrior. The fuse was lit with a simple message, understood by a select few, but impacting the lives of all Americans. It read:

On the day of the feast of Saint Sylvester,
Tear down locked,
Green light burning.
Love, MM

And so it begins …

In *Doomsday: Apocalypse*, all events occur on New Year's Eve

New York City

It was New Year's Eve, and New York City was the center of the annual celebration's universe. Over a million people had crowded into Times Square to bid a collective farewell to the old year and to express hope and joy for the year ahead.

There were some, however, who had other plans for the night's festivities. A clandestine meeting atop the newly constructed One World Trade Center, ground zero for the most heinous terrorist attack on the United States in history, revealed that another attack was afoot. One that sprang from a meeting in a remote farmhouse in Maryland and was perpetrated by a shadowy group.

In New York, Tom and Donna Shelton, retirees from Charleston, South Carolina, belatedly celebrated their fortieth anniversary atop the Hyatt Centric Hotel overlooking Times Square. Caught up in the moment, they made the fateful decision to join the revelers on the streets for a once-in-a-lifetime opportunity to be part of the famous ball drop and countdown to New Year's.

However, terror reared its ugly head as a squadron of quadcopter drones descended upon Midtown Manhattan, detonating bombs over Times Square and other major landmarks in the city. Chaos ensued and the Sheltons found themselves fighting for their lives.

After an injury to Donna, the couple made their way back to their hotel room, where they thought they were safe. However, Tom received a mysterious text, one that he was afraid to reveal to his wife. It came from a sender whom he considered a part of his distant past. It was an ominous warning that weighed heavily on his mind.

The text message read:

The real danger on the ocean, as well as the land, is people.
Fare thee well and Godspeed, Patriot!
MM

Six Flags Great Adventure, New Jersey

Dr. Angela Rankin and her husband, Tyler, were in the second leg of their educational vacation with their two children, Kaycee and J.C., although the New Year's Eve portion of the trip was supposed to be the fun part. They had arrived at Six Flags Great Adventure, the self-proclaimed scariest theme park on the planet.

Following a trip to Boston to visit historic sites related to our nation's founding, they were headed home to Richmond, Virginia, with planned stops in Philadelphia and Washington to see more landmarks. The planned stop at Six Flags was to be a highlight of the trip for the kids.

The night was full of thrills and chills as they rode one roller coaster after another. Young J.C., their son, wanted to save the *wildest, gut-wrenchingest* roller coaster for last—Kingda Ka. The tallest roller coaster in America, Kingda Ka, in just a matter of seconds, shot its coaster up a four-hundred-fifty-six-foot track until the riders reached the top, where they were suspended for a moment, only to be sent down the other side. Except on New Year's Eve, some of them never made it down, on the coaster, that is.

When the Rankin family hit the top of the Kingda Ka ride, an electromagnetic pulse attack struck the area around Philadelphia, which included a part of the Mid-Atlantic states stretching from Wilmington, Delaware, into northern New Jersey. The devastating EMP destroyed electronics, power grids, and the computers used to operate modern vehicles.

It also brought Kingda Ka to a standstill with the Rankins and others suspended facedown at the apex of the ride. At first, the riders avoided panicking. To be sure, they were all frightened, but they felt safe thanks to Tyler's reassurances, and they waited to be rescued.

However, one man became impatient and felt sure he and his wife could make their way to safety. On his four-seat coaster car, with the assistance of a college-age man, they broke loose the safety bar in order to crawl out of the coaster. This turned out to be a bad idea. The young man immediately flew head over heels, four hundred feet to his death.

The man who came up with the self-rescue plan and his wife attempted to shimmy down a support post to a safety platform within Kingda Ka but lost their grip. Both of them plunged to their deaths.

Safety personnel finally arrived on the scene, and they began the arduous task of rescuing the remaining passengers, leaving the Rankins for last since they were at the front of the string of coaster cars. Unfortunately, as the safety bar was lifted, J.C. fell out of the car, only to be retrained by a safety harness that had been affixed to his body.

Despite the fact that he was suspended twenty feet below the coaster, held by only a rope, the family worked together to hoist him to safety and an eventual rescue. But their night was not done.

The Rankins made their way to the parking lot, where their 1974 Bronco awaited them. Tyler pulled Angela aside, retrieved his handgun that was hidden under the chassis of the truck, and explained. The EMP had disabled almost all of the vehicles around them. Thousands of people were milling about. Most likely, they had the only operating vehicle for miles. And the moment they started it, everyone would either want a ride or would want to take their truck. When they decided to leave, it would be mayhem. So they waited for the most opportune time—daylight.

Mobile, Alabama

Michael Cortland split his time between his home in Mobile—with wife, Meredith, and daughter, Hannah—and Washington, DC, where he served as the chief of staff to powerful United States Senator Hugh McNeil. Congress had remained in session during what would ordinarily be the Christmas recess due to the political wranglings concerning the President of the United States and attempts to have him removed from office. But that was not the reason Cort, as he was called by his friends and family, was taking the late evening flight home.

He had been summoned by his father-in-law, George Trowbridge, to his East Haven, Connecticut, estate. Trowbridge was considered one of the most powerful people in Washington despite the fact he'd never held public office. Cort was the son Trowbridge never had, and as a result, he had been taken under the patriarch's wing and groomed for great things.

The conversation was a difficult one, as the old man was bedridden and permanently connected to dialysis. However, as they conversed, Cort was left with these ominous words:

Either you control destiny, or destiny controls you.

Cort was consumed by what his father-in-law meant as he waited for a connecting flight from Atlanta, Georgia, to Mobile, Alabama. The flight that should have been routine was anything but. On final approach to Mobile, the plane suffered a total blackout of power. Nothing worked on board the aircraft, including battery backups, warning lights, or communications.

The pilots made every effort to ditch the plane in the Gulf of Mexico, but the impact on the water caused the fuselage to break in two before it sank towards the sandy bottom of the gulf.

Cort leapt into action to help save his surrounding passengers, including an important Alabama congressman from the other side of the aisle. His Good Samaritan efforts almost killed him. He almost drowned on that evening and was fortunate to be rescued and delivered to the emergency room in Mobile.

After a visit from Meredith and Hannah, Cort began to assess the devastating events around the country and then hearkened back to the words of his father-in-law regarding destiny. Deep down, he knew there was a connection.

Atlanta, Georgia

On the surface, Will Hightower appeared to be a man down on his luck although some might argue that he'd made his own bed, now he had to sleep in it, as the saying goes.

Will's life had changed dramatically in the course of two years since a single inartful use of words during a stressful situation caused his family's world to come crashing down. He had been a respected member of Philly SWAT, one of the most renowned special weapons and tactics teams in the nation. Until one night he lost that respect.

During the investigation and media firestorm, his ex-wife, Karen, turned to the arms of another man, one of his partners. His son, Ethan, and daughter, Skylar, were berated in school and alienated from him by their mother. And Will made the decision to leave Philadelphia to provide his family a respite from the continuous attacks from the media and groups who demanded Will be removed from the police force.

With a new start in Atlanta as part of the security team at Mercedes-Benz Stadium, Will looked forward to a new life in a new city, where his children could visit far away from his past. Ethan and Skylar arrived in Atlanta for a long New Year's weekend that was to begin with a concert, featuring Beyoncé and Jay-Z, at the stadium.

A poor choice by his son landed the kids on the field level of the concert in front of the stage, and then the lights went out. Saboteurs had infiltrated the stadium and caused all power to be disconnected. The thousands of concertgoers panicked, and the kids were in peril.

Will was able to find an injured Ethan and frightened Skylar. He whisked them away to the safety of his home; however, their evening was not over. Will was able to pick up on the tragic events occurring around the country. The collapse he'd feared was on the brink of occurring manifested itself.

Then he received a text. Four simple words that meant so much to his future and the safety of his children. It read:

Time to come home. H.

He'd been asked to come home. But not in the sense most would think. His home was not back in Philadelphia with an ex-wife who'd made his life miserable. It was in another place that he'd become a part of since he left the City of Brotherly Love.

It was time for him to go to the Haven, where he was simply known as Delta.

Washington, DC

Hayden Blount was young, attractive, and a brilliant attorney. She also represented the President of the United States as he fought to protect his presidency. After winning reelection, the president came under attack again, but this time, it was from his own side of the aisle.

Making history, his vice president and members of his cabinet invoked a little-known clause of the Twenty-Fifth Amendment to the Constitution to remove him from office because they deemed him unfit for the job.

Using Hayden's law firm to represent him, the president counterpunched by firing all of the signers of the letter and installing a new cabinet. This created chaos within Washington, and many considered the machinations to have created a constitutional crisis.

The matter was now before the Supreme Court, where Hayden once clerked, and she was putting the final touches on a brief that had to be filed before midnight on New Year's Eve. After a conversation with the senior partner who spearheaded the president's representation, and a brief appearance at the firm's year-end soiree, Hayden left for home.

Trouble seemed to be on the horizon for the young woman when she got stuck on the building's elevator for a brief time. After enduring two drunken carousers, the elevator was fixed, and she happily headed for the subway trains, which carried people around metropolitan Washington, DC.

She was headed south of the city toward Congress Heights when suddenly, just as the train was at its lowest point in a tunnel under the Anacostia River, the lights went out, and so did all power to the train.

A carefully orchestrated cyber attack had been used to shut down all transportation in Washington, DC, including the trains, public buses, and the airports. The city was brought to a standstill, and Hayden was stuck in the subway, in the dark, with a predator stalking her.

She got away from the man who would do her harm, using her survival skills and Krav Maga training. Then she helped some women and children to safety by climbing up a ladder and through a ventilation duct.

Once at home with her beloved Maine coon cat, Prowler, Hayden began to learn of the attacks around the country. She was shocked to learn the Washington transportation outage wasn't the lead story. It was far from it.

Monocacy Farm, South of Frederick, Maryland

The story ended as it began. The people who had initiated these attacks came together for a toast at the Civil War–era farmhouse overlooking the river. They weren't politicians or elected officials. They were spooks, spies, and soldiers. Government officials and bureaucrats—accountable to no one but themselves.

They shared a glass of champagne and cheered on their successes of the evening, hurtful as they were to their fellow Americans. They acknowledged their task had just begun. Standing before them, the host of the gathering closed the meeting with the following words:

"One man's luck is often generated by another man's misfortunes. I, for one, believe that we can make our own luck. It will be necessary to achieve our goals as laid out in our carefully crafted plans.

"With this New Year's toast, I urge all of you to trust the plan.

Know that a storm is coming. It will be a storm upon which the blood of patriots and tyrants will spill."

He raised his champagne glass into the air, and everyone in the room followed suit.

"Godspeed, Patriots!"

And so it began …

Book Two: *Doomsday: Haven*

The story continues with the introduction of Ryan and Blair Smart, and their four-legged kids, Chubby and The Roo.

My mother taught me a German proverb that goes like this — *Wer im Spiel Pech hat, hat Glück in der Liebe.* Or something like that (My German is a little rusty). This translates to mean *he who is unlucky in game or gambling, is lucky at love.*

Well, Ryan and Blair Smart were lucky in both. The married couple from Florida spent each day of their lives together and loved every minute of it. They were not gamblers, but on one fateful night before Halloween, they decided to take a stab at winning the largest Megaball lottery in history.

They won. Now, they faced the daunting task of what to do with their money.

The Smarts were genuinely concerned about the direction their country was taking and vowed to never let outside influences disrupt their happiness. They wanted to find peace and serenity in their daily lives while preparing for the eventual collapse of American society.

Over the next two years, their lottery winnings were transformed into the Haven, a community developed on the site of the Hunger Games movie set located at Henry River Mill Village in North Carolina, an hour or so west of Charlotte.

The community was designed to use the existing structures on the land, plus modern ones specifically purposed for creating a preparedness community. The Smarts set about to assemble a team, all of whom had an important skill to contribute to the Haven. Through direct contact and the recruitment of like-minded thinkers they met on social media, the Haven became a reality.

And it was just in time. In the midst of a quiet New Year's Eve celebration, the proverbial crap hit the fan.

OUR OTHER CHARACTERS

As a new day dawned on a new year, our characters found themselves in various states of disarray. As the reader found out in book two, they all had a common goal—get to the Haven. The journey was not easy for any of them.

HAYDEN BLOUNT was in a state of limbo. She was scheduled to appear before the United States Supreme Court on behalf of the President as he fought the 25th Amendment action taken against him. She was self-reliant and confident in her capabilities, but by the same token, she wasn't going to risk her life unnecessarily by staying in the metropolitan Washington, DC area as society collapsed around her.

Hayden prepares for either eventuality and travels to a nearby Walmart to purchase additional ammunition and supplies. After stopping by the gun range to retrieve her firearms, she sees a group of people spray-painting graffiti on a bridge support. The drawing of a fist raising a black rose high into the air was unknown to her, but left an indelible mark nonetheless.

TOM and DONNA SHELTON had survived the chaos of New Year's Eve with the only injury coming to Donna's ankle. As they rested in their hotel room, they are startled by loud knocking at their door. The police were evacuating the area around Time Square due to a dirty bomb scare.

With the assistance of a wheelchair, Tom and Donna made their way through Midtown Manhattan to a staging area where buses were provided for refugees to flee the city. One of the destinations to choose from was East Haven, Connecticut, a place that Tom knew well.

While Donna slept by his side, Tom decided to call upon a resident of East Haven whom he'd met in the past — George Trowbridge. During this meeting in which Tom asked for assistance to get closer to home, it was revealed that the two had been connected for many years.

Trowbridge was rich and powerful, and he'd purchased the loyalty of Tom Shelton with a handsome stipend in exchange for seemingly mundane tasks related to his command at Joint Base Charleston. The relationship had been hidden from Donna but she accepted her husband's explanation as their benefactor assisted them to Norfolk.

During the meeting at the Trowbridge residence, the sickly man provided Tom a letter to deliver to Meredith Cortland. Tom did not know anything about her, but Trowbridge assured him that their paths might cross.

MICHAEL "CORT" CORTLAND, wife MEREDITH, and daughter, HANNAH

The Cortland family had to make a decision. Cort had recovered and was released to go home. After seeing the news reports and speaking with his boss, a powerful Washington Senator, Cort knew that he had to take his family to the Haven.

There was just one problem. They knew nothing about it. Following an emotional scene in which Cort revealed some, but not all, of what he knew about the state of affairs and his reason for becoming involved in the Haven to begin with, Meredith acquiesced to their leaving Mobile.

Her bigger concern was now for her husband who wanted to fly. Gasoline shortages had struck the nation and societal unrest was rampant on the first day following the terrorist attacks.

DR. ANGELA RANKIN, TYLER RANKIN, and their children, KAYCEE and J.C.

The Rankins were caught in the midst of a region decimated by an EMP attack. Electronics were destroyed, the rural parts of New Jersey where they were located had no power. But the Rankins were fortunate that Tyler had an old Ford Bronco that was not susceptible to the electromagnetic pulse.

This would become both a blessing and a curse for the family. Having the only operating vehicle for miles, they immediately became a target for their desperate fellow man. Their first challenge was to get away from the Six Flags parking lot that was packed with dazed and confused New Year's revelers.

Then, they had to traverse the back roads through New Jersey toward their home in Richmond, Virginia. Except for a few skirmishes along the way, the family was almost in Virginia when they came upon the Chesapeake Bay Bridge-Tunnel. They entered the dark tunnel not realizing that trouble lay ahead.

Tyler gets ambushed by thugs who were robbing travelers in the darkness of the tunnel, but Angela came to the rescue. The family persevered and eventually made it home to Richmond where they came to the realization that they needed to wind up their affairs and head for the Haven.

THE HAVEN

Delta blended in with the team and he tried to reassure his kids, Skylar and Ethan that they would be safe. Skylar took to the community immediately, but Ethan had his doubts. He was more focused on reaching out to his mother and possibly bringing her to the Haven than assimilating with the other residents.

Around the Haven, preparations were being made. Security was established, duties were assigned, and the Smarts tried to implement the detailed plans they'd created over the prior two years. They hoped for the best but prepared for the worst.

It turns out, as the conspiracy surrounding George Trowbridge, his associates and the Schwartz family deepened. Trowbridge began to have his doubts about what happened to Cort on the ill-fated Delta 322 flight. Meanwhile, György Schwartz and his son, Jonathan, plot the further demise of the United States by inserting themselves into the chaos.

Jonathan was the henchman of the family while his father played global financier. One of the Schwartz family's favorite tools to manipulate financial markets was to fabricate societal unrest. To further their goals of collapsing the U.S. dollar, and destabilize American society, Jonathan calls upon the anarchist group known as the Black Rose, or Rosa Negra.

Well-financed by the Schwartz family organizations, the grassroots movement around the country was known for wreaking havoc on cities during political events. Now, they'd be called upon to take the fight to Main Street USA, America's heartland, where we all live in our neighborhoods, with two-car garages, and parks for our children to play in.

Book Three: *Doomsday: Anarchy*

THE SCHWARTZ FAMILY

On New Year's Eve, the fuse had been lit and now others were interested in joining the fray. One politician infamously said that you never let a good crisis go to waste. For the Schwartz family, this was their opportunity to bring down the house of cards known as the United States monetary system.

Markets like stability and financial profiteers like György Schwartz had the ability to disrupt that stability when a financial opportunity arises. However, the events of New Year's Eve were different. Making money was one thing. Collapsing a mighty nation like the United States was another.

It had been a dream of Schwartz's for many years to bring America to its knees, and now somebody had started the process for him. While the terrorist attacks were disruptive, they didn't accomplish his goal of collapsing the economy and the U.S. dominance over world financial markets. He didn't care if Russia, China or the hapless Europeans stepped into America's shoes, as long as the U.S was cut off at the knees.

Jonathan calls upon his minions in the Black Rose, also known as Rosa Negra. He believes that one man's anarchist is another man's patriot. As a result, it was easy for Jonathan to justify the violent methods employed by the Black Rose federation of anarchists.

He frequently likened their actions to those of the Sons of Liberty who opposed British rule in the pre-Revolutionary War days. Others saw them as a band of rabble-rousing thugs, loosely made up of groups from Occupy Wall Street, Antifa, and Black Lives Matter who were willing to use the disruption of society as a means to a political end.

Regardless, the Schwartz's devised a plan that would not only disrupt the psyche of Americans who chose not to engage in the fight brewing on the streets, but also enable them to profit from the societal collapse as well.

Using their vast financial resources, and the passions of the Black Rose movement, in the midst of the chaos that was initiated on New Year's Eve, the father and son threw gasoline on the fire. And, like the North Viet Cong soldier who would toss a grenade inside a village hut, only to run away and not observe the aftermath, the Schwartzes rushed to their jet for a planned escape to their safe place in New Zealand.

Their nemesis, George Trowbridge, had other plans for the father and son team. Using his contacts within the Federal Government, Trowbridge orchestrated a hastily obtained warrant for the arrest of the Schwartz's with the intent to have them detained indefinitely following the martial law declaration. In Trowbridge's mind, this would put an end to the feud between the power political opposites.

As the FBI closed in on the Schwartz jet sitting on an obscure tarmac, ready for departure, Jonathan saw the handwriting on the wall and narrowly escaped arrest. As he lay in the cold, wet grass, he vowed revenge.

Meanwhile, Trowbridge had another score to settle. He had become skeptical of his long-time associate, Hanson Briscoe, who was spearheading the events of New Year's Eve. The fact that Trowbridge's son-in-law, Michael Cortland, was nearly killed troubled the old man. He'd been around too long to get one-upped by Briscoe.

After a meeting in the Trowbridge home, Briscoe was allowed to leave but Trowbridge had made his assessment—the man who orchestrated the New Year's Eve attacks had to die. Trowbridge had big plans for Cort, and the attempt on his life could not be tolerated.

THE HAVEN

Meanwhile, back at the ranch, as they say, the Haven was busy implementing its survival game plan that had been a couple of years in the making. Ryan and Blair Smart had spent many months picking the right property for their prepper community and then planning to provide its residents with safety, sustenance, and medical treatment, all while trying to maintain some sense of normalcy.

WILL HIGHTOWER had been the first to arrive and was immediately rotated into a security shift. This left his children, Ethan and Skylar, alone during the day. Alpha, the head of the Haven's security team, had incorporated drone technology into their perimeter monitoring. His plan included using older kids to operate the drone's that continuously fed surveillance footage back to a series of monitors in the Smart residence, known as Haven House.

During Alpha's orientation of Ethan, the teen learned that his father had made no effort to locate a battery charger for his son's cell phone. This angered Ethan and he immediately devised a plan to leave the Haven and return to his mother and boyfriend in Philadelphia.

Using one of the drones as an aid, Ethan discovered a nearby home that was occupied by an elderly couple. He put the drone away, snuck over the wall, and stole the couple's car without saying goodbye or *arrivederci*.

The fifteen-year-old was sailing along, singing and allowing the wind to blow through his hair without a care in the world, until he reached Richmond. Then the old Oldsmobile ran low on fuel, and patience with the high-speed it had endured for hours, and the engine seized.

Ethan was naïve to the ways of the world. He thought he would be welcomed anywhere, anytime. He was wrong. At the end of his journey to Philly, he was badly beaten, stripped of his shoes, jacket, and cell phone, and left for dead next to a dumpster at a gas station.

Ethan's sudden, unannounced departure from the Haven caused more drama than Ryan and Blair wanted to put up with. The other important members of their team, the Cortlands, the Sheltons, and toward the end, the Rankins and Hayden Blount, arrived safely at the Haven by the end of the day.

Michael Cortland was tapped to be Ryan's right-hand man from an administrative standpoint.

As America descended into societal collapse, Ryan needed to focus on the safety and operations of the Haven. Cort, who was well organized and had fought trench warfare in DC, was the perfect man for the job.

In addition, Ryan called upon Tom Shelton to act as his advisor from a security standpoint. While Alpha was the warrior that the Haven needed under the circumstances, Tom was a seasoned commander whom Ryan could trust.

And, as it turns out, so could George Trowbridge. The Sheltons and Cortlands were astonished to find one another and when Tom presented Trowbridge's letter to his estranged daughter, Meredith, some tears were shed. The letter also contained a suggestion to his daughter—you can trust Tom Shelton, and no one else. Time will tell if the advice from her father was sound.

The Sheltons had something in common with another important member of the Haven, although they didn't know it yet. As they traveled through Richmond, the Black Rose anarchists were up to their dastardly deeds and blocked the southbound lanes of the interstate. While the thugs were attacking motorists, a young woman fought back and cleared the path for the Sheltons to escape too. During the melee, they even noticed how some creature mauled the face of one of the attackers.

Unbeknownst to them, the young woman was Hayden Blount who arrived later that evening and the creature that mauled the face of the anarchist was her Maine Coon cat, Prowler.

The mauled marauder crossed the path of another of our characters—Dr. Angela Rankin. She and her husband, Tyler, made the decision to leave their jobs and home in Richmond to go to the Haven. While Tyler was purchasing a truck and trailer, Angela went to the VCU hospital where she worked to negotiate a leave of absence. While she was there, she worked on the patient whose face had been mauled by Prowler.

Also, while she and Tyler were making their arrangements to leave, their kids, Kaycee and J.C. were left home alone to do some chores and gather the family's things for a road trip. However, the Black Rose federation had different plans for the neighborhood. After gathering at a Schwartz owned-property to the west of the Rankin home, the thugs began to march toward downtown Richmond and the State Capitol with the intent to destroy everything in its path.

They broke into homes, terrorized residents, and generally wreaked havoc along the Rankin's street. When they approached the house to break in, Kaycee and J.C. devised a plan. J.C. found a space in the old house to hide and Kaycee locked herself down the hall in her parent's bedroom.

Armed with a shotgun, she waited. Two of the marauders found her locked away and threatened her. They started pounding on the bedroom door in an attempt to break it down. Kaycee didn't hesitate.

She racked a round into the shotgun and sent a blast of buckshot through the door and into the bodies of her assailants. The two bad guys scrambled to leave the house, begging for their lives as they went.

Tyler and Angela eventually arrived to comfort their kids and the family made their way to the Haven where they were late to arrive. Now, everyone who had purchased property or had been invited into the community was within the safe confines of the Haven.

But there was one among them who had a dark secret. He'd been unknowingly recruited into a conspiracy that might lead to the demise of everyone at the Haven, including himself. He too had been the recipient of mysterious texts.

X-Ray was an introverted, techno-geek who could have been a valuable asset to Ryan and Blair Smart. As it turns out, he was someone else's asset as well. He'd done as instructed by the anonymous benefactor who paid him well enough to buy the electronics gear he so desperately craved.

When the shock wore off from meeting the man he was instructed to watch out for, Michael Cortland, he found the burner cell phone that he'd procured before arriving at the Haven. He issued the required text message, careful to get the words just right.

The eagle's mark is in sight.

Then X-Ray waited, unsure of what this meant and how he was supposed to proceed. Then he received a response.

Tell no one.
Will advise.
Godspeed, Patriot.
MM

X-Ray was beginning to lose his nerve. He considered running away from the Haven as fast as he could. He wished he had a drink. He stared at the cheap flip phone, wishing it would malfunction. But then, it buzzed to life with another text message.

From Doomsday Anarchy …

X-Ray quickly pulled the phone out of his pocket and flipped it open. He pushed the select key to change the display to the text function. He read the message and then collapsed back into his swivel office chair.

Beware of those around you.
All is not as it might seem.
Godspeed, Patriot.
MM

"What?" he shouted again. "Beware of who? You? Jesus!"

In a rare show of anger and raw emotion, X-Ray flung the phone across the room, where it careened off a lampshade and landed safely on the leather couch in front of the fireplace, its light-blue screen continuing to illuminate despite the attempt to kill it.

Book Four: *Doomsday: Minutemen*

THE SKULL AND BONES

Legends were not born, they were created. So was the case of the *The Order of the Scull and Bones*, later modernized to simply, *Skull and Bones.* Arising as a secret society at Yale University in 1832, the mystery surrounding its members, coupled with the clandestine meetings which they held, gave rise to a legend that has continued to this day.

Doomsday Minutemen begins with the backstory of the *Bonesmen*, as the members were known, and how they relate to the principal characters in the story. As the story goes, one summer day at Yale in 1984, the Bonesmen gathered at their private retreat on the St. Lawrence River, Deer Island.

Divisiveness grew within the ranks and in a rare of showing of political animus, the arguments became so heated that the Bonesmen were forced to separate to opposite side of the island until emotions died down.

Although, on the surface, a truce had been reached, some members of the Skull and Bones, led by George Trowbridge and Hanson Briscoe, used the rift as an opportunity to plan for the future. That foresaw the collapse of America, following the path of all great empires before it. They vowed that, when the time came, they would take whatever steps were necessary to preserve America and the principles upon which the nation was founded.

THE FUSE HAD BEEN LIT

Trowbridge provided the means, and Briscoe the muscle, to push America into an internal struggle reminiscent of the Civil War. The political and cultural war that had been brewing in America for decades was now turning into one in which property destruction had become expected and killing commonplace.

As was true in any story of historical significance, there was the big picture, the coming of a Second American Civil War, and then there was how these events impacted the lives of everyday people.

Jonathan Schwartz was on the run. His father had been unceremoniously arrested on the tarmac of the Danbury, Connecticut airport. Out of self-preservation, Schwartz ran, stole a pickup truck, and made his way to a remote hunting lodge that had been in the family's real estate holdings for decades. Off the grid, but without friends, Schwartz hid and regrouped.

Meanwhile, Hanson Briscoe, the polar opposite of Schwartz from a political perspective, had troubles of his own. You see, he'd tried to assassinate Michael Cortland, the heir-apparent to the George Trowbridge legacy. He'd shot and missed, and now, he was fully aware that Trowbridge had discovered his betrayal.

Just as Briscoe was implementing another phase in the Minutemen's plan to instigate a Second Civil War, Trowbridge's operatives arrived at Monocacy Farm to kill him. Using the secret tunnels built beneath the home and grounds of the antebellum mansion, Briscoe narrowly escaped the assassination attempt and sought refuge.

He descended upon his caretaker's home, a loyal couple who'd watched over Monocacy Farm for decades. Briscoe, after thanking them for their hospitality, murdered the older couple and stole their vehicle. Hoping to escape to Canada, Briscoe travelled north into Pennsylvania and then came up with an idea.

THE ENEMY OF MY ENEMY IS MY FRIEND

Briscoe was aware that György Schwartz had been arrested. He knew Jonathan Schwartz was a smart guy and likely presumed that Trowbridge was behind it. Briscoe wanted revenge against Trowbridge and he expected Jonathan would be seeking it as well. So, he reached out to one of Jonathan's top henchmen, the anarchist—*Chepe.*

Chepe had terrorized Richmond, Virginia and had been reassigned by Jonathan to do the same in Charlotte, North Carolina. Jonathan wanted to take the battle to Main Street USA, not just the usual locales for anarchist activity on the West Coast or cities like Chicago, Detroit, and Washington D.C.

Briscoe was convincing and Chepe put the two powerful men together by phone. Hours later, they sat in the hunting lodge outside Kutztown, Pennsylvania, sharing a bottle of brandy and plotting the demise of George Trowbridge, or the next best thing, the powerful man's family.

Meanwhile, there were lots of enemies in the story as Ethan Hightower, who had survived the brutal beatdown administered in South Richmond thanks to some good Samaritans who took him in, was reunited with his mother. Karen, Will "Delta" Hightower's ex-wife, and Frankie Scallone, Will's ex-partner. There was no love lost between the two exes and Will, who'd fully adopted his new persona as Delta, member of the Haven's security team.

Ethan led his mother and Frankie directly to the front gate of the Haven where the trio attempted to gain entry. After a confrontation in which Blair Smart laid down the law, Ethan was readmitted, Karen was invited in, with conditions, and Frankie was unconditionally sent on his way.

This didn't set well with the ex-partner and now ex-lover, and he angrily made his way to Charlotte to look up an old acquaintance. He found an old acquaintance, all right, but it was not who he expected. Instead, it was Chepe and his band of anarchists.

You see, Frankie had arrested Chepe years before while the two were in Philadelphia and now, fate had brought them together. Fearing for his life, Frankie acted on instinct and played up to Chepe. Through quick-thinking and smooth-talking, Frankie went from being the anarchist's next victim to a member of the club. *The enemy of my enemy is my friend.*

The two men soon learned that they had common interests and the Haven suddenly became their mutual target. They compared notes, sent out a scout team, and then devised a plan of attack.

THE HAVEN

The Haven had settled into a routine now that all of its residents had arrived. Jobs were assigned, relationships were formed, and the Smarts implemented the plans for surviving Doomsday that had been formulated over the years.

But, as was often the case, even the best laid plans can go awry because of a single reason—the human factor. People had a way of changing any dynamic and the same was true at the Haven.

The Haven's perimeter was threatened by passers-by and at one point, two men attempting to cross the Henry River into the former movie set of the Hunger Games got entangled in some fallen trees. One man was badly injured, and both suffered from hypothermia. Through the efforts of Tyler Rankin, and his trauma physician wife, Angela, the men were resuscitated and saved. One of them, however, in a particularly ungrateful move, chose to escape the Armageddon

Hospital, prompting a manhunt.

He was later captured, and when the two intruders' loved ones appeared at the main gate, the whole lot of them were expelled from the premises.

The security team at the Haven beefed up their monitoring of the river portion of their perimeter, a fact that didn't go unnoticed by Chepe's scouts who'd observed the activities. When they reported back to their leader in Charlotte, coupled with Frankie's knowledge surreptitiously obtained from Ethan, a plan was formulated.

Chepe would eliminate his target, the Cortland family and Frankie would exact his revenge on Will Hightower, Karen, or both.

The assault upon the Haven began during the security shift change was taking place. Chepe's men hurdled the walls using ladders stolen from Lowe's and several teams of two entered the Haven in search of their prey.

When the breach was discovered, gunfire erupted. Several of the anarchist's were killed, but the Haven suffered losses as well. Two well-placed snipers across the river were designated to locate and kill Cort. He and Tom Shelton were patrolling the riverbanks near the cabins when the hyperaware former Naval Commander caught a glimpse of light on the hill across the river.

Instinctively, he shielded Cort from view and took a bullet in the back for his efforts. Members of the Haven security team closed ranks around Cort and Tom which enabled Tyler to rush Tom to the Armageddon Hospital.

In the woods, Frankie and Chepe worked together to get into position. Chepe opted to stakeout Haven Barn as he knew it was a center of activity for the security team. Frankie chose to approach Haven House, where he presumed women and children would be kept. He suspected that Will would focus on protecting Karen, Skylar, and Ethan.

Frankie was right, except he never expected that Ethan would be back on duty as a drone operator. Ethan had successfully convinced Ryan and Alpha that he was remorseful. He wanted to help the Haven and with the security team shorthanded, he was put in charge of the kids operating the drones.

This turned out to both fortuitous and cursed. Ethan recognized Frankie through the high-definition camera lens of the drone. He followed the former boyfriend through the woods and when he saw that Frankie intended to shoot Will, Ethan manned-up to protect his father.

He knocked Frankie into some large rocks, causing the man's head to bleed profusely. Blinded by the blood in his eyes, and lashing out like a cornered animal, Frankie fought back, landing blow-after-blow against the teenage boy's head and body. With one final swing, he knocked Ethan hard against the boulders, causing his skull to crack open, killing the boy instantly.

As this battle between man and child came to an end, the security team at the Haven successfully repelled the larger attack. The leaders of the Haven gathered at Haven Barn to check on one another and compare notes. That's when they discovered that one of the children was missing.

During the melee and confusion, the drone brigade, which now included Hannah Cortland, split apart in fear. Hannah was last seen running toward Haven Barn, but a quick search yielded nothing.

As Cort and Meredith melted into despair over their missing a child, the buzzing sound of a drone could be heard.

From *Doomsday Minutemen* …

The others heard it too. They wandered around the gravel area in front of the barn, looking skyward in all directions for the drone. Both Hayden and Alpha fanned out, scanning the woods in search of any threats.

The high-pitched sound emanating from the four motors of the quadcopter grew even louder, until it suddenly sailed over the roof of the barn and down the gravel road toward Haven House. Then, it suddenly stopped and swung back around.

Slowly now, the quadcopter returned to the barn. Moving painstakingly slow, it inched closer and lowered its altitude as if it was an airplane preparing for landing.

The group stared at the device. Some were confused, others pointed their weapon at it, anticipating that the machine might attack them in some way.

Cort hesitated, and then he began to walk toward the drone. Meredith quickly caught up to them until they stopped. The operator smoothly set the drone a few feet away from them and the motors suddenly shut off.

The rest of the group gathered around as the four propellers stopped, leaving them in complete silence.

Meredith began to wail as she pointed at one of the arms of the drone. Tears poured out of Cort's eyes as he lowered himself to pick it up. Attached to the arm was the double-cross pendant necklace Meredith had given Hannah earlier that day for protection.

Also wrapped around the arm was a note, affixed with one of Hannah's colorful hair ribbons. Cort wiped the tears and sweat out of his eyes. He tried to regain his composure long enough to read and comprehend the words.

"The King needs to come to the Queen City and we will turn over his Princess. Frankie knows where to find me. Come alone."

Scores will be settled as the Doomsday series concludes with—*Civil War …*

DOOMSDAY: Civil War

The Doomsday Series
Book Five

PART ONE

CHAPTER 1

The Varnadore Building
Uptown Charlotte, North Carolina

"Dammit!" Chepe slapped his hands against the dashboard out of anger and frustration. The pounding caused dust to billow through the air vents designed to defrost the windshield and prompted Hannah Cortland to shriek in fear. "Shut her up! I told you I wanted the kid gagged!"

"She was having trouble breathing," replied one of the guys who'd participated in the raid upon the Haven. "The way she was hyperventilating, we'd lose our bait before we got back to the Varnadore."

Chepe shook his head and turned around to stare at Hannah, whose eyes grew wide. Chepe scowled, causing her to whimper. His death stare was sufficient to calm the child down, or at least keep her quiet.

Almost unconsciously, Chepe reached into his torn shirtsleeve and found the dark ink of his tattoo, the black rose, indicative of his involvement in Rosa Negra. It was his reminder that he fought for a greater cause than engaging in the kidnapping of children.

The entire attack on the compound where Michael Cortland and the others were holed up was necessary. He had the tools to blast them all off the face of the earth, yet he didn't. It wasn't because he had scruples. Chepe had lost those years before. Somehow, the thought of using the advanced military weaponry provided by Jonathan Schwartz was overkill for the task at hand—assassinating Cortland.

His mind wandered as he recalled when the black rose tattoo had been etched onto his body. He was in Greece at the behest of Schwartz. At the time, Occupy Wall Street was all the rage, and their successes in garnering press attention changed Chepe's life.

Springing up under the counterculture of the 1960s, anarchists in Europe actively participated in student and worker revolts. Conferences were held to form groups that spread throughout the Old World. Soon, anarchist enclaves sprang up throughout Western Europe, especially Greece.

The Schwartz family had funded and supported Greek Prime Minister Alexis Tsipras's leftist group, SYRIZA. Chepe embedded with the urban guerilla group known as the Conspiracy of the Cells of Fire, which was known for its letter-bomb campaigns and packaged explosive devices. The leaders of SYRIZA taught him how to mobilize his followers into a formidable force that could easily overwhelm law enforcement if necessary.

None of his training, however, schooled him on how to raid a compound, assassinate a man, or kidnap a little girl. Now he found himself in a quandary as to how he should proceed.

He had to make a decision. Putting it off wouldn't make it any easier, though, and returning the girl was certainly not an option. After the raid, he doubted the people at the Haven would shrug it off and be thankful the girl was returned.

He reached for the satellite phone and contemplated calling Jonathan and his new pal, Hanson Briscoe. He pressed the first three numbers on the dial pad and then quickly hit cancel repeatedly. His anger built up again and he slapped the dashboard twice. Naturally, this prompted Hannah to begin crying.

"You know," Chepe began with an eerily calm voice, "we could just drop the kid on the side of the interstate. We'll gather the troops and find another place to conduct business. Hell, we could just move on to another city. Savannah could burn again, right?"

Chepe made reference to the swath of destruction toward the end of the Civil War when Union General William Tecumseh Sherman did more than defeat his enemy, he savagely punished Southerners and their way of life. He pillaged and burned the majestic plantations and antebellum homes of the Old South, from Chattanooga to Atlanta to Savannah. Sherman was no gentleman.

None of Chepe's lieutenants responded to his statement. The driver, who hadn't participated in the raid, remained stoic. The two men who flanked a whimpering Hannah in the back seat were tired or partially wounded themselves.

"Jesus," he muttered. The layers of emotions Chepe felt could be conveyed with just one word. He continued to chastise himself for the reckless attack, one that looked good on paper, but had easily been repelled by the security team at the Haven. He glanced to the back seat again and reminded himself of the one success he had achieved. *I have a bargaining chip.*

"Or we let it play out," he continued. "The Varnadore is built like a fortress. We've got at least a mile of unobstructed views in three directions. The houses in the neighborhood behind us have been cleared out for the most part by either our people, or because the residents took off."

One of his lieutenants offered encouragement. "We can post snipers and spotters on the roof. We've got the heavy artillery plus a few guys who are good shots. And I think we outnumber them."

"How would you know that?" asked Chepe.

"Well, I don't know for sure," he replied. "I do know, however, that they'd have to bring everybody they've got to come close to matching us man for man. I know they want the kid back, but they're not gonna abandon the safety of those walls. Not all of them anyway."

Hannah's eyes darted around the interior of the SUV, listening to the men debate her fate. She suddenly grew quiet, calming her emotions.

"Good point," said Chepe. "I mean, let's say that Cortland is stupid and comes alone. Then this is a piece of cake. Even if he brings six, hell, a dozen of their best guys, we've got him outnumbered by a few dozen."

"That's right," said the driver, speaking for the first time.

The fourth man in the vehicle, who was nursing a gunshot wound where a wildly fired shot had grazed him as he climbed over the wall, offered his opinion. "I think some of their people are ex-military. They could come at us in a way we never expected. I mean, we're trained to break things, not defend—"

Chepe scowled and turned to stare at his lieutenant. "It doesn't matter. It's a numbers game. We've got them by at least six to one. Plus, we'll hide the princess in the castle really good. I'm a chess player. We'll lay out a nice gambit that traps them."

"So we play it out?" asked the driver.

Chepe smiled, confident in his decision for the first time.

"We play it out."

CHAPTER 2

Haven Barn
The Haven

Sweat poured off Cort's brow and down the sides of his face. He'd kept in shape after his years as a college basketball player at Yale, but it wasn't the type of sweat released to cool the body down from overexertion or exposure to heat. Stress sweat was different. It was milkier, full of fatty acids and proteins, and was released from glands around a person's brow or armpits. The chillier temperatures did nothing to prevent Cort from soaking his shirt and drenching his face.

"Who could've done this, and why?" asked Alpha. "I can't imagine they attacked us to kidnap Hannah."

Cort kicked at the rocks beneath his feet. He paced rapidly back and forth, his eyes darting between the ransom note, the quadcopter, and his wife's trembling hands holding the double-cross necklace.

"They were after me," Cort replied. "I just don't know why. I mean, for sure, anyway."

"What does that mean?" asked Alpha.

Blair stepped in because Alpha wasn't privy to all of the information they'd received from Tom, Cort, and more recently, X-Ray. "Listen, for now, it doesn't matter who's behind it. We'll deal with that another day. Personally, I think that Hannah was taken because she was readily available to the guys who staged this raid."

"I agree with Blair," interjected Ryan. "She wasn't the target, and the note pretty much says that. They're after Cort. We'll have to figure out why, later."

"What are we gonna do?" Meredith's question came out more as a despondent wail than a series of words.

"Honey, we're gonna get Hannah back. I promise." Blair moved in to comfort her, but Meredith pulled away. She was too distraught to be touched, yet she needed someone to help her through the pain of losing her child.

"You don't know that!" Meredith shouted. "We know nothing about these people! All we know is that this guy Frankie is our only hope. And he's lying half dead on the porch back there." She turned and pointed in the direction of the hospital.

Cort set his jaw and spoke through gritted teeth. "I'm gettin' some answers." Before anyone could stop him, he raced toward the Armageddon Hospital, where Blair had dumped Frankie's body earlier.

"Cort, wait!" shouted Ryan. "Let's talk this through first."

Cort ignored Ryan's plea, and Meredith took off after him, at one point stumbling on the gravel and ripping open the skin on both of her knees. She recovered, raced forward again, and then fell harder.

Blair turned to Alpha. "Call Tyler and tell him they're coming for Frankie. We can't let Cort get there first."

Angela and Tyler had remained at the hospital with their two kids and Skylar. Frankie had been taken into the hospital by the Rankins while the kids were being watched by Donna.

Ryan jumped in his Ranger, with Alpha crawling into the passenger seat at the same time. Ryan floored the gas pedal and spun the vehicle around in pursuit.

Blair was left alone, staring at the children's dead guard. By her count, the Haven had lost three men during the attack, with several others seriously injured, including Tom Shelton. She walked around the man's body, which had been ignored by the group in the urgency to find Hannah. She knelt down next to him and closed his eyelids.

"I'm sorry," she said apologetically. "This was never supposed to happen. At least, not like this."

Blair jogged to her Prairie and took off down the gravel road, full throttle. She wanted to personally extract the information out of Frankie, but she suspected she'd have to stand in line.

*****

Cort was the first to arrive at the front porch of the hospital, followed closely by Ryan and then, Blair, who pulled the lever for the rear brakes of her four-wheeler, skidding to a stop and throwing gravel in all directions. The Rankin kids scrambled out of the way to avoid being hit.

Tyler was waiting for Cort, holding his hands up to stop his entry. "Cort, wait, you can't go in there. The guy's still unconscious."

"I'll wake him up!" Cort shot back.

"No, you can't," said Tyler. "Please calm down. I heard what happened, but you gotta let Angela do her best to keep him alive."

Cort ignored Tyler's request and tried to push past him. The much taller Cort was manhandling Tyler, causing the Rankin kids to cry for help. Blair jumped off her four-wheeler and ran to the front door, blocking Cort's access. She drew her pistol and held it toward the ground, but in a way that Cort could see it.

"Out of my way, Blair!" Cort snarled.

"Trust me, I want to beat it out of him, too, Cort. But let's talk to Angela first and see what we're dealing with here."

"C'mon, Cort, you gotta calm down," plead Tyler, who was still wrestling with the distraught dad.

Suddenly, the door opened and Angela emerged from the building. The white lab coat given to her as the sole doctor of the Armageddon Hospital was drenched in blood. She was wearing a surgical mask and sterile gloves. Her appearance startled Cort, causing him to stop struggling against Tyler's grasp.

Angela removed the mask and gloves and began to speak just as the rest of the group arrived. She paused, caught her breath, and waited for everyone to approach.

As she arrived out of breath, Meredith's eyes grew wide at the amount of blood on Angela's clothing. She began to weep but managed to ask, "Is he still alive?"

Angela took a deep breath and sighed.

CHAPTER 3

The Armageddon Hospital
The Haven

Angela glanced at her husband and then nodded towards their children. Tyler turned to Kaycee and J.C. "Kids, I need you to go inside for a moment, okay?"

"We're fine out here," replied Kaycee.

"No, I wanna see the bloody guy," countered J.C.

Angela stood a little taller and placed her hands on her hips. "Both of you, inside. Now! And go into my office, close the door, and don't touch anything. Understood?"

"Yes, ma'am," mumbled a dejected J.C. He and Kaycee slipped inside as Angela returned her attention to the group.

"What's the story, Doc?" asked Alpha.

Angela grimaced before explaining Frankie's condition. "Well, he's still alive, but barely. It appears that he suffered another head trauma recently. A fair-sized gash on his forehead was treated with 3M Steri-Strips to close the wound. They weren't sufficiently strong enough to withstand the additional beating he received."

"What happened to him?" asked Alpha.

Blair replied, "He snuck up on the back of Haven House. There was a scuffle and he apparently hit his head on a rock. During the fight, Delta hit him in the side of the head with the butt end of his rifle."

"A direct blow to the temple, I might add," said Angela.

"This is all his fault!" groaned Meredith, who became emotional again. "He and his tramp wife. They're the ones who brought this, this animal to our doorstep."

"I'll deal with them later," growled Cort, who remained angry over his missing daughter.

"Hold on, guys," Blair interrupted. "It was Ethan who attacked Frankie, preventing him from shooting Will."

"Lucky him," said Meredith sarcastically.

Blair stepped closer to Meredith. "Ethan is dead."

"What?" Meredith asked.

"You heard me," replied Blair. "Ethan was killed during the fight. Lots of people have lost loved ones today. After this, I've got to explain to three wives why their husbands are lying facedown in the Haven."

"I didn't know …" Meredith's voice trailed off as a few remorseful tears flowed from her eyes.

"I'm sorry, Blair," said Cort. He reached for his wife, who fell against his body. "Angela, please continue."

Angela smiled. "Anyway, in a short period of time, Frankie had multiple blows to his head. While the last one, delivered by Delta's rifle, wasn't enough to kill him, it did knock him unconscious and close to being comatose."

"He's in a coma?" asked Ryan.

"Without the proper equipment, it's impossible to provide an accurate diagnosis of his neurological state. A coma is a state of unconsciousness when a person cannot be wakened with touch, noise, or even a strong respiratory inhalant like ammonia inhalants. It's different from sleep or even unconsciousness. Sometimes a body slips into a coma to aid its survival."

"So you're not sure if he's in a coma?" asked Meredith.

"Initially, it was hard to tell because he was unresponsive. Without a PET scan, um, a positron emission tomography, it's impossible to give you a definitive answer."

Cort released his wife and stepped forward. He had calmed down and was speaking unemotionally. "Where is the closest place to get a PET scan?"

"Who knows at this point?" replied Ryan. "Before the news blackout, it appeared that most hospitals were overrun, and some were even shutting down in fear for their staff's safety."

"Well, there's more," interjected Angela. "I didn't know what the situation was when I began to treat him." She glanced over at Blair.

"Yeah, I kinda dumped him on her and left," said Blair.

"Anyhow, I tried to save his life, which is what I do," Angela continued. "Donna had some Ativan, a form of lorazepam—a common sedative. It was my only alternative to the barbiturates that are normally used. Because Frankie was unresponsive, I had to inject the sedative into his body. The first thing I did was reconstitute the Ativan by dissolving it in a calcium-free solution of glucose—"

Meredith interrupted her with a question. "If he was unconscious, or even in a coma, why did you need to sedate him?"

"Because the body's best way to recover from a serious head trauma like Frankie endured is to be in a comatose state," replied Angela. "I used the Ativan to medically induce a coma."

"What?" asked Cort. "You intentionally put him into a coma?"

"That's right," replied Angela defensively. "It was the only way to save his life."

"He deserves to die!" Meredith raised her voice, prompting Blair to step forward.

"Well, it's a good thing he didn't, right?"

Meredith sheepishly looked at the ground and fiddled with a few rocks at her feet. The group stood silently for a moment as they contemplated Angela's treatment and Frankie's condition.

"How long?" asked Cort.

Angela looked at the hopeful eyes of the group. She understood they all had mixed emotions. All of them couldn't care less if Frankie Scallone lived or died. At this point, he was nothing more than a source of information. She also knew that the minute they had the location of Hannah, Frankie would be killed. The only question in her mind was who'd get the honor of doing it.

"Cort, it's hard to tell. There are three stages of disordered consciousness, which includes coma, the vegetative state, and a minimally conscious state. At this point, his body is battling to survive, and the sedative-induced coma will hasten that recovery, odd as that might seem. If I take away the sedative, he might recover and enter a minimally conscious state. Then I'll be able to see if he opens his eyes and is capable of responding to basic commands."

Ryan asked, "What are the ramifications of bringing him out of the artificial coma too soon?"

"At this point, the medically induced coma, coupled with keeping his body temperature reduced by positioning his gurney away from the fire and close to a partially cracked window, is preventing his brain from swelling. The coma reduces the energy requirements of the brain, which reduces the blood flow and pressure, thus allowing the brain to rest."

Cort shook his head and Meredith became impatient. "Angela, please. How long will it take to bring him out of the coma so we can find out where my baby is?"

"Every patient is different. A quick withdrawal could have deadly consequences or possibly put him into a vegetative state. Under most circumstances, I would wean a patient off the sedative. Then I'd monitor the intracranial pressure and his seizure activity to decide if he should be placed back into a medically induced coma."

Meredith began to cry again and buried her head in her husband's chest. "No. No. No. This can't be happening." Her muffled voice could barely be heard by the group.

Cort comforted her but then matter-of-factly stated the bottom line. "He could die if she pushes him too hard. Then we'll never know where Hannah is."

CHAPTER 4

The Armageddon Hospital
The Haven

A solemn Cort and Meredith entered the hospital after promising not to disrupt Angela's care of Frankie. They were now keenly aware that their daughter's life might depend upon keeping the man alive.

The entire group entered, causing a sizable crowd in the space that already contained Tom Shelton, who was recovering from a gunshot wound; his wife, Donna, who periodically checked on all of the patients under their care; and several members of the Haven who'd received relatively minor injuries.

"Meredith, please, come take a seat and let us take care of your scrapes," said Donna in a soothing voice. The two women had bonded since the moment they met. Under these unusual circumstances, they'd learned that they shared a common thread—both of their husbands had secretive, close relationships with George Trowbridge.

"Okay, thanks," muttered Meredith as she found her way to a seat next to the wood-burning stove. As she sat down, she couldn't take her eyes off Frankie, who was located at the far end of the room.

Cort helped his wife sit, and then he moved out of the way as Donna lovingly used fresh water to remove the dirt and debris from Meredith's wounds. Angela knelt down to take a better look at Meredith's knees and shins. Then she reached out to take her hands, injured when Meredith tried to break her fall.

"These aren't serious, Donna," started Angela. "There's no need to use stronger cleansing solutions such as hydrogen peroxide, iodine, or rubbing alcohol. They might serve to irritate the wound. Cool, clean water should be fine for now."

"She's still bleeding a little around the knees," Donna observed.

"Yes, I see." Angela looked up to Meredith. "We're going to apply some gauze on your knees. Can you hold it in place, applying firm, direct pressure?"

Meredith nodded.

Angela continued. "Meredith, I know you're distracted, but I need you to concentrate on yourself for a moment. Don't raise the gauze to check on your wounds because that could start the bleeding again. If you feel blood seeping through the dressing, just let us know. Okay?"

"I will, um, and thank you, Angela. You know, for explaining everything to me so calmly. I mean, I know I was rude out—"

Angela smiled and rubbed Meredith's arm. "Are you kidding me? I'd be out of my mind if it were one of my kids. You're a far better mom than I am."

Meredith managed a smile. "I doubt that, but thanks."

Angela turned her newest patient back over to Donna and approached the rest of the group, who were hovering over Frankie's gurney.

"I thought I saw his eyes move," said Cort as Angela approached them.

"Well, that's a good thing; however, it's not what you're hoping for," she began. "The good news is that eye fluttering, or movement, as you called it, means that the patient's brain is still functioning. He's most likely dreaming rather than reacting to external stimuli. It doesn't mean that he's about to wake up."

"Let me guess, the next thing you're about to tell us is that standing over him like this isn't gonna bring him out of the coma, right?" asked Ryan.

"That's right," replied Angela with a wink.

Blair was the first to step away from Frankie's gurney, and she wandered over to Tom, who was sitting upright in a chair next to a couple of other wounded security personnel.

"How are you guys doin'?" she asked.

"I'm the worst of the bunch," replied Tom, who was older than the other two men combined.

"The doc said we can go back to our cabins soon," one of the other men offered. "We're ready, but I think she's worried about infection."

Blair smiled. "Here's what I've learned about our Dr. Rankin. This is her domain, and it's not a good idea to argue with her. I'd follow her orders."

"Oh, yeah," one of the men added. "She read us the riot act already. Heck, Tom had to argue with her just to get off the bed and sit with us."

"How did you win the argument, Tom?" asked Blair.

Tom laughed and replied, "Oh, I made a promise to talk American history with J.C. He's really a smart kid and it's my pleasure to do it."

Blair glanced over her shoulder and noticed two people approaching from the direction of Haven House. "All right, guys, get better." She quickly turned and headed toward the front door unnoticed. She slipped onto the front porch into the cooling early evening air to confront the new arrivals—Will and Karen Hightower.

It only took a moment for Blair to realize the grieving parents had arrived at the hospital to exact their revenge on Frankie.

"Blair, is he still alive?" Delta demanded answers. "I wanna see the murdering son of a—"

Blair stood fast and held her hands up to force Delta to stop. "No, you can't. At least not now. Please hear me out."

"Why?" countered Karen. "He killed our son. He doesn't deserve to be treated by a doctor."

Blair had her hands full and backed up a couple of paces, instantly wishing she had one of the guys as backup. "It's complicated. We need him."

"Why?" asked Will aggressively.

"Hannah Cortland was kidnapped by the attackers, and Frankie is the key to finding her. Apparently he knows where their hideout is, or whatever."

Delta stopped Karen's progress toward the door. "Frankie? Why would he even be involved with people like this? And why would they kidnap Hannah?"

"There are a lot of unanswered questions, but all we know, for now, is that they are holding Hannah, and a note they sent to us via drone read that Frankie knows where to find her."

"What do they want? Money?" asked Karen.

"Cort," replied Blair. "Listen, like I said, there are a lot of unanswered questions. Angela has to keep him alive and bring him out of a coma so that we can get information from him."

"Coma? Is that because I hit him?" asked Will.

"Look, seriously, you guys," began Blair as she moved closer to them both. "There are two parents inside who are frightened for their little girl. You guys have lost a son and have a daughter who needs you. Please take her back to your cabin and hold her tight. She's a precious child and needs you right now. Okay?"

Karen nodded and pulled at Delta's arm. "Let's go, Will. There'll be time to deal with him later."

Before they walked away, Blair asked one more question. "Listen, can you guys think of anyone Frankie might know around here? I mean, anywhere in North Carolina. A relative, friend, ex. Anyone?"

Delta responded, "We had a buddy on Philly SWAT who moved to Charlotte, but I don't know anything other than that. Well, wait. Maybe he got a job with the county. I'm not sure."

"Got a name?" asked Blair.

"Yeah, Kenny Williams. That's all I remember."

They left and Blair breathed a sigh of relief. She'd defused another potential confrontation. The stress was beginning to get to her as well, and with so many unanswered questions, she really needed to take Ryan back to the house and sort it all out. She walked back inside to gather up Ryan and Alpha.

"Listen, guys, it's getting crowded in here, and I just turned the Hightowers away, who were determined to deal with Frankie themselves. Let's go outside, okay?"

The men followed her, and after discussing Angela's treatment plan, Blair bottom-lined it. "If Angela moves too quickly, Frankie could die. If she doesn't try, Hannah could die."

"Wonderful," added Ryan sarcastically. "All we can do is wait."

CHAPTER 5

Haven House
The Haven

Alpha agreed that the waiting game was all they had at the moment. In the meantime, there was a lot of gunfire that had probably attracted the attention of the locals. He left the Smarts at the front of Haven House and went down to the front gate to make sure their security team remained on the lookout for law enforcement. He also suggested that Blair and Ryan prepare to meet with the families of the three residents who had died repelling the attack.

Ryan and Blair entered their home in a state of exhaustion. Intuitively, the princesses of the palace could tell that it was not playtime. They remained on the sofa, studying Ryan and Blair's demeanor. The Roo, who was especially in tune to the Smarts' state of mind, studied them both as first Ryan and then Blair flopped on the overstuffed sofa next to her. Her eyes followed them and attempted to read them. Somehow, *she knew. She always knew.*

Neither of them uttered a word as they both snuggled a pup. Their lives had changed dramatically since that fateful night when they'd won the lottery. All of their carefully thought-out plans had come to fruition. However, they were barely a week into the collapse of society, and they'd lost three of their own; plus a young girl had been kidnapped.

"Well, jeez, Ryan. I don't know where to start."

"Me neither," he said, gently scruffing his fingers along the underside of Chubby's mush. The pup, completely unaware of what was going on, twisted and turned her head so that Ryan could hit every spot. "The problem you and I face is what to do next."

Blair grimaced and nodded. The two were on the same page, as always. "I feel terrible for Hannah, and we need to find her, but Alpha's reminding me that we have families of dead loved ones to visit really struck a chord."

"I know. I feel responsible for these people. Sure, they're grown adults and they made their choices to come here. By the same token, I know they looked to us for protection. I mean, in a way, didn't I kinda promise them that?"

"Sort of, but not really," replied Blair, who sat a little taller on the sofa so she could face Ryan. "They all knew the risks and, if it becomes an issue, I'll be glad to remind them that their alternative is to be out there." She pointed her thumb over her shoulder.

"Okay, we'll do the best we can to console them. But here's the thing. We don't know what's coming next. This whole drone message-delivery thing could be a trick. You know, to draw us outside the walls and leave our security weakened in the process. We have all the residents to consider, not just the Cortlands."

"I agree, but Cort and Meredith won't see it that way," added Blair. "If we can get Hannah's location out of Frankie and if we can come up with a viable plan to rescue her, then we have to decide how much of our security manpower we assign to the task."

"That's a lot of *ifs*," said Ryan, shaking his head. "I can feel where they're coming from. If one of our girls got hurt or killed, I'd be madder than a hornet. Nothing could stop me from going after the people responsible."

"Okay, but would you expect everyone to join in, regardless of how dangerous it was?"

Ryan's shoulders visibly slumped with the realization that not everyone would join the hunt. "I guess not."

"Neither should the Cortlands," said Blair. She tried to lift the mood. "I'm not saying that we won't try. That little girl was adorable, and she was also helping us defend the Haven. That makes her a soldier, in my opinion. We don't leave anybody behind, you know?"

"Yeah, I agree."

Blair continued. "That said, we can't send the entire cavalry and leave the fort unprotected."

Ryan sighed and lifted himself off the sofa. He walked toward the fireplace and mindlessly adjusted picture frames that held photos of Blair and the girls. There were images of Christmas celebrations as well as one of the entire family sitting on the front porch of Haven House. He smiled at the fond memories and reminded himself as to how lucky they were. He turned to Blair.

"We've got to do what we can, but we need more information. If Frankie dies, we've got nothing. Heck, he could lie or try to escape before he talks."

"I'll torture him myself," interrupted Blair.

"I have no doubt," said Ryan with a chuckle. He thought for a moment and then made a suggestion. "We've got an asset who could help. Maybe X-Ray can access some kind of cameras or satellite or something? Anything that can keep us from relying on Frankie waking up and telling the truth."

Blair threw her hands up. "How do we know we can trust that little weasel? After I had him locked up in the toolshed out back, he'll say anything to get loose."

Ryan shrugged. "For now, he's all we've got. Do you wanna give it a try or not?"

"Here's the thing, he isn't doing us any good tied to the hitching post in the shed," she replied. "We have to decide what to do with him anyway. If I stand over him and watch him work, I can learn a little about the computer equipment he has. If we kick him out or execute him, we'll still have his stuff."

"I vote we try to use him."

Blair stood and adjusted her clothes. "Yeah, might as well, but you and I've got some families to see. This has been a rough day, but it's nothing like what they've gone through."

CHAPTER 6

Haven House
The Haven

Ryan and Blair had not dealt with the type of loss that the families of the Haven were experiencing who had lost their husbands and fathers in the raid by Chepe. They were keenly aware that tragic death and loss was a fact of military life, whether the nation was at war or not. However, the contribution of the Haven's residents toward the security of all who resided there was far from military enlistment, but their job was similar, nonetheless.

Without having experienced the violent death of a loved one, it was difficult for the Smarts to express their condolences. Naturally, Ryan tried to offer hope and even tried to find the words to fix their grief. Some were open to his sympathy; others were bitter and closed off. They certainly weren't ready to embrace hopeful statements about the future.

By the time they reached the third family, Blair realized that it was best to simply say "I'm sorry for the loss of your husband." This enabled her to get on a personal level with the grieving family.

Above all, the Smarts offered words of reassurance. The families of the fallen warriors who defended the Haven were now part of the Smarts' family, and all of the others who resided there. Their loss had become the community's loss. The loved ones were promised that everyone would be there for them if needed.

Tears were shed and hugs were exchanged as the harsh realities of life in the apocalypse hit home. It wasn't about some fantasy of playing soldier with your buddies or rummaging around your neighbors' homes looking for stuff you could use. A post-apocalyptic world was about real people and whether they lived or died.

It was against that backdrop that Blair and Ryan went directly to the toolshed where Echo was keeping a watchful eye on X-Ray. The Smarts couldn't return the dead heroes to their families, but they could find a way to return a frightened little girl to her distressed parents.

"Hey, Ryan and Blair," greeted Echo after the Smarts exited the Ranger. The solemn looks on their faces spoke volumes. Echo was a man who understood sacrifice because he'd lost the life of a daughter during her service as a law enforcement officer. The Echols had been visited by a police notification team, a moment in their lives that had left an indelible mark on Echo. He walked up to them both and gave them a genuine, heartfelt hug. "Are you guys okay?"

Blair smiled and nodded. "That was one of the hardest things I've done in my life. But, honestly, Echo, after our last visit, looking at that wife and her two young kids, I just got angry. I'm furious that this happened to us. I realized that we have a huge responsibility to all of these people. And now we have a chance to save one of our own if we can just find her."

"How can I help?" asked Echo.

"First off," Ryan started to answer. He pointed toward the toolshed. "Has he said anything?"

"No, not really," replied Echo. "He's not aware of everything that's happened. Remember, he was locked up just as everything went south. He peed himself because a few stray rounds stitched holes along the back of the shed. I got him some pants and helped him change. That's about it."

"You went to his place?" asked Blair.

"Yeah. It looks like a Radio Shack in there. He barely has a place to sleep with all of that computer crap."

Ryan wandered toward the shed, turning his back to Echo. "Did it look like he was trying to pack up? You know, like he planned on leaving."

Echo shook his head. "No, not at all. In fact, all of his monitors were still turned on. He has spiral notebooks lying open on several folding tables. It just looked like a messy office space for six secretaries, but of course, it's just him."

Blair motioned for Ryan to come closer. She began to whisper, "I have an idea."

"What's that?" asked Ryan.

"Let's play good cop, bad cop," she replied. "We'll work as a team and break him down."

Ryan chuckled. "Let me guess, you wanna be the bad cop."

"No, not this time. Although, if my plan doesn't work, then I'll turn into the worst kind of cop Eugene O'Reilly ever imagined. You're the bad cop this go-around."

"Me? I don't know …" Ryan's voice trailed off with uncertainty.

Blair eased closer to him and looked up into his eyes. "This will work. I want you to go in there like you've lost your damn mind. He has to fear for his life. Do you understand me?"

"I am pissed off and I'd love to take it out on somebody," said Ryan. "The guy who snatched Hannah is whom I had in mind, though."

Blair patted her husband on the chest. "I think X-Ray can help us find Hannah and whoever's behind all of this. You go in there and pound the crap out of him emotionally. Hell, slug him if you have to."

"I can pull his long hair," interjected Ryan.

"Hubs, you can kick him between the legs for all I care. Just scare the crap out of him and I'll come to his rescue."

Ryan nodded. "He'll be just as afraid of you."

"Good, and he should be. I'll take him back to his cabin and put him to work. But know this, my hand will be resting on my pistol grip the whole time. I'll put him down like a dog if he screws up."

Ryan took a deep breath and conjured up the visions of the grieving families and the anger he felt when he thought of wrapping his hands around the throats of the people responsible for their husbands' deaths. He suddenly turned and stormed away from Echo and Blair.

Playing his role, Echo shouted after him, "Ryan, wait! You can't do that to him! Doesn't he have the right to a trial or—"

"Hell no!" Ryan shouted, cutting off Echo's question. Simultaneously, he kicked open the old wooden door, slinging it open until it slammed against the wall and nearly off the rusty hinges.

Light filled the darkened space, illuminating X-Ray hugging a round support pole in the middle of the shed, his hands tied together with two sets of zip-tie cuffs.

"Wait. Ryan, what's the matter?" asked X-Ray, fear in his eyes.

Ryan stormed toward him, reached down and removed his Morakniv blade from its sheath. He raised it high over his head and plunged it toward the much shorter X-Ray, barely missing the man's ear as the tip of the knife embedded in the wood post.

"Oh my god!" X-Ray shouted as he slid down the pole to avoid Ryan's attempt to skewer his skull. "What? Why are you doing this? Help! Echo!"

"Shut up!" Ryan screamed in X-Ray's face so loud that spittle flew out of his mouth and drenched the man's cheeks. He wrestled with the knife to extract it from the post. Ryan's anger had caused it to go more than an inch in the wood.

"Ryan, please. Please. Don't kill me!" X-Ray twisted back and forth in an effort to put the pole between him and Ryan. This only served to give Ryan another method of intimidation.

He grabbed X-Ray's longish hair and slammed his head against the pole. He reached around the pole with his right hand and pushed the blade up against X-Ray's throat.

Ryan's voice was low, guttural, animalistic. He was no longer acting or playing a part. "I'm gonna watch you bleed out. This is for the people who died today. And the little girl they stole from us! This is all on you, pal!"

"No! No! I didn't know, um. Come on, Ryan. I can—arrrgggh!"

X-Ray screamed in agony as Ryan got a little too close to his throat with the knife, breaking the skin just below the Adam's apple. Ryan's grip on the knife loosened somewhat as X-Ray began to sob and beg for his life.

"Puhleeze, Ryan. I can fix this. Help!"

Blair rushed into the toolshed, leaving Echo outside to prevent anyone from responding to X-Ray's pleas for help. "Ryan! Ryan, stop! Don't do this!"

"Why shouldn't I gut him?" he shouted back to her. "This guy, this piece of crap, got three of our people killed. And now Hannah has been kidnapped. What do you think they're gonna do to that poor little girl?"

Ryan jerked X-Ray's head back against the post with a thud. He then jerked it to the side, exposing the prisoner's carotid artery. Back in control of his emotions, he sneered as he brought the knife up against X-Ray's neck once again. X-Ray tried to crane his neck to pull away, but Ryan's grip was too strong.

"I understand that," Blair said in a calming voice. She circled around to face X-Ray, which was when she saw the steady trickle of blood emanating from the wound in his neck. Her eyes grew wide in surprise before she continued. "We need to have a trial. We're not barbarians here."

"Those guys who killed our people didn't offer up a trial first. That's BS. What about Hannah? Do you think they're giving her a trial? What are they gonna do—?"

"Hannah? They took Hannah?" X-Ray repeated the question.

Ryan made eye contact with Blair. The two understood each other completely without uttering a word or twitching an eye. It was time for Blair to take over.

Good cop, for now.

"Yes, Eugene, the men who attacked us killed three, wounded several others, and kidnapped Hannah. That darling little girl was practically yanked from the arms of her mother and whisked away."

"All because of me," mumbled X-Ray. In that moment, he took full responsibility for what had happened at the Haven that day. He realized his seemingly innocent response to a text had had dire consequences for the Cortland family. Tears began to flow down his cheeks, mixing with the blood that now covered his sweatshirt. "Please let me help you find her. I can. I promise."

He was broken.

CHAPTER 7

X-Ray's Cabin
The Haven

It was dark when Blair escorted X-Ray back into his cabin at gunpoint. Two guards were assigned to the perimeter along the riverfront, so Blair was confident she could call for backup if X-Ray tried to make a move. She didn't trust him and assumed he had weapons stashed throughout his living space. While he changed out of his bloody clothes, she didn't turn her head to provide the young man some privacy. Instead, in an act of intimidation, she watched him carefully, pointing her sidearm at his chest as he undressed.

"Eugene," began Blair, who no longer considered the young man a part of the Haven and therefore refused to recognize his nickname of X-Ray regardless of who had given it to him. "Do not mistake my kindness for weakness. Are we clear?"

"Yes, I understand," he replied, holding his hands in the air as he made his way into his living room.

"Seriously, I will shoot you. In fact, I want to."

"Please don't. I promise you. I want to make this right, even if it means I'm expelled from the Haven. I owe it to those people who died. I owe it to the Cortlands and Hannah, whom I genuinely like."

"I'm sure you do," said Blair with a hint of snark. She motioned with the barrel of her gun for X-Ray to sit down at the computer and get to work.

He pulled the small office chair out from under the folding table he used as a desk. He nervously wiped the sweat off his palms. He took a deep breath and studied his monitors that displayed various screensavers. One home screen showed a painting of George

Washington in a skiff, crossing the Delaware River on Christmas night in 1776.

"Nice touch," said Blair, complimenting X-Ray for his choice.

X-Ray spoke calmly as he prepared his workspace. "It was a masterful attack, one that surprised the drunken Hessians. The biggest mistake an adversary can make is to let their guard down."

Blair couldn't resist. "Like we did with you?"

X-Ray closed his eyes and shook his head. "Fair enough," he replied. He then turned in his chair and asked, "May I address something that you said at the dining table when we spoke?"

"Might as well," replied Blair.

"You obviously have a knack for internet research, which explains how you came across some of my alternate social media handles. I want you to know that it's not what you think."

Blair laughed. "Well, Eugene, what should I think? You have an alter ego that likes to troll the web, engaging in chat rooms with high school girls. Let me get right to it. Are you a pedophile?"

This riled X-Ray, who set his jaw and sat taller in his chair. "No, I am not, obviously."

"Doesn't seem so obvious to me," Blair shot back.

"I'm not, Blair, and you know it. Otherwise, you wouldn't have let me within a hundred miles of this place."

Blair sniggered. "Just because I couldn't prove it to be true doesn't mean I can't have my suspicions."

"You are aware, of course, that was several years ago. At the time, I was nineteen."

"Twenty," interrupted Blair.

"Fine, for a while, I was twenty," said X-Ray defensively. "I was immature for my age and couldn't relate to college girls. I was only comfortable interacting with younger women."

"They were teenagers! High schoolers, for Pete's sake."

"True, and they were only a few years younger than me. Think about it. How much older is Ryan than you?"

"Fourteen—" Blair began to respond before catching herself. This conversation was irrelevant to the task at hand. "There's a huge difference. We were both adults when we met. You were trolling for kids."

"Teens, and they were just a few years younger than me."

"Jeez, Eugene, who cares. I don't, or you wouldn't be here, like you said. What I do care about is finding Hannah. Now, get on the stick or you'll be of no use to us. *Comprende?*"

He nodded and swung around to his keyboard. He banged away, deftly switching from window to window on his multiple monitors. At one point, he stopped, flexed his fingers and exhaled.

"Good. I'm not locked out."

Blair looked over his shoulder and saw the official seal of the National Security Agency. "You're on the NSA website?"

"Sort of, I mean, not the public NSA.gov that you might expect. This is their encrypted interagency domain that can be accessed by the Defense Department and the FBI."

"Hold up," cautioned Blair. "Can they trace that back to here?"

"Their servers think I'm in the Dallas office of the FBI. I used a VPN, virtual private network, to mask my identity and location."

"Did you hack in?"

"Oh, no. I have a user name and password, provided by my handlers."

Blair shook her head in disbelief. This young-looking, still pimple-faced young man, who just a few years ago was flirting with teenage girls online, had access to the NSA's databases and surveillance tools.

"What's your plan?"

"I'm going to access their satellite footage. I'm hoping that, under the circumstances, they devoted more resources to the U.S. mainland in order to assist law enforcement and the National Guard as they deal with the uprisings."

"Makes sense," said Blair as she leaned over his shoulder to get a better look. For the first time, she holstered her pistol, but kept her hand resting on the grip, just in case.

"From what you guys just told me, there had to be at least four vehicles bringing the attackers and their ladders to the Haven. There may have been one or two on the other side of the river, but we won't concern ourselves with that just yet."

X-Ray began to navigate through the NSA's subwebs in search of satellite footage from the last twenty-four hours. It took fifteen minutes, but he eventually found two feeds that covered North and South Carolina.

"All right, as we know, traffic from the interstate toward the Haven is sparse. Any cars or trucks coming down Henry River Road, especially with extension ladders strapped on the roof, are important. I'm gonna start the feeds on both of these monitors. You watch the left and I'll watch the right."

"Got it."

X-Ray set the speed of the feed replays at 2x, fast enough to cut their viewing time in half, but also not so fast that they'd miss the approaching vehicles. After forty minutes, they had struck out.

"Do you have any other ideas?" asked Blair as she stood upright from her hunched-over position to crack her back.

"We have to stick with it," replied X-Ray. "It's possible they waited until the last minute to get set up. When exactly did the attack occur?"

"Right about the time the morning meeting was breaking up. The morning shift was coming—"

"That's it!" exclaimed X-Ray. "They must've been watching us prior to the attack. Hang on."

He adjusted the speed to 4x, causing the camera to zip along faster, but still allowing them to notice vehicles heading south toward the Haven.

The time stamp on the footage registered five in the morning when Blair pointed at her monitor. "There! There's the first one. It was a white van. There were four ladders strapped to the top."

X-Ray paused his monitor and focused entirely on the footage that Blair pointed out. The two of them watched as five trucks or vans, separated by five minutes, drove down the road and eventually turned off into the woods in various spots.

"That's them," X-Ray declared as he leaned back in his chair and clasped his fingers behind his head. "Now we have to follow them back to their nest after the fight's over."

Blair breathed a sigh of relief and pulled her radio off her jean's waistband. "Ryan, you copy?"

"Go ahead."

"We've got something."

"On my way."

Blair and X-Ray continued to watch the footage, which didn't allow them to see any of the attack due to the extensive tree cover. However, when the battle was over, X-Ray zoomed in to see everyone gathering in the clearing in front of Haven Barn. He paused the camera replay until Ryan arrived.

CHAPTER 8

Armageddon Hospital
The Haven

Alpha stood vigil over Frankie's body, much to the chagrin of the comatose man's attending physician, Angela. The hulk-like man towered over the gurney and frequently got in the way as Angela was trying to attend to the other injured patients. Gradually, as the evening progressed, everyone was sent back to their cabins except for Tom, who remained under the watchful eye of Donna.

Angela had tried repeatedly to send Alpha out the door, encouraging him to get some rest, check on his team, and even attempted to fool him into running an errand. He didn't fall for any of it.

Finally, an exhausted Angela rolled a gurney into her office and stretched out on it to catch a few winks. Before she did, she made sure Tom had a pistol tucked under his sheets. She instructed him to shoot Alpha if he tried to harm Frankie, although she wasn't sure if he'd do it.

"You know," Alpha began, breaking a long period of silence in the large open space within the hospital, "stupid people are like glow sticks. You just wanna snap them and shake the crap out of them until the light comes on. This guy, lying there in a coma, isn't much different. Maybe if I jerk him around a little bit, he'll magically wake up?"

The tone and tenor of Alpha's voice concerned Tom enough to reach for the handgun for the first time. Before it came to threatening Alpha, Tom tried the diplomatic approach. "Hey, I get it, big guy. I could do it with one good arm, but I don't think it will work."

"So the doc says," grumbled Alpha. "Still, we've got to do something to get this thing off dead center. Every hour that passes is bad news for the kid, you know?"

Donna stood and walked over to Alpha. She gave him a grandmotherly hug. "Why don't you come sit with us?" she asked, encouraging the big man to stop being fixated on Frankie.

He dropped his head, revealing his mental and physical exhaustion for the first time. "Thanks, but I don't wanna miss the opportunity to question this clown. He may only come alive for a second. I need to get the name of the place where those asshats hang out. Just one word. A street. Anything."

Suddenly, the door opened, and Delta entered the hospital. He'd stayed away since the earlier encounter with Blair and Karen. Donna moved to stand between Delta and Frankie. If Will went into a rage and attacked Frankie, she wasn't sure Alpha would stop him.

Delta gently closed the door behind him and stared in Frankie's direction. His face was sullen and withdrawn. He'd been losing weight since he'd arrived at the Haven, a combination of more exercise and a leaner diet. His clothes hung on him, and the stress caused him to look many years older than he was.

"Anything new?" he asked calmly.

"Nada," replied Alpha. "Hey, man, I'm sorry about what happened to your kid. I'll be honest, I was kinda put out with him before. Today, he really stepped up."

Delta smiled and acknowledged Alpha's kind words. "He saved my life. By doing so, however, he put the other kids at risk when he left them alone."

Donna moved to console Delta. "Things happen, and it doesn't make any sense to point fingers of blame or take on the burden of guilt. It wasn't Ethan's job to protect the children. It was all of ours, and especially the two guards who left their post."

"Yeah, but if Frankie hadn't been here, and if I'd just taken everyone and left." Delta's voice trailed off.

"Woulda, shoulda, coulda," said Tom in all seriousness. "There are a lot of things we'd like to have a do-over on, including the events of the last twenty-four hours. Now, we regroup, heal as a family, which is what we are now, and get Hannah home. Back to the Haven."

Delta looked down to Donna and gave her a reassuring smile. He walked toward Frankie's gurney, and Alpha hesitated before stepping aside. His baritone voice whispered to Delta, "You good, buddy?"

Delta nodded. He walked up to Frankie's lifeless body. "He used to be my partner. We had each other's backs, once."

Alpha said, "Things change. People change."

"Yeah, I guess so." Delta turned and rubbed his hands through his disheveled hair. "Has Ryan talked about what we're gonna do with him when he gives up the location of his new friends?"

Tom answered, "We haven't gotten that far yet. Our focus has been on keeping him alive."

"I suppose they'll call the police," Donna suggested. "I mean, technically, he is a murderer and should be arrested."

"That's not gonna happen," said Delta as he cast a steely glare at Frankie's body. "I'll kill him myself before he leaves the Haven."

Donna tried to calm down the former law enforcement officer. "I don't think that's a good idea. I mean, you could be charged with murder."

"I don't trust the system anymore, Donna. I can't have Frankie possibly walking free and coming back here. It's better to be judged by twelve than carried by six."

Delta's words hung in the air when Alpha exclaimed, "Hey, I saw his fingers move. No doubt about it. His fingers just wiggled."

"I'll get Angela," said Donna as she gently tapped on the office door and opened it.

"I want him to see my face first," Delta insisted. "He needs to know he murdered Ethan."

CHAPTER 9

George Trowbridge's Residence
Near Pine Orchard, Connecticut

For patients suffering from end-stage renal disease, or ESRD, the most common cause of sudden death was hyperkalemia that resulted from missed dialysis or an improper diet. Overall, death for those on dialysis was caused by cardiovascular failure. Over time, George Trowbridge had progressively lost the function of his kidneys. Commensurate with his advance toward ESRD, his cardiovascular system weakened, making him susceptible to a heart attack, angina, and stroke.

Trowbridge was nearing the end of his life. The pumping power of his heart muscles was decreasing due to the fluid buildup around the most vital organ in the human body. In recent days, he'd begun to experience a persistent, chronic cough, nausea, and some swelling around his ankles that was diagnosed by his caregivers as edema.

The once healthy, virile man was approaching the end of his life on earth, and it became a cause of concern for Harris, the man who'd stood by Trowbridge's side for years. He paced the floor as the medical professionals finished up their testing and made Trowbridge more comfortable. When they completed their examination, Harris followed them out of the master bedroom suite and closed the large solid wood door behind them.

"He's getting worse, and now he's slipping in and out of consciousness," began Harris as he expressed his concern to the medical team.

The physician, who'd cared for Trowbridge from the beginning, was frank in his response. "He's held on longer than most in his condition, a testament to the man's inner strength and resolve. That said, however, the mortality rate for someone who is this advanced with ESRD is around seventy-five percent. Yes, he will most certainly die, as will we all."

"When? Imminent?" asked Harris.

"No, not necessarily. To be sure, he is nearing the end of his life, but I believe what you have observed over the last day or so is as much a reaction to stress as a product of his condition."

"Are you positive?" Harris was not convinced. Then he got to the crux of the matter. "Mr. Trowbridge, as you know, is a powerful man. Arrangements need to be made. Also, he has a daughter and a granddaughter. He's very close to his son-in-law."

"I am aware of his family," the doctor interrupted.

"In the past, Mr. Trowbridge has instructed me to keep his daughter in the dark about the condition of his health. Only his son-in-law is fully aware, and he's been asked to keep it confidential."

"Yes. Again, I'm aware of his wishes."

"It'll be a travesty if he doesn't have the opportunity to reconcile with his daughter before his death. Do I need to summon them to his bedside or not?"

The doctor wandered over to the large windows that looked out over the Trowbridge estate and beyond to Long Island Sound. Several patrol boats meandered along the shoreline, and a couple of two-man patrols traversed the soggy grounds.

Without taking his gaze away from the security team's activities, the doctor finally responded, "No, not yet. Unless he requests it, of course. George and I have discussed this at length in the past, and I am very much aware of his wishes. I am also cognizant of the fact that a decision will need to be made at some point to gather the loved ones around the deathbed, to be blunt."

He turned to Harris, smiled, and continued. "To ease your mind, we're not at that point yet. The best thing you can do to help your boss is to take away his stressors. Mr. Harris, I know you well enough to say that you can handle just about anything, and George would give you his blessing. Give him good news if you have any. Deal with the bad on your own."

Harris furrowed his brow as he considered the doctor's advice. The doctor was suggesting that Harris undertake a course of action that was tantamount to treason in Trowbridge's mind. But if it kept the old man alive a little longer, then treason it shall be.

Harris saw the doctor and his team to the door before stopping by the head of security's temporary office on the main floor of the mansion. Trowbridge hadn't entertained more than a couple of guests at a given time in the two years since his kidney disease had progressed. Just prior to the New Year's Eve attacks, Harris had increased security with a handpicked team of operatives capable of both defending his boss and eliminating any threat through assassination or other means.

As a result of the increased security presence, the main floor more closely resembled the lobby of a major financial institution, heavily guarded with a constant influx of armed personnel. Gone were the days of entertaining politicians and foreign dignitaries. Now the only activity was related to Trowbridge's protection and keeping him alive.

"What's the latest on Briscoe's whereabouts?" asked Harris as he marched into the security chief's temporary office in the keeping room adjacent to the kitchen.

"His escape was inexcusable," he began in response. "I've just learned that he murdered the caretaker of the property and his wife. We have a lead on a vehicle he stole, and ordinarily, I'd alert police in the tristate area."

"No cops! We don't want him alive," Harris ordered. "The last thing we need is Hanson Briscoe trying to save his hide by snitching out all of his associates. There's too much to lose."

"I understand, and that's why we're monitoring all police frequencies. If they pick him up, we'll take him out. Although, the last thing we want is any cops losing their lives in the process."

Harris shook his head and shoved his hands in his pants pockets. "That's regrettable, but it can't be helped."

"Yes, sir. I agree." The security chief motioned for Harris to sit down, but he declined.

"What about Jonathan Schwartz? He never struck me as being very resourceful, but he is his father's son."

"He's a ghost, sir," replied the former U.S. Marshal hired by Harris many years ago. "At first, we relied upon the FBI to canvass the area around the airport and to seal off the Schwartz estate. Then we called upon our own resources to look under every rock."

"Well, he certainly has resources of his own, but I suspect he's quite paranoid under the circumstances," said Harris.

"Sir, he could be holed up anywhere, hoping to weather the storm."

Harris sighed. "Okay, keep me informed."

He walked into the kitchen, retrieved a small bottle of Perrier, and then suddenly stopped.

The head of security noticed his abrupt turn back toward the keeping room. "Is there something else, sir?"

Harris thought for a moment and then replied, "Write this down. *Hunger Games* movie set. It's in North Carolina. Find it on a map and then dispatch one of our choppers down that way, but not too close. I don't want it to be seen."

"Yes, sir. Will do, but it'll take a couple of days to make the arrangements."

Harris added to his request. "That's fine. Also, I want a trusted team. They need to be pilots, but also soldiers, understand?"

"Yessir. What else?"

"This op needs to be discreet," replied Harris. "Let me think." Harris paced the floor for a moment and then scrolled his smartphone, studying his contacts.

While he did so, the head of security placed a phone call. "Okay, day after tomorrow, I'll have a crew ready."

"I'll need them to pick up two passengers along the way," said Harris as he picked up a pad and pen off the desk. He began to write as he added, "Here are their names and location. Give them this note to deliver." Harris continued to write and then exhaled.

"Will do, sir."

"After they've touched down at a nearby, secure landing area, I want the men being picked up to deliver this message to Tom Shelton, who is residing at this location. They must only speak with Shelton."

"Of course, sir. What's the message?"

Harris backed toward the door. "Simply advise Shelton that the chopper and its crew are at his disposal if needed. It's all explained in the note I gave you."

"That's it? How long will the crew be assigned to this operation?"

"As long as necessary, but if you're worried about manpower, prepare to rotate another crew in and out."

Harris loitered for a moment and then left without another word. He didn't want to overstep his boss's orders, but he wanted a helicopter available in the event he needed to rush the Cortland family to the estate. Shelton could be trusted to make levelheaded decisions, so he entrusted the keys to the chopper, so to speak, to him.

Trowbridge's right-hand man made his way up the marble stairs toward the landing that overlooked the sound. He turned to take in the large ornate grand foyer, which had hosted so many rich and powerful people over the years. He wondered what would become of it after his boss's death. Would it die along with the old man's legacy?

CHAPTER 10

X-Ray's Cabin
The Haven

While Blair and X-Ray awaited Ryan's arrival, the computer geek continued to watch the footage to determine if as many cars left the area outside the Haven's walls as had initially traveled down Henry River Road. They were both relieved when the satellite feed indicated that all of them had left together, racing at a high rate of speed onto Interstate 40 eastbound.

Blair turned her back on X-Ray for a brief moment as she heard the sound of a four-wheeler approaching. She walked to the windows at the front of X-Ray's cabin to confirm it was Ryan.

X-Ray glanced over his shoulder and saw that he was not being monitored. This was the moment of truth, and his mind raced to weigh his options.

At this point, his decision was not based upon loyalties but, rather, self-preservation. Who was more likely to kill him? Those within the Haven, who believe he betrayed them all, or his handlers, the ones with powerful contacts and even more powerful weapons, capable of dropping a bomb on his head with a push of a button.

His handlers, the leaders of the Minutemen, had orchestrated the greatest attack on America in its history. However, he was but a small cog in their wheel. On the other hand, he was now a prisoner in the hands of people who held him responsible for the attack on their home, the death of several within their community, and now the kidnapping of a young girl.

Who would I rather piss off? If I can't follow where the cars went, will these people know my failure was intentional? Will the handlers know if I help recover

Hannah? What's the safest thing for Eugene O'Reilly?

"Come on in, Ryan," said Blair, who held the door open for her husband, allowing a rush of cold air into the cabin. In their haste to get started, Blair and X-Ray hadn't built a fire in the fireplace.

"What've you got?" asked Ryan as he motioned toward X-Ray.

Blair followed him and was about to respond when she noticed the monitor had gone blank. She reached for her sidearm and demanded, "What the hell?"

"Oh, sorry," X-Ray replied. "Um, I turned the monitor off just in case it wasn't Ryan. Here, I'll power it up again."

Ryan and Blair exchanged skeptical looks. When the display reemerged, the satellite feed was paused on the barnyard again, showing the group milling about as they realized Hannah had been kidnapped.

"Come on, Eugene," said Blair angrily. "We're way beyond this point. We'd found the vehicles and you were tracking them back to the interstate. Why did you start over?"

"Um, well, I thought Ryan would want to see it all for himself." He nervously stammered over his words as he responded. He was buying time. He wasn't sure which side to choose.

"Out with it!" Blair suddenly shouted, startling both men.

"Honey, I don't understand. Why is this important?"

"Because he's jackin' us around, that's why!" She ripped the pistol out of her paddle holster and cocked the hammer. She pointed it at the back of X-Ray's head, who was now trembling in utter fear.

"No. No," he continued to stammer. "I can bring us back to where we were. Hold on." X-Ray rapidly moved his mouse around the screen and used the arrow keys on his keyboard to reposition the camera's orientation on the vehicles as they headed up the ramp to Interstate 40.

Blair leaned forward and growled into X-Ray's ear, "Don't try me or you'll never walk out of here alive. Make no mistake, I'm your judge and executioner."

With X-Ray sweating profusely, he expertly followed the vehicle caravan down back roads toward Charlotte and ultimately to the

Varnadore Building. The process of tracing the steps of the retreating attackers took nearly an hour, but the Smarts were satisfied they'd found the location where Hannah was being held.

"Can you get an address for this place?" asked Ryan before adding, "It looks like an office building. Weird, though. It's all by itself off the highway."

X-Ray tapped a few keys, producing a map overlay of the satellite video feed. He reached across the table and pulled one of his spiral notebooks closer. He jotted down the street names, mumbling them aloud as he did.

"North side of East Independence Boulevard. West of Pierson. South of Winfield." He paused and then turned around to the Smarts. "Okay, with this information, if I can access the Mecklenburg County Property Assessor's records, I can get a physical address and ownership information, if you're interested."

Ryan didn't say anything for a moment, and then he leaned into Blair. "We need to think about this and talk."

"Okay, but I'm not leaving this squirrely guy alone."

Ryan nodded and raised Alpha on the radio. At first, Alpha objected, but Ryan insisted. If a rescue was going to be mounted, Alpha would be leading the teams. He was the one who needed questions answered regarding this office building and its surroundings.

After Alpha arrived, Ryan and Blair brought him up to speed, and he quickly got to work with X-Ray to learn about where Hannah was being held. After saying their goodbyes, the Smarts walked to the Ranger, but Blair suddenly paused before leaving.

"Listen to that," said Blair. "What do you hear?"

Ryan slowly turned in a circle, straining to listen. "I'm sorry, honey. I don't hear anything."

"Exactly. This is the way it was supposed to be. Quiet. Serene. A place to ride out the storm without drama. Now look."

"Hey, as the old song goes, I never promised you a rose garden. In fact, if you recall, Mrs. Smart, I said you'd, A, never be bored and, B, be treated to a never-ending supply of adventures."

"But …" Blair folded her arms and feigned a pout. She was just glad to be alone with her husband again.

"You were warned, missy," said Ryan as he drew his wife close to him.

"Yeah. Yeah. Kiss me before I beat you."

CHAPTER 11

Haven House
The Haven

Ryan and Blair's quiet moment alone was short-lived. When they returned to Haven House, the Cortlands were sitting on the front porch in the Adirondack chairs. They both stood in unison as the Ranger came to a stop, headlights still illuminating the parents as Ryan shut off the motor.

Blair was the first to exit. "Hey, are you guys okay?"

Meredith rushed towards Blair, and the two hugged. Tears rushed out of Meredith's eyes as her emotions took over once again. "I'm sorry, Blair. I thought I'd stopped crying. I don't know, it's just—God, this really sucks and I'm so frightened."

"Hey, of course you are. We all are. We might have a breakthrough." Blair's words comforted Meredith. Wiping away the tears, she appeared hopeful.

"What have you learned?" asked Cort.

"I have an idea," said Ryan. "If there was ever a time for an adult beverage, today is the day. Wouldn't y'all agree?"

"How about a glass of wine, Meredith?" asked Blair.

"Maybe two?" Meredith replied with a laugh that was coupled with a long sniffle.

"Scotch for me," said Cort.

"Come on in, Cort. I've got a bottle of Glenlivet that was given to me by a fellow from Boston. Let's bust it open and try to relax while we tell you the latest."

Within seconds of entering the house, they were greeted by the princesses, who were followed closely behind by Handsome Dan.

The unconditional love shown to them by their furbabies warmed their hearts before the first glass of alcohol was poured.

While Ryan poured the drinks, he checked in with Angela to get an update on Frankie's condition. With no change, he quickly provided the Cortlands details of what Blair and X-Ray had discovered via the NSA website.

The two couples discussed their various options, and Ryan cautioned there was still a lot to learn about the location where Hannah appeared to have been taken to. He completely trusted in Alpha to formulate a rescue plan, but Frankie's recovery would help even more because he'd likely been inside the building.

Blair invited Meredith into the kitchen to put together a tray of munchie-type foods, which allowed Ryan to spirit Cort away to the study, where they could speak in private.

Cort had a concerned look on his face. "Is there something else? Something you can't say in front of Meredith?"

"No, it's not that," replied Ryan, who continuously glanced at the doorway to make sure they were alone. He didn't want to close his door, as that would draw unnecessary curiosity. "Cort, I have to ask this question. And let me say that your answer in no way affects our decision to rescue Hannah."

"Okay. What is it?"

Ryan took a swig of the scotch and grimaced at the strong taste. There was a reason the bottle had never been opened since his trip to Boston a year ago. He didn't really like the hard stuff.

"I understand about the situation between Meredith and your father-in-law. But maybe we should consider asking for his help. I mean, clearly the man has resources we could only dream of."

Cort wandered around the study, contemplating Ryan's question. "You've got a point, Ryan. However, I'm not sure whom I can trust. Think about it. These people have eyes and ears everywhere. X-Ray was on their payroll. Tom Shelton used to work for Trowbridge. For all I know, you guys are old pals with him."

"I wish," said Ryan. "We'd be up at his place, most likely surrounded by Navy SEALs or Delta Force."

"You see my point, right? The tentacles of these people reach far and wide. I could make matters worse if I'm not careful."

Ryan nodded his agreement. "Listen, I have a lot of confidence in our people. We brought them on board because they have a variety of skills, but most importantly they are loyal. Not only to one another, but to all of us who live here at the Haven. I trust them with my family's lives, and I know they're capable of getting that darling little girl back to her parents."

Cort finished off his scotch and raised his glass to show his agreement with Ryan. "Okay, if they're on board, so am I. I'll speak with Alpha as soon as we're done here. I'm going with the team."

"No." Ryan shocked Cort with one word.

"What? Yes, I absolutely will go to rescue my daughter."

Ryan was adamant as he too finished off his drink. "No, Cort. No way in hell. You're too emotional and untrained. Let the professionals do this."

Cort rubbed his forehead. "How can I possibly stay here and let someone else rescue Hannah?"

"Because it's the smart thing to do, and I'm gonna need you here," answered Ryan. "We'll be sending our best security personnel out of the Haven to rescue Hannah. What if this whole thing is a ploy to draw away our resources and attack us again? I'm gonna need you to help me defend this place."

Cort's shoulders drooped, indicating his acquiescence. "Of course, you're right. It's just … It's gonna be hard. You know, the waiting."

"The reward will be when you guys are reunited with that adorable child."

CHAPTER 12

Armageddon Hospital
The Haven

Midnight had arrived and Angela was awakened from her long nap by Tyler. He'd dropped the kids off at the Haven House, along with Skylar Hightower, who was distraught over the death of her brother. The Rankins thought Skylar could use the help of kids her own age as they worked through the death of Ethan and the sudden disappearance of Hannah. Kids had a way of talking with one another that adults didn't understand.

What Angela hadn't anticipated was that the thoughtful gesture of grouping the kids together would free up the Hightowers to descend upon the hospital to hover over Frankie, who was still in a coma. She knew a little bit about their history, and although the death of a child should bring an estranged couple closer together, everybody reacted differently.

She rolled her head on her shoulders and stretched to work out the kinks received courtesy of the uncomfortable gurney. Tyler had offered to bring one of the kids' twin-size mattresses on the back of his medical cart for her to sleep on, but she didn't want to trouble him. Her stiff body was telling her that she'd made a poor choice.

"Hey, where did Tom and Donna go?" she asked as she entered a room suddenly empty except for the Hightowers.

"Well, Tom was complaining that he couldn't get comfortable," replied Tyler. "It got so bad that Donna threatened to maim him if he didn't stop. I took a look at him, changed his dressings, and sent them home so he could rest in his own bed."

"Babe, he was shot barely twelve hours ago," admonished Angela. "You can't send a GSW victim home that quickly."

"Agreed, but I'm tellin' ya, he was gonna go regardless. At least I checked him out before he left."

Angela sighed and then smiled. Crusty old codger.

"Angela, I hope you don't mind that we're here," said Karen. "We won't be any trouble, and I'll help out any way that I can."

"That's okay. I appreciate the offer. For now, we're just in a holding pattern. Excuse me while I check his vitals."

Will and Karen stepped away from the gurney, and Angela noticed that they were arm in arm. She furrowed her brow as she tried to make sense of the interesting family dynamic. Frankie had been an important part of their lives, first as Delta's respected partner on Philly SWAT and, later, as the man who occupied an angry wife's bed.

"Well, there's been no change. His heart rate and blood pressure are still lower than I'd like. We'll keep him hydrated and just keep a close eye on his recovery."

"He lost a lot of blood, didn't he?" asked Delta.

"Yeah. He had a previous head trauma, likely within the last several days. When that was reopened, the wound gushed blood. That, coupled with the blow to the temple, which likely tore the miniscule arteries that ensure blood flow to the brain, has placed his cardiovascular system in a perilous position."

"When will he wake up?" asked Karen.

Angela wasn't sure how she should answer the question. She was a doctor and, as such, she'd sworn to uphold the highest ethical standards when treating a patient. That said, she was fully aware there were competing interests within the Haven as it related to Frankie's health.

Some wished him dead. Others wanted him alive long enough to give them information. The Hightowers were a potential mixed bag. Delta most likely wanted Frankie to live just so he could kill his ex-partner himself. Who knew with Karen? Maybe she would take her old boyfriend back in.

After her nap, Angela was prepared to make a decision regarding Frankie's medically induced coma. As a woman and a mom, she empathized more with the plight of the Cortlands and the need to find Hannah. If he was stable, she'd planned on cutting back on his sedatives. Hannah's life was more important than Frankie's.

This was a secret she wouldn't even share with Tyler. It was one course of action she planned on doing alone, during the middle of the night, and without an audience. And now she was surrounded by onlookers.

"I have no idea," Angela finally responded. "The body does what the body wants. Guys, I appreciate your concern, and I know you both have reasons to be here, but please, go home. Let me do my job without distractions, okay? I'm all Frankie's got, and regardless of what he's done, he deserves my undivided attention."

Will nodded and pulled Karen away from the gurney. "She's right. Let's get some rest. There's nothing we can do except hover and get in the way."

Karen reluctantly agreed. "I know. Yes, you're right. Thanks for taking care of him. I mean, I'm with Will now, but, um—"

"I understand, Karen. Now, please. Let me take care of Frankie, and I'll send word the moment something happens. I promise."

The Hightowers agreed and quietly exited the hospital, leaving Tyler and Angela alone. Angela wandered around the open space, enjoying the emptiness while she could.

Tyler sensed she was distressed. "Babe? Is there something else?"

"Nah, I mean, well, maybe," she replied. "He needs to be in a hospital, but I don't think anyone here is willing to risk their life to take him there."

"Do you want me to do it?"

"No! No way. He's not worth it." Angela ran her fingers through her hair. "God, listen to me. I'm a doctor. I can't think like that."

"You're human, too, babe," said Tyler, who moved to embrace his wife. "Don't overthink it. Just keep him in a coma and see what happens."

Angela pulled away and walked toward the window behind

Frankie's gurney. Suddenly, she needed fresh air. She hated lying to Tyler.

"That's just it, Ty," she began. "I hadn't planned on giving him any more sedatives. In fact, nobody else knows this, but he's three hours overdue now. He could wake up anytime."

As if on cue, Frankie began to convulse. His body was shaking uncontrollably as his eyelids opened, revealing only the sclera.

"What's happening? Seizure?" asked a frantic Tyler.

"Stroke," said Angela as she moved into position to help her patient. Then, suddenly in a surreal moment of clarity, Frankie Scallone became still and breathlessly said his last word before he died.

"Chepe."

Part Two

CHAPTER 13

The Varnadore Building
Uptown Charlotte, North Carolina

Chepe intended to take a deep breath, hoping to revel in the ordinarily clean, crisp air as he strolled the rooftop of the Varnadore Building. However, the smell of smoke lay heavily in the cold air, as many parts of Charlotte had been set ablaze, in large part due to his activities. The rank odor of burning chemicals created a pungent taste in his mouth. It was the unmistakable perfume of anarchy.

The faraway sounds of sirens responding to pleas for help could be heard throughout the city. First responders, or at least those who still bothered to show up for work, were completely overwhelmed as the collapse took its toll on Charlotte. Chepe had been confronted by a firefighter while his group of anarchists was looting Lowe's. The man had admitted he was gathering supplies before his family left for East Tennessee.

The man had said that the cops and firefighters he knew had opted to protect their families first rather than risk their lives to defend a lost cause. He confirmed to Chepe that looting was rampant in all parts of the city, and those responsible were from all walks of life. Desperation and panic had set in as America descended into the abyss.

"I think we have everything in place, Chepe," announced one of his top lieutenants, who'd just emerged through the roof access stairwell. He stepped over a series of pipes and half walls to get closer to the undisputed leader of the Black Rose Federation. "I've got people posted throughout the building and within radio distance of our perimeter. When they come for us, we'll know it."

Chepe motioned for the man to join him next to the parapet wall overlooking the front entrance. "Did you put everyone out there like I asked?"

"Ten-four. They're already grumbling about the long shift, and all I promised the outsiders is that we'd rotate them inside, you know, to be fair."

"They'll be coming for us soon," said Chepe as he stared up and down Independence Boulevard. He was pensive, trying his best to put himself in the shoes of a distraught father who'd be desperate to recover his child. "I don't think it'll be during the day, but we have to be ready."

"Are you sure the guy won't come alone? You know, be the great dad and give himself up for the sake of his kid."

"He'll bring his wife for sure," replied Chepe. "I mean, there has to be somebody to hand the kid over to, right?"

"And that'll be it?" His lieutenant appeared skeptical.

Chepe abruptly turned to him. "Think about it. He knows he's gonna die. He'll make the ultimate sacrifice for his kid. Now, once we make the exchange, that's when the trouble will begin. They'll risk his life to try to get him back because they know he's a dead man anyway."

"What if they try to rescue the kid?"

"That would be real stupid, but I've thought of that. First off, we'll know they're coming, and even if they were to get into the building, I'll have some surprises for them. I call it the King Koopa defense."

"Huh?"

Chepe laughed and slapped his man on the back. "Come on, let's head inside and I'll explain."

The two made their way back into the attic access stairwell and walked down one level to the top floor of the Varnadore Building. It was the only floor in the building that hadn't been at least partially gutted.

Chepe explained, "King Koopa was the dragon-monster guy who had to be defeated in order to complete the *Super Mario* video game. I used to love playing classic Nintendo games as a kid, and in order to beat Bowser, or what most people called King Koopa, you had to get through a ton of bad guys and challenges. That's what I have in store for them if they think they're gonna rescue their little princess."

He and the lieutenant walked down the hallway, and Chepe pointed out features of the rooms that would be awaiting any potential rescuers.

"It's like a maze on this floor," commented the lieutenant.

Chepe laughed. "More like a house of horrors. They're gonna have to search each of these rooms after they enter the hallway through the stairwell. We'll have traps laid for each of them. If they manage to make it to the conference room at the end, they're gonna be surprised."

"Why's that?"

"Come on, I'll show you."

Chepe led the man into the large conference room, which doubled as an executive dining area. A professionally designed kitchen was located behind a set of double doors at the rear of the room. It was pitch black inside, as the power was not on and the kitchen had no windows. Chepe reached into his pocket and retrieved his lighter. He used the flame to look around.

"I can't see anything," said the lieutenant.

"Good. Now, they'll probably have flashlights, but they'll be hyped-up and anxious. They're not gonna check what's behind these cabinet doors."

The lieutenant slowly walked through and opened the cupboard doors above the countertops.

"Let me show you," said Chepe as he moved past the cooktop toward the end of a long stainless-steel table. He reached a two-door cabinet and knelt next to it. "Dammit!"

They were suddenly thrust into darkness.

"What?"

"I burnt my finger," complained Chepe, who switched hands and flicked his Bic once again. "Look, check this out."

He opened the doors, revealing a bottomless void inside. The lieutenant crawled on his hands and knees and looked inside.

"It's kinda dark down there. Is that a hole in the floor?"

Chepe replied, "Yeah. It's a laundry chute to a large basket below. We'll gather up all of our bed linens and blankets to fill it up. If they get this far, I'll take the girl down the chute and double back to the stairs. They'll think we were never here."

Chepe released the lighter and felt his way through the darkness into the conference room again. Once they were back in the hallway, he stopped and counted the office doors.

"What do you want me to do?"

"Gather up eight of your best people. I want them armed and ready to fight. I'll work with them on how to stage an ambush. If they do attack us, this floor will be where it ends."

"I'm on it," said the lieutenant. He turned to hustle toward the stairwell. "Oh, hey, Chepe. Where's the kid?"

"Nobody will know that except me. It's better that way."

CHAPTER 14

Haven Barn
The Haven

The mood was solemn as the bulk of the Haven's security team gathered at Haven Barn that morning. A skeleton crew, coupled with drone surveillance, monitored the perimeter while the residents buried their dead. Three men and Ethan Hightower were laid to rest in an emotional scene that left everyone in tears.

However, in the apocalypse, life goes on despite the death of a loved one, and everyone quickly pulled together in order to survive. Alpha gathered up his available personnel, and Ryan had the Sheltons, Rankins, and Cortlands join him at Haven Barn to discuss Hannah's rescue. Blair, who'd already been working with X-Ray on gathering information, was there with the young man who'd suddenly become an important part of saving Hannah, despite his previous poor choices.

The chatter rose to a crescendo as everyone discussed the events of the prior day. Ryan checked with Alpha and Blair to make sure they were ready to get started, and then he moved to quieten the crowd.

"Okay, everybody, listen up."

The chatter dropped to a low murmur, and eventually the group gathered in the barn to give Ryan their undivided attention.

"Thank you. Okay, first let me thank you all for keeping your chin up throughout this ordeal. We never expected to get attacked like we did yesterday. Well, at least not that soon, anyway. Sadly, I can't promise you that it'll be the last time, either."

"We'll be ready for the next bunch!" shouted a woman from the rear of the group.

Ryan pointed in her direction. "That's exactly right. We learned a lot yesterday, albeit the hard way. As a result, we'll be better prepared for an organized attack on the Haven if and when that might happen. That's part of the reason I've called all of you in this morning. The next twenty-four hours are critical to our safety and the life of a little girl."

"Are we gonna go get Hannah?" asked a man in the front.

"Yeah! We need to get her and then get even for what happened!" shouted another.

Ryan raised both hands and motioned to tamp down the enthusiasm. "That's certainly what we have in mind, but we have to be extremely careful. For one thing, we can't gut our security here. Hannah's kidnapping could be a ploy to induce us to weaken our defenses. The Haven needs to remain well protected for the benefit of all our people."

"What about Hannah?" asked the first woman who spoke up.

"We're going to put that plan into effect today. It will be carefully thought out and executed with precision. For that reason, I'm going to leave the planning and team selection up to Alpha. He will use his military experience and knowledge of you guys to determine who goes on the rescue operation."

Ryan stepped to the side and allowed Alpha to address the group. "Okay, I need the following people to meet me in the conference room. Bravo. Charlie. Delta." Alpha reeled off his top people who had military or law enforcement experience. He also selected six extra personnel to act as drivers and backup when the rescue operation was initiated. They all made their way into the conference room. The Cortlands, X-Ray, and Blair followed them.

Ryan took over once again. "Today and this evening, I'll be asking a lot of you guys. We're short of manpower because of the losses yesterday, and the fact that we've got to spend a considerable amount of time going over our rescue plan. Everybody will be pulling double shifts until we bring Hannah home tomorrow. I know it will be taxing on you physically and emotionally."

One of the men spoke up. "Don't you worry about us, Ryan."

"Yeah, we've got this," encouraged another before adding the sentiment of the entire group, "You make sure that little girl comes home safe and alive."

Ryan smiled and said thank you to those who'd keep the Haven safe while the others ventured outside the walls. He addressed the Rankins and Sheltons before he entered the conference room.

"Tom, shouldn't you be in bed resting?" he asked and then he turned to Angela. "Is he supposed to be up and about?"

She replied, "Yes, as to bed rest, and no, as to up and about."

"He's not good at following orders," interjected Donna.

"I was, back in the day," said Tom with a grin. "Now, not so much. Ryan, what can we do to help?"

Ryan looked at his loyal team and became emotional. "You guys are incredible. Thank you."

Angela was the first to hug the man who'd conceived of the Haven and carried the burden of protecting all of its residents. "Don't be stressed. We're here to help in any way we can."

Ryan smiled and thanked her. "Well, I've gotta spend the day planning this rescue, and then I'll be pacing the dang floor while it's going on. Blair won't let me go."

"Good," said Tom. "I saw whom Alpha chose, and he picked a good team. Your job is right here."

Ryan reluctantly agreed, and then he assigned duties to them. Angela would remain in charge of the hospital, but she'd check on Tom frequently, who was to stay at Haven House. Ryan asked him to constantly monitor the drone surveillance. He still wasn't positive that the kidnapping wasn't a form of misdirection.

He asked Tyler to take charge of the drone brigade in Alpha's absence. The Rankins agreed that their kids were able to resume their duties, and Tyler jumped at the chance to monitor their activities. Donna was asked to be a roving ambassador, of sorts. Her job was to check in with the injured personnel from the firefight, including her husband. Also, she was to stay in contact with the grieving families.

Ryan believed the first twenty-four hours were critical to holding the group together. The last thing he needed while they were shorthanded was unexpected drama. He'd already dealt with the sheriff that morning when he'd showed up with two deputies at the crack of dawn. Front gate security personnel hailed Ryan on the radio, and he sped down the gravel driveway to address the sheriff. When the sheriff said he'd been alerted to gunfire at the compound, Ryan deftly explained it away as target practice. The sheriff was skeptical, but legally, he had no basis for entering their private property without a warrant, which were in short supply, as no judges were reporting to their courtrooms.

After everyone finalized their new assignments, Ryan made his way into the conference room, where Alpha was laying out the basic approach he wanted to take to rescue Hannah. After he finished his initial remarks, Ryan added a few thoughts and told the group about their timetable.

Ryan was careful to choose his words wisely so he didn't unduly frighten Meredith and Cort. They were putting on a good front, but he knew they were torn up inside.

"Like Cort and Meredith, I'm very anxious to bring Hannah home to the Haven. Planning and execution are more important than rushing headlong into a firestorm, one that would most likely get people hurt."

Alpha took the floor. "If we were organizing this rescue through law enforcement or the military, we'd take days or even weeks to get ready. We'd create a mock-up of the building where Hannah is being kept. The teams would make multiple dry runs and then discuss tactics, strategies, and potential pitfalls."

"We're not going in there blind, are we?" asked Bravo. The seasoned military veteran was more than capable of taking down half of the anarchists by himself. "Not that I'd mind. Charlie and I'll kill every last one of 'em!"

He and Charlie exchanged fist bumps. "Oorah!"

Alpha continued. "Under normal conditions, both LEOs and the military personnel would have eyes in the sky, intel, and lots of fun hardware to give them an advantage. We have some things that will help us."

"Like what?" asked one of the backup security personnel.

"For one thing, we're smarter than they are, and we've got combat and law enforcement experience. The jerks we're up against, based upon what we've learned, are nothing more than a bunch of thugs who like to destroy other people's property. They're anarchists who rely upon fear and intimidation to succeed."

"We don't scare easy!" exclaimed Charlie.

Bravo quickly corrected her. "Hell, we don't scare at all!" The two high-fived and adjusted their tactical vests as if they were getting ready to attack at that moment.

"You're right," added Alpha. "We don't scare at all, and powered with the information X-Ray has for us, we're not going in blind either. Tell 'em, kid."

CHAPTER 15

Haven Barn
The Haven

X-Ray sheepishly took the floor. He was timid anyway, and in many respects unsure of himself. After betraying the group and giving information on Cort's whereabouts, he had a huge sense of guilt plaguing him, making it very difficult to face the people whose trust he'd broken.

He began by reminding them what his initial value was to the Haven—access. He had the ability to look inside the government's computers. While Blair prided herself on the ability to conduct background research using private investigative tools, by virtue of his role within the Minutemen network of hackers, X-Ray had been given the keys to the kingdom.

"I was able to access the servers at the NSA and FBI, which enabled me to further research records for Charlotte-Mecklenburg County. Can I summarize my findings?" he asked, turning toward Ryan.

"Yes, please. Regarding our approach to the building, however, we'll need to spend more time on the details of the property and its surroundings."

X-Ray nodded and continued. "Using the NSA satellite video archives, I was able to trace the attackers by their vehicles. I saw when they came in, and I followed them back to Charlotte after they left."

"Did you see Hannah?" asked Meredith.

"No, ma'am. Because of the tree cover, most of the grounds

around the Haven are obscured. I was only able to pick up the vehicles coming and going."

Meredith turned to Cort and he hugged her. "Thanks anyway," said Cort.

X-Ray moved to his laptop and powered on one of the television monitors mounted on the wall behind him. He used the television remote to find an open input, and then he returned to his laptop.

"Right now, using Bluetooth technology, I'm pairing the laptop with the monitor so you can have a look at what I found. Just give me a moment for the devices to hook up."

The group positioned themselves to have an unobstructed view around the monitor. Within seconds, the screen came to life and an aerial view of the Varnadore Building appeared.

"This is an abandoned office building that has been vacant for many years, according to property records. It's owned by a 501(c) charitable trust that was established by the Schwartz family in the eighties. It has changed hands a couple of times, but all within their vast network of charities or real estate entities."

"Why would they take her there?" asked one of the drivers.

X-Ray banged away on the keyboard and produced a mugshot that filled the screen. "Because of this guy. His name is Joseph Jose Acuff, also known as Chepe. When Frankie died just after midnight, the last word he uttered was *Chepe*. I spoke with Delta about this."

"That's right," said Delta as he raised his voice to get everyone's attention. "This guy was known for his anarchist activities in DC and Philly back when I was on the SWAT team. Frankie had arrested him on behalf of the feds. I didn't know they'd kept in touch."

X-Ray walked closer to the monitor. "Chepe is connected to the Schwartz family, the owners of the Varnadore Building. He's heavily involved with the Black Rose Federation, aka Rosa Negra."

"I saw their logos in DC and Richmond," interrupted Hayden. "There has to be a connection."

Ryan provided some more background. "Based upon my conversations with all of you, we believe that Chepe, using resources and direction from Jonathan Schwartz and his father, has been organizing unrest along the East Coast since the New Year's Eve attacks."

"Are they the ones responsible for what started all of this?" asked one of the drivers.

"I knew it! Schwartz is a liberal scumbag. Of course this is all his fault!" proclaimed another.

Ryan's eyes darted from Blair to Cort and then back to the group. "We don't have all the facts on what happened on New Year's Eve, and for now, we're focused on getting Hannah back." He paused and then gestured for X-Ray to continue.

The young man returned to the screen that displayed a satellite view of the building. "We are very fortunate to have this static perspective of the Varnadore. Ordinarily, the NSA satellites move in a synchronous orbit around the planet. However, it appears that due to the attacks, the ECHELON surveillance satellites have been placed into a stationary orbit."

"Echelon?" asked Bravo.

"Yeah, it's old technology, dating back to the cold war days of the sixties and seventies, but is still widely utilized by the NSA. For our purposes, it enables me to continuously monitor the Varnadore Building and its surroundings, but unfortunately, I don't have the control capabilities like zoom and infrared that are available to the operators within the NSA."

Bravo asked another question. "You were able to follow the vehicles back to the nest, right?"

"Yes, in the archived videos. That won't help us with the rescue. We're gonna need real-time footage so I can guide the teams in."

"What do you have in mind?" asked Blair.

X-Ray fidgeted and glanced over at Alpha. "We're gonna deploy our two infrared drones to help. Two of our drivers are also experienced drone operators. After the teams are dropped off to mount the rescue, they will operate the drones with my guidance."

"Wait, won't this guy Chepe and his people hear them? I mean, as quiet as it is, and with a lack of traffic, they'll be noticed as soon as they get close."

Alpha addressed Blair's concerns. "We're gonna create a loud diversion—one that leads their attention away from the point of insertion and also generates noise to mask the sound of the drones."

"The two teams will only need a few minutes to get past their perimeter defenses," added X-Ray. "The diversion will give them time, and the drone cameras will give them a set of eyes."

"Plus, we have our own night vision to assist," added Alpha.

He moved to a table behind him and picked up two black-zippered pouches. He opened one of them and pulled out a square device that resembled a small camera. He continued. "This is a night-vision monocular. It doesn't have the capability of those used by the military and private contractors, but for the money, it'll do for our purposes. It has six-times magnification, digital zoom, and is also capable of recording onto a micro SD card. Each team will have one of these that, coupled with X-Ray feeding us information from the drone, will allow us the ability to see in the dark."

X-Ray paused as Alpha finished discussing the benefits of night vision and also the two-way communications system the teams would use to keep in contact with X-Ray. Once he was finished, he turned his attention to the more difficult aspect of the operation. He returned to his laptop and, with a few keystrokes, pulled up a set of blue-lined drawings from the early sixties. They were the original schematics of the Varnadore Building when it was permitted for construction.

He explained as he flipped through the pages of the drawings using a program called *Scribd*. It was a digital library subscribed to by the NSA and embedded within their secured website.

"Although it won't be easy getting the two rescue teams inside the building, the real challenge begins with finding the needle in the proverbial haystack," began X-Ray. He caught himself as he made eye contact with Meredith. "Um, I'm sorry, ma'am. I meant no disrespect."

Meredith gave him a reassuring smile. "It's okay, X-Ray. Thank you for doing this. Please go on."

He nodded and continued. "Anyway, the building has been empty for over ten years, and during that time, vagrants and now Rosa Negra has occupied the space. I sat down with Echo just before our getting together this morning. He did business with the Varnadore company many years ago when they wanted to buy a part of his farm for a subdivision development. I learned a lot from him regarding the layout of the building. We'll plan the rescue operation based upon his recollection of the floor plan, and our expectations of how that might have changed over time."

One of the drivers raised his hand. "I noticed that you've referenced just two teams. Is that gonna be enough? I mean, we have lots of people capable of stormin' the place."

Ryan took the question. "Hannah's life would be in danger if we took the building head-on. We've got to be stealthy in our approach, but once inside, based on Alpha's plan, we'll use what these people fear the most—anarchist tactics."

CHAPTER 16

Haven Barn
The Haven

"Anarchists utilize tactics that instill intimidation and fear in those they oppose," explained Ryan. "They dress in all black and often cover their faces to obscure their identity because, after all, they're breaking the law when they engage in protests accompanied by property destruction."

Alpha picked up on Ryan's thought. "We plan on blending in with them, relying on the fact that this hastily assembled group in Charlotte may not be entirely familiar with one another. All we need is the slightest hesitation, a brief moment during which our enemy tries to process who we are, in order to have the upper hand."

Charlie added to his statement. "I take it we're going in weapons hot, but we'll try to use alternative methods to take them out first."

"Initially, during our approach to the building, we'll use X-Ray's overhead sets of eyes to identify targets for us. We'll eliminate them using blades until we're inside the Varnadore. Then I'll take Foxy up the service elevator shaft to start a top-down sweep of the building. I expect the stairwell to be well guarded. Based upon the drawings he found, and Echo's input, the former executive offices on the top floor are the most likely location of Chepe and Hannah."

"What's the plan for us?" asked Bravo.

"Target practice," replied Alpha. "You two will be equipped with our AR-15s with multiple sixty-round magazines."

"Why not the hundreds?" asked X-Ray. "I've got two drum magazines that—"

"Hold a hundred rounds, but they'll jam after twenty or thirty," interrupted Bravo. "We've tested every brand made, and the failure rate is ridiculous. They're a bulky toy and I wouldn't trust them in battle. I like the Schmeisser sixties, made in Germany. They resemble the Surefire sixty-rounder, but they're made out of polymer."

"Pricey," added Charlie.

Alpha pointed toward Ryan. "Well, thank Ryan for them. When he asked my opinion, he didn't hesitate to pull the trigger and buy a couple of dozen."

Bravo got back to the mission. "I'm gathering you want us to light it up."

"Absolutely!" exclaimed Alpha. "Shock and awe. These jerks break windows and cop cars. We break bodies. When they attacked the Haven, the rules of engagement changed. Now we're at war."

"Aren't you afraid they'll hurt Hannah when the shooting starts?" asked Cort.

"That's where our communications come in," replied Alpha. "Foxy and I will get into position to sweep the top floor, and then we'll give Bravo-Charlie team the green light. During the chaos, I expect two things to happen. The entire building will panic because these thugs aren't used to pushback. They're flamethrowers who know the cops will stand down because they don't want to make a scene for the media. They'll cower in the corner when we come at them. Most importantly, Cort, I firmly believe that Chepe will opt for self-preservation. He'll use Hannah as a bargaining chip to gain his freedom. Otherwise, he knows he'll take a bullet like the rest of the cowards."

"What about cover?" asked Charlie. "When we walk in the lobby, they'll make us immediately."

Alpha gestured to Ryan, who answered the question. He picked up a box bearing the yellow and black logo for the EG Grenade Company.

"P-40s," said Delta. "I trained with those when I was brought aboard Philly SWAT."

"That's right, Delta," said Ryan. "EG, which stands for Enola

Gaye, started their company in England. I like them because they have a low-heat formula. The stick doesn't produce an external flame, and the casing doesn't get hot. You can hold it longer and place it exactly where it has the maximum impact."

"These things can be pretty toxic," added Delta. "If the teams are going to use them inside, they'll have a helluva time breathing."

Alpha began to toss plastic bags to Bravo, Charlie and Hayden. "These are Holulo full-face respirators. They're designed to prevent the inhalation of paint and pesticides, but the activated carbon respirator prevents smoke inhalation, too."

"What made you think of these?" asked one of the drivers.

Ryan took that one. "Well, certainly not for this mission, to be honest. Actually, all you have to do is look around the Haven to realize we live in a huge tinderbox of hundred-year-old wood. These homes weren't built with fire-retardant materials. They're all in their original condition and vulnerable to fires. The masks were purchased to aid us in dealing with structure fires."

"And now, the rescue of Hannah," added Alpha. "Once you enter the lobby of the Varnadore, you'll ignite the stick grenades, which produce black and gray smoke. Scream fire and try to flush people toward the front entrance, which will act as a choke point."

"What about the rear exits?" asked Charlie.

"They'll be locked off with chains and disk locks. Do not forget this. You'll only have one way out as well."

"What about you guys?" asked Bravo.

"Rear fire exit," responded X-Ray. "The wrought-iron structure has a drop-down ladder that can be extended from the second floor to the ground."

The room grew quiet as they contemplated the plan.

Finally, Ryan spoke up. "Alpha, are you certain that we can't add another team or two? You know, to supplement you guys on the inside."

"Thanks, Ryan, but no. We need seasoned gunners who can handle weapons and threats. If we have too many people in the building, we run the risk of friendly fire. Truthfully, and I've already discussed this with Foxy, so she knows where I'm coming from, having Delta on the inside on my team made more sense than her. That said, we've trained together at the Haven in the past and understand each other's movements. Plus, when we find this little girl, I believe a female voice and her gentle touch will be more likely to keep her calm."

"Yeah," added Hayden. "She'd probably run as fast as she can from Alpha the way he'll be dressed."

The group shared a laugh and then Bravo raised a point. "You guys talked about blending in. Why don't we dress in all black like they do? That will buy us another few seconds for that whole recognition thing you mentioned."

"Bandannas. Trench coats. The whole nine yards," added Delta, who then appeared solemn. "Sadly, my son had a lot of clothes and accessories that might help. I can check."

"I like it," said Alpha. "If we go in there with camo and our chest rigs on, it'll be obvious."

Blair spoke up. "I'll speak to our residents and see what they can provide us."

"Good, thank you, darling," said Ryan.

*****

Throughout the day, the teams researched every minute detail of the Varnadore Building and its surroundings. They identified and debated points of insertion for the teams. They strategized about the potential countermeasures Chepe and his group might take. Most importantly, they talked about extraction methods once Hannah was retrieved.

Dinner was brought into Haven Barn for the group, and as they ate, Cort addressed them. With Meredith by his side, he spoke from the heart.

"Meredith, Hannah and I are a close family. Because of my responsibilities in Washington, we're apart a lot during the week, but when we're together, we're inseparable.

"Hannah is a warm and loving little girl. Well, you know, I see her as little. She really is more mature than what I give her credit for. I think she'll be tough and hold on until y'all can rescue her.

"I know the danger that you're walking into to save Hannah. Your bravery is incredible, and your sacrifices will never be forgotten. Please know this. Meredith and I, and Hannah, will be forever in your debt for what you're doing for us. Thank you and Godspeed."

CHAPTER 17

The Varnadore Building
Uptown Charlotte, North Carolina

The teams arrived near the Varnadore Building from different directions. X-Ray needed to position his van close enough to the building to have his drones in range and to be able to communicate with the teams on their two-way radios. He also wanted eyes on the front entrance, albeit using long-range binoculars. The task of finding a location where he could park to avoid detection by Chepe's people was not easy. Ultimately, he found a hillside near the east on-ramp to the Independence Expressway, east of the Varnadore. He expected Chepe to focus his surveillance toward the west, in the direction of the Haven.

There were several stalled cars on the ramp, and he hoped pulling his van onto the grassy hill wouldn't be noticed in the dark. Delta dropped off Bravo and Charlie at the Pierson Drive underpass, a tunnel-like stretch that crossed from south to north under the expressway and a stretch of Albemarle Road that ran parallel with the wider highway. He then parked his car below the tree-lined expressway and out of sight of any curious eyes atop the Varnadore Building.

The tunnel gave Bravo-Charlie team cover as they made their way to a position at the side of the building. Once they were in position, they could advise Alpha-Foxtrot team, who were approaching from the adjacent neighborhood located north of the Varnadore.

By two in the morning, all teams were in position, and two vehicles were strategically placed within a half mile of the building to aid in the extraction of the teams and Hannah. Alpha believed in redundancy. If one of the drivers or escape vehicles was disabled, then they needed options. As he put it, "It would be a crying shame to rescue that little girl only to have no way to get the hell outta Dodge."

Delta arrived at X-Ray's van and slipped inside. This was his first glimpse of the vast array of equipment at the much younger man's disposal.

"Impressive," Delta said as he took in X-Ray's domain. "How can you monitor all of this stuff?"

"Trust me, it won't be easy," he replied with a sigh. He cracked his knuckles and relaxed in his chair. "I have the NSA satellite feed open, just for reference, and I have our people ready with their drones. It's the comms that will prove the most difficult to keep up with."

Delta pointed to a radio on the table to his left. "A scanner?"

"Yes. In fact, that's for you. Here's where I need your help."

Delta picked up the portable Bearcat scanner, a device he was thoroughly familiar with, as he kept one at his home in Atlanta. He focused on X-Ray. "Talk to me."

"As three o'clock approaches, I'm gonna run through a radio check with all the teams. I need you to determine if Chepe and his people have two-way communications. If they do, monitor the channel for chatter. Here's a list of the most likely frequencies."

Delta studied the list. "It appears the higher-powered radios use frequencies in the four-six-two range. The lower-wattage types are in the four-six-sevens."

"That's right. Most people have Midlands, so I'd focus on the four-six-twos. Once you've locked in on the frequency, keep me posted, and I'll relay it to the team. They only need to hear one voice, you know what I mean?"

"You're the quarterback," replied Delta. "What else can I do?"

X-Ray handed him a felt pouch marked FLIR. "This is mine, so please be careful with it."

Delta studied the Pulsar Helion thermal monocular manufactured by FLIR. He slipped his hand through the strap and felt the weight. "Nice," he muttered.

"Yes, it is. I offered it to Alpha, but because it has a range in excess of a mile, he thought you could use it to monitor the entrance as well as the highway in case Chepe has the ability to call for reinforcements."

"Anything that I need to know about it?"

"Not really," replied X-Ray. "It's point and shoot. You'll be able to view in real time and so will I. The built-in video recording will simultaneously appear on this small computer monitor to my right as long as you stay within Bluetooth reception. Don't wander too far away from the van or I'll lose the feed."

"Got it."

"Okay, it's 2:45. In five minutes, our team is going to use the diesel fuel and Tannerite to cause an explosion at an oil-change station a couple of miles to our southwest. The used oil stored in the containers will create a lot of black smoke, drawing their attention to it. We want their eyes on the front of the building while our people quickly make their way inside from the back."

"X-Ray, I'm partially responsible for what happened to Hannah because Frankie came after the Haven to get at me."

X-Ray shrugged. "Well, Chepe wouldn't know that Cort and his family were at the Haven if it wasn't for me. I guess we both need to redeem ourselves."

Delta patted the young man on the back. "Let's do this, then!"

CHAPTER 18

The Varnadore Building
Uptown Charlotte, North Carolina

The driver parked nearly a mile away to the north of the Varnadore Building, ensuring that Alpha and Hayden could get suited up without detection. They both preferred to make the trek through the neighborhood streets and yards, using the sparse tree cover to avoid detection from observation scouts on the rooftop. Once the battle ensued and Chepe's people were distracted, the driver was instructed to take up a position just to the west of the office building, behind a closed-down pool-table store. This would leave his teams a quick sprint across the parking lot and then easy access to the westbound lanes of Independence Expressway.

As they zigzagged through the backyards, they spread apart, using a leapfrogging tactic known as bounding overwatch. It's a military technique used when enemy contact was expected during an assault on a fixed target. Bounding overwatch allowed the forward-moving soldier to engage and suppress an enemy before the remaining members of the squad came under fire.

This buddy system was especially effective under the cover of darkness the recent power outage provided them, and the other fortunate stroke of luck—a new moon. Using the night-vision monocular, Alpha took the lead as they traveled into an especially tight area. Hayden caught up and continued with the next leap forward, or if Alpha considered it too dangerous, he'd take that leg himself. As a team, they quickly moved the mile to get into position, where they awaited the detonation of the explosives at the oil-change facility.

By 2:30, they were on Sheffield Drive with an unobstructed view of the roof of the seven-story office building. Periodically, someone would walk along the northern edge of the roof, glance around the surrounding neighborhood, and then move on.

"You'd think they'd have enough people to monitor the entire perimeter at once rather than a single patrol," Hayden observed.

"Yeah, it's the same guy every time," added Alpha. "They may have people positioned in the windows, but your vision can be distorted looking through glass."

"Alpha, I know we're supposed to wait for the distractions to kick in, but we're gonna need to scale the wall that separates that row of houses from the back of the building."

Alpha thought for a moment. Without the benefit of Google Earth, they'd been unaware of the wall that appeared when they surveilled the houses with their night vision. He wasn't sure how far it extended, and if they tried to circle around it, they'd find themselves right on top of Bravo-Charlie team, clustered together. That would make them a big target. The success of their assault from the rear was to have each of the teams covering the other as they crossed Bamboo Street to reach the base of the building.

"We could move in sooner. I'm not saying that we'll scale the wall before the diversion, but at least we could be there when the time comes."

Hayden reached for the night-vision monocular. She focused on the five houses within her field of vision. "Hey, I've got movement."

"Let me see," said Alpha. He stood and walked out of their hiding place between a hedgerow and a parked car. "Dogs. Two of them. They're tied to a tree near a house at the end of the road."

"They're being used as warning devices," said Hayden.

"What?"

"I think they're strategically placed so they'll bark if someone approaches. Folks in the country do it all the time. If a burglar approaches their house, the dog goes nuts, warning the homeowners."

"It's a force multiplier," concluded Alpha. "That's why they've only devoted one man to the rooftop. He's got eyes on the ground and they're attached to four-legged hounds."

"Exactly."

"We have to neutralize those dogs," said Alpha.

"Or cut 'em loose," said Hayden. "We need to get movin'. We'll circle around and then I'll bribe them with some beef jerky I have in my pockets."

"Then what?"

"We're gonna free Hannah tonight, and I'm gonna free these dogs, too."

Without hesitation, Hayden darted across the street into the backyard of the homes facing the Varnadore. Alpha chased behind, glancing at the building's rooftop to confirm they were undetected. Once Alpha caught up to her, she made the next bold move by crossing the street a few houses down from where the dogs were now lying in the yard. They weren't asleep, but they certainly weren't on high alert.

Alpha caught up to Hayden, who was crouched behind some trash cans. "How do you plan on doing this?"

"I'll play on their curiosity rather than their sense of protection," she began. "I doubt these two have been fed. Look at them. They're hounds, not somebody's AKC champion. They'll have a great sense of smell."

"Okay, so how're ya gonna sneak up on them?"

"I'll toss the jerky just outside their reach. They might notice the pieces of meat hit the ground and become curious. Then their noses will take over and make them ravenous. They won't bark at something like that, and they'll be too distracted to pay attention to me."

Hayden pulled her knife out of the sheath wrapped around her leg.

Alpha was impressed. He had to ask, "Are you gonna gut 'em?"

"No, no way. While they're stretching to get at the jerky, I'll cut through their ropes from the back side of the tree. Once they're loose, I'll toss another piece farther into the street, and we'll sneak into the backyard once they go after it."

Hayden made her way through the shrubs to the back of the tree, keeping the large oak between her and the resting dogs. She carefully stepped through the grass, wary of any fallen twigs that might give away her position. When she was in position, she threw the first pieces of jerky just beyond the ropes tied around the dogs' necks as leashes.

Hayden focused on the dogs, analyzing their reaction so she didn't raise their suspicions, wholly unaware of what was happening behind her.

*****

As Hayden moved forward, Alpha noticed movement in the house behind her. It was just a shadow that crossed in front of a window. He inched forward to get a better look and then raised the night-vision monocular to his right eye. There was a faint light emanating from a bedroom window. It flickered, either from the distortion of the sheers or it was a candle. Either way, there was someone in the house.

Then he saw the signature of body heat as an arm appeared through a crack in the front door. Four fingers slowly pulled the door inward, exposing more of the man's body, which was crouched low to the floor. In the darkness, Alpha couldn't determine whether the man had a weapon, but under these circumstances, his voice could be just as deadly as the report of a gun.

Alpha moved quickly toward the garage door and then slid with his back against the cedar shake front façade of the mid-century rancher. He held his breath, expecting the man to shout at Hayden or the dogs, or even someone else in the house with him.

He reached inside the black coat provided to him by Blair and retrieved a throwing knife from his utility belt. The one-piece, black-coated blade was barely five inches long, but it was lethal when it found its target.

He'd practiced with it many times. It was fairly balanced but leaned toward being heavy in the handle. Alpha gripped the blade and focused on the spot where the man had emerged through the front door. He determined his throwing line. Alpha had practiced with this knife for years, and instinctively, he was able to draw back and release the handle with one fluid motion.

It sailed through the cold, damp air, slicing unimpeded with barely a whisper, until it plunged into the man's throat. Almost simultaneously, Hayden finished sawing through the nylon ski rope used to tie off the dogs. It wasn't until she heard the man's body fall down the short flight of steps leading up to the front porch that she realized how close she had been to being exposed.

In a flash, Alpha was upon the dying man and reached for his knife, twisting it several times in the man's neck before removing it. Hayden slowly retreated from the tree and looked down at the man's dead eyes, which stared skyward.

The two never said a word, but rather, nodded and gestured toward the side of the house. While the dogs sniffed around the yard and street for more of the delicious beef jerky, Alpha and Hayden reached the brick wall that separated the neighborhood from the noise that used to emanate from the once busy expressway.

Tonight, it was deathly silent, with the only sound being a slight breeze rustling the oak tree's limbs.

CHAPTER 19

The Varnadore Building
Uptown Charlotte, North Carolina

Alpha and Hayden found a stack of cinder blocks near a storage shed in the backyard. They quickly set the blocks in place to use as steps to reach the top of the wall. First Hayden and then Alpha scaled to the top, where they remained perched under the tree's protective canopy. They were fortunate to be under a red oak, a tree whose leaves turned brown as fall turned to winter but stayed on the tree during the cold season.

"Why did we get stuck patrolling the outside?"

The man's voice startled Alpha team, causing them both to draw their sidearms. The voice appeared to come from their right.

"Man, I don't know, but they promised we could rotate inside at four," another man responded. "Look here, man. This isn't what I signed on for. I like to break stuff, you know. Really, I was hopin' to fill my place with some new furniture. Maybe snag a Mercedes or somethin' like that."

"Dude, I know. We're bustin' into these rich neighborhoods and comin' out empty-handed. What's the point?"

Alpha leaned into Hayden and whispered, "They're coming closer. We gotta take them out or they'll walk right into Bravo team."

Hayden slipped her handgun into its holster and removed her rifle from her shoulder. She quietly placed it on top of the brick and block wall. Then she slowly removed her knife from its sheath and whispered to Alpha, "Lie flat on top of the wall. When they're directly underneath, roll off and plunge your knife into the base of their skull. It's the best way to get a silent kill."

Impressed, Alpha nodded and emulated her position after removing his rifle. The two assassins lay prone on the top of the wall, face-to-face, waiting for their marks. The men stopped talking, but their lazy, shuffling footsteps gave them away as they got closer. They were mere feet away from death when an explosion rocked the quiet of the night.

The detonation of the oil drums to their south occurred right on time. Alpha and Hayden, rather than being ready to breach the rear of the building, found themselves with two previously bored sentries who were now frightened, looking in all directions for the source of the explosion.

Alpha nodded to Hayden and they both flipped over the wall, landing on their feet in a crouch. The two patrolling guards turned, but it was too late for them. With catlike quickness Hayden had picked up from Prowler, she thrust herself out of the crouch and drove the blade of her knife into the throat of the man closest to her.

"Hey!" the other man exclaimed before Alpha slashed the man's face, ripping the flesh off his cheekbone. Before he could scream in agony, Alpha whipped his hand back, deftly repositioning the blade so that it carved a gash across the man's carotid artery. Any words he attempted at that point came out as a garbled mess.

Alpha turned to Hayden. "Guns, fast."

"We gotta get back up there."

He clasped his fingers together and held them low near the wall. "Step in here. I'll hoist you."

Hayden moved in front of Alpha, placed her hands against the wall, and put her foot in the makeshift catapult. With his massive arms, Alpha flung her too high up the wall, almost causing his hundred-and-twenty-pound partner to fly over the other side.

"Jeez, big guy," whispered Hayden as she struggled to stay on top of the wall. She gathered herself and located their rifles, quickly tossing them down to Alpha.

"Jump. I'll catch you."

"I've got this." The fiercely independent woman rejected his offer.

Once they were reunited, they raced across Bamboo Street and joined the Bravo-Charlie team, who were huddled under the canopy of a former bank drive-thru window. Out of breath from the sprint, Alpha fist-bumped the two former soldiers.

"Nice of you to join us," said Bravo.

"I had to drag Foxy away from playing with a couple of puppies," whispered Alpha as his eyes darted in all directions.

"Shut up," said Hayden under her breath. "Let's get our girl."

Alpha led the way, hiding under the canopy of the building, which had a slight inset around its entire perimeter. The design was beneficial to the two teams, as they were able to access the rear of the building without being seen from above.

The two teams flanked the rear service entrance to the building. The steel doors had been left ajar with a brick, allowing the patrols to come and go as necessary. Alpha leaned over to Bravo and asked, "Where is everybody?"

"It was like a magnet. When the explosion went off, the foot patrols ran to the front to see what happened."

"How many were back here?" asked Alpha.

"Three sets of two, but you eliminated one and we took out another," replied Bravo. He looked back and forth, then added, "I'm not saying this is gonna be easy, but we're not up against people with training. Hell, they're not even wannabes."

Alpha shouldered his rifle and drew his sidearm. He motioned for Charlie and Hayden to lean in as he spoke. "The drawing shows the service elevator directly behind this wall. Foxy and I are gonna enter the shaft through the roof of the elevator, and then we'll scale the walls until we reach the top floor. Once we're there, I'll key the mic with three steady bursts. That's your *go* signal. Lead with the smoke; flush them out or take them out, your choice. Then move up the stairs to the next floor."

"Roger that," said Bravo. "You hit the elevator; we'll lock up the rear exits and wait for your signal. See you on the outside!"

Alpha took a deep breath and flung the door open, leading with the barrel of his sidearm in search of a target. The roar of excited voices rumbled through the concrete ground floor of the building, but all their attention was focused toward the front of the building, where people had exited to see the black smoke obliterate the stars on the clear night.

Alpha pointed his hand to the right, indicating that the Bravo-Charlie team was safe to go in that direction. Hayden was the last to enter and followed Alpha to the elevator that stood open in the dark hallway. Just as they approached the elevator cab, they heard the barely audible metallic click of the disk locks closing off the rear exit to the building.

"Are you ready for this?" asked Alpha as he put on his Energizer headlamp and flicked on the LED light.

"Hoist me up," Hayden said in response. She illuminated her headlamp as well. "The hard part will be dragging you through the trapdoor."

Just like the two had worked together when Hayden scaled the brick wall moments ago, Alpha created a stirrup for her to step in, and she was easily raised into the opening. She turned and looked down to her partner.

"Pass me your gun." Alpha quickly obliged, and then he waved her out of the way.

"Is the frame of the opening steel? X-Ray said the newer elevators require it for stability."

"Yeah."

"Good, stand back," he instructed.

Alpha, exhibiting an athleticism that Hayden hadn't seen in a man of his size, took a running start toward the side of the elevator, placed his left foot against the steel handrail bolted into the cab, and then pushed off so that his body moved upward and toward the ceiling near the emergency hatch. With his arms raised overhead, he gripped the steel frame that held the hatch door, and swung like a child hanging onto monkey bars. Finally, with a grunt, he hoisted his two-hundred-forty-pound frame of muscle through the hatch and onto the top of the elevator cab.

"You're nuts," said Hayden dryly as she replaced the hatch door to mask their intrusion.

"Yeah," he said with a deep breath. "I always liked doing pull-ups. Now for the fun part."

Alpha pulled out his tactical flashlight and lit up the interior of the elevator shaft. Hayden looked up with him and asked, "Sixty feet?"

"Seventy-two, per the drawings," he replied. "It's like climbing a ladder. Follow my lead and footing. Sometimes you'll need to stretch, and I might need to grab you by the hand to pull you up."

She gestured for him to get started. "We'll knock it out. Let's go."

The team worked together to scale the inside of the Varnadore's service elevator shaft, which was wider than the office elevator servicing the building. The additional width provided ample room to move and a variety of plates, connections, and braces to use as footholds. It was somewhat like scaling a climbing wall at a gym, only the opportunities to step were far apart at times.

It took them ten minutes to climb to the top floor. As they moved upward, they listened for voices near each of the floor's elevator doors. It was remarkably quiet.

Once they reached the top, Hayden and Alpha got a foothold on the threshold on the back side of the elevator door. This was their moment of truth. They were in a precarious position, barely holding onto the steel frame around the door. Alpha would be required to drive the blade of his knife into the crack separating the closed doors in order to pry them open. Hayden, using her handgun, would have to be prepared to shoot any threat on the other side.

Both would have to hold on until the hostile was eliminated, and to keep their balance in case they were surprised by gunfire.

"Ready?" asked Alpha.

Hayden nodded and pointed her pistol toward the opening. Using his left hand, Alpha carefully inserted the blade between the doors and then twisted it ninety degrees to create a two-inch opening. He slowly removed his knife, hoping that the doors didn't automatically close. When they remained open, he allowed a big grin to come over his otherwise serious face. He held his hand up and leaned toward the opening he'd created.

"Clear," he whispered barely loud enough for Hayden to hear, but his body language said it all. She holstered her weapon and mimicked Alpha as he pulled his rifle off his shoulder.

Alpha reached up to the collar of his jacket and keyed the microphone to his radio. He pressed the button three times, indicating to everyone on the channel that the battle was about to begin. He adjusted his earpiece, which was connected directly to the two-way radio. He was ready to accept advice and instructions from X-Ray.

With a nod to Hayden, they put on their respirator masks and slowly readied their AR-15s. Each inserted their fingers into the crack and pulled the elevator doors open, careful not to lose their balance and fall backward into the shaft. A rush of fresh air enveloped their bodies, replacing the dank, stale air that had surrounded them during their brief time inside the elevator shaft. It was a welcome relief and provided them a boost of adrenaline as they entered the dark hallway together.

CHAPTER 20

The Varnadore Building
Uptown Charlotte, North Carolina

"Alpha team in position. Over." Alpha's voice spoke in a hushed tone over the radio. Despite the activity outside the building, the top floor of the Varnadore was eerily quiet and still.

"Roger that, Alpha-Foxtrot. Bravo-Charlie, you're a green light." X-Ray came across the radio as calm and professional.

"Roger, X-Ray. Deploying smoke."

Alpha leaned over to Hayden and whispered, "Follow my lead. I'm gonna clear one room at a time. You cover my six in the hallway."

"Lead the—" Hayden began before being interrupted by the sounds of gunfire traveling up the elevator shafts from the ground floor.

Her body tensed as she lowered herself into a crouch and began to scan the dark hallway for movement. Then she heard it—the muffled scream of a child.

"Did you hear that? It was Hannah."

"Yeah," replied Alpha, whose adrenaline was now pumping through his body. "End of the hallway."

Hayden rose out of her crouched position to move forward, but Alpha grabbed her arm.

"No, they've set up a gauntlet," cautioned Alpha, breathing heavily through the mask. "There could be a gun behind every one of these office doors."

"But she's—"

"She'll be there when we get there, too. We've gotta clear this floor first, Foxy."

He paused for a moment and keyed his mic. "X-Ray, possible confirmation of the princess. Over."

"Roger. They're scurrying out the front doors like rats. Bravo-Charlie report that the ground level is clear and they're moving to the next floor. Over."

Alpha thought for a moment and responded, "Should you redeploy Delta to mop up the rats? Over."

X-Ray replied with confidence, "Not necessary. They can't run away fast enough. Over."

"Roger that," replied Alpha with a grin. "Advise Bravo team the princess is here. Use caution as they clear each floor. Bogies in the offices. Out."

Alpha made eye contact with Hayden and nodded his head toward the hallway. "It's on."

Alpha approached the entry door of the first room, ignited a smoke grenade, and tossed it into the center of the former executive secretary's office. He dropped to a knee and scanned the room for movement, using his trained eyes to detect the slightest change in his surroundings. Their challenge was to take out the anarchists without getting Hannah caught in the crossfire.

The dimly lit offices only received ambient light from the outside. While the new moon phase benefited the rescue teams in their approach to the building, it was a significant handicap once inside. Alpha had cautioned the team not to use their flashlights inside the building, as the light would give away their position. Also, while the smoke grenades helped to create confusion amongst the anarchists, it also rendered their night-vision monocular useless.

"Arrgh!" a man growled at Alpha as he lunged off a tabletop toward the steely-nerved former operator. Alpha brought his rifle around and plugged two rounds in the man's chest. The sound of gunfire had detonated a panic bomb on the seventh floor.

"Alpha!" shouted Hayden as she opened fire. Several people scurried out of the offices and into the hallway. She couldn't make out whether they were men or women, but she shot at their upper torsos. Hannah was less than five feet tall, so Hayden was comfortable shooting high.

Alpha backed out of the room and led the charge down the hallway. He began to shout as he fired rounds into the anarchists who lay writhing in pain on the concrete floor.

"Hannah! Hannah!" Hayden shouted.

There was no response.

"Cover me," shouted Alpha as he swung right in the next room. He ignited another smoke grenade and tossed it toward the back of the room. He waited several seconds, and when nothing moved, he backed out of the space. "Next!"

They moved in tandem down the hallway. The next office door was twenty feet from the conference room. Alpha eased against the wall and prepared to enter the first door on his left. Suddenly, Hayden turned and fired several rounds in the direction of the service elevator.

"Get down," she shouted, as a gunman had slipped in behind them and opened fire on their position. But as is often the case when an untrained shooter is involved, the adrenaline-fueled gunman aimed high and peppered the ceiling with his bullets.

Hayden caught a glimpse of his muzzle flash. It was a slight orange glow, but it was enough to provide her a target. She quickly adjusted her aim and squeezed the trigger, allowing the powerful weapon to bounce against her shoulder. She sprayed half a dozen rounds in the direction of the shooter, and some of them found their mark. The man screamed in agony and fell to the floor in a heap.

"Plug him again," instructed Alpha.

Hayden walked slowly toward the body and, when she had a good view through the smoke, fired two more rounds into the man's torso. He was dead. She dropped her magazine, stowed in her vest, and slapped in another.

A woman ran into the hallway and caught Alpha by surprise. Just as he swung his rifle in her direction, she shouted, "Please don't shoot!"

His training ignored her empty plea. He shot her anyway, her limp body dropping a handgun as it hit the floor.

Hayden joined his side again as they moved forward, stepping over several dead bodies in their path. The space, devoid of ventilation, began to reek of smoke and the metallic smell of blood.

Alpha counted the kills in his head. "Nine," he mumbled to Hayden and then pointed to the double doors of the conference room at the end of the hallway.

They arrived together and pressed themselves against the walls flanking the entrance, using the doorjambs as cover. They made eye contact, and then Alpha shouted, his deep voice reverberating off the walls.

"Chepe! This ends now. Let us have the girl, and I promise you'll walk out of here alive."

An evil grin came across his face as he spoke. Of course, he was lying.

CHAPTER 21

The Varnadore Building
Uptown Charlotte, North Carolina

Chepe pulled Hannah off the floor and dragged her into the kitchen through the stainless-steel swinging door. His plans of making a last stand were abandoned as he listened to his top people's screams of pain. He'd handpicked his fighters to defend the top floor and their hostage, and his pursuers had killed them all, including the woman who begged them not to. At this point, Chepe didn't like his chances, even with the hollow promise to let him go. He knew better.

"Come on, kid," he snarled at Hannah. "I'm getting out of here, and I'll hold you in front of me until I'm out the door. Get up!"

Hannah wrestled against his grip, but Chepe, nervous with anxiety and fright, was much stronger. He grabbed her by the arms with a death grip and shoved her toward the cabinet doors that led to the laundry chute. Hannah lost her balance and fell forward onto the hard floor, groaning in pain through the bandanna used to gag her.

Chepe dropped to his knees and opened the doors. He glanced down into the dark space below but couldn't see anything. The utility room on the sixth floor didn't have any windows and was empty except for the eight-foot-square laundry basket on casters centered under the opening. Earlier, he'd gathered up pillows and linens from the offices-turned-bedrooms to create a soft landing spot in the event an emergency escape was necessary.

"Go on, jump down there!" Chepe ordered Hannah, who fought him again. She looked down toward the floor ten feet below them.

"Uh-uh," she grunted, apprehensively shaking her head.

"Yes, you will. Now go!"

Chepe forced her into the cabinet and pushed her headfirst into the basket below. Hannah dropped into the basket with a thump, followed by a moan.

"Come on out, Chepe!" Alpha yelled again through the door. "Your people downstairs have all run off. Everyone here is dead. I'm giving you a chance to walk out of here. We just want that little girl back!"

Chepe was distracted by Alpha's booming, bellowing voice taunting him through the conference room doors. He'd heard the gunfire from below. Then the mayhem in the hallway outside the conference room had rattled him to his core. He had one chance to escape, and it was now.

He backed into the void within the stainless-steel cabinet and dropped through the hole leading to the laundry basket below. Only, it wasn't there.

Chepe was expecting a soft landing, and instead, his body crashed onto the concrete floor. His ankle turned unnaturally, sending pain shooting through his leg and into his back.

Hannah had recovered from the fall and crawled out of the laundry basket. Then she'd shoved it out of the way so Chepe didn't have it to fall into.

"You little—!" Chepe's last words were cut off as Alpha boomed from above, "We're done fooling with you, Chepe!"

The sound of the conference room doors getting kicked in and furniture being tossed about caused Chepe to panic.

He frantically called out for Hannah, who'd hidden in the dark recesses of the laundry room behind a broken-down commercial washing machine.

Chepe yelled for her under his breath. "Where are you, kid! Come out or I'll kill you!"

Hannah didn't respond, but Alpha's voice was getting closer. "Chepe! It's time to give it up. Bring her to us safely and you live. If you don't, the torture you'll suffer will make you beg for death!"

"Dammit!" muttered Chepe in frustration. He tried to stand and then groaned in pain as his injured ankle caused his legs to buckle. He crawled toward the utility room door and found the handle. He pulled himself up and hopped through the exit into the hallway of the sixth floor.

Chepe abandoned his hostage and opted for self-preservation instead. He knew the building and bounced down the hallway on one leg until he reached a short hallway leading to the fire escape. Once there, he struggled with the old fire door, which refused to open.

Wrought with paranoia, he thought he heard footsteps in the hallway behind him, so he pulled his fist back and slammed it into the top half of the door, which was glass. The first punch didn't break it out, but the second one did. Large shards of glass crashed onto the fire escape, and one piece ripped open his knuckles.

Frantic, he crawled through the opening, disregarding the damage done to his hand as he tumbled onto the steel mesh landing outside. He subconsciously took in the fresh air, and a feeling of freedom came over him.

"Almost there," he mumbled as a smile came across his face.

Still hopping on one leg because his left ankle was most likely broken, Chepe made his way down the rusty fire escape stairs until he reached the second floor. At that point, he had to release a ladder that would fall to the ground.

Chepe pulled a piece of glass out of his hand and fumbled with the latches that held the ladder in place. Over the years, from lack of maintenance, the rust had taken hold and created a weld. Chepe pounded the steel mesh floor, causing his hand to bleed further.

He looked over the rail. The drop was over twenty feet. He was down to one ankle and couldn't afford to lose the other.

He violently shook the ladder, hoping to break the rust weld loose. It seemed to give. He dropped to his knees once again and worked with the latches. Finally, one latch broke loose.

Chepe mustered all of his strength and tore at the other latch, trying to force it open as he could feel the pressure of his pursuers. Once again, in his paranoid state, he thought he heard someone on the stairs above him. He kept shaking the latch where it held the ladder in place, constantly looking upward to see if he'd been discovered.

His efforts paid off, much to his surprise, and chagrin. While he was focused on the people after him, the latch released and the heavy steel ladder flew down its rails toward the ground, ripping two fingers off in the process.

Chepe couldn't control his agony as he yelled in pain. He immediately grasped his right hand and saw that his pinky and ring fingers were missing. Blood poured out of the wound and all over his body. The pain was so bad that he nearly passed out, but he managed to get control of himself.

He looked down to confirm that the ladder had reached bottom and began to climb down. With his broken ankle, he couldn't put any weight on his left leg. He had to use his hands to lower his body—one bleeding profusely and the other still with smaller shards of glass embedded in it.

But Chepe persevered. He looked up the fire escape as he made his way downward. Blood poured out of his hand and drenched his face, obscuring his view. He was halfway down when he heard the sounds of sirens in the distance. The distraction caused him to instinctively turn toward the source, and when he did, he lost his grip.

Chepe tried to hold onto the rails as he slid downward. To slow his descent, he desperately searched with his right foot to find a rung, but he was unable to. His face, however, was more successful.

Only ten feet from the ground, Chepe's open mouth caught a rung, knocking out several of his upper and lower teeth. The jolt was too much for him to endure and he lost his grip on the ladder's rails. His body fell the final ten feet in a contorted twist, landing face-first on the concrete pavement.

Now his nose was broken. Chepe lay on the ground, motionless, prepared to die. The pain shooting through his body was so intense that he couldn't focus on which part was the worst.

Despite the brutal beating he'd taken, Chepe was a survivor. He was still alive and had a chance.

He crawled under the canopy of the ground floor and looked for a way to pull himself up. A stack of crates, similar to the ones he'd used to stand tall and direct his anarchist army from, was just ahead. He crawled over to them, leaving a bloody trail like a slug crawling across hot pavement in the dead of summer.

With each motion forward, his hopes lifted. He felt for his car keys. He managed a bloody, toothless grin when he found them in his jeans pocket. He reached the crates and hoisted himself upright. Then, like a pogo stick, he quickly hopped toward his white Chevy Avalanche.

The pain was forgotten for now, as he used all of his strength to get into the tall pickup truck. He settled into the driver's seat and caught a glimpse of himself in the rearview mirror. Blood mixed with mucus poured out of his nose and over his chin. It was a ghoulish sight, reminiscent of a horror flick, but it didn't faze him.

"You should always kill the bad guy," he said with a laugh. "Never let them live to fight another day."

With a guttural laugh followed by a coughing fit that spewed blood and spit all over the dash, he inserted the key into the ignition and raced out of the parking lot. Chepe had escaped the bedlam at the Varnadore.

CHAPTER 22

The Varnadore Building
Uptown Charlotte, North Carolina

Alpha took one set of doors into the kitchen, and Hayden took the other. With their headlamps illuminated, they simultaneously kicked them open and burst into the darkened space. They searched the room, using the barrels of their rifles to pan the former kitchen in search of Chepe and Hannah. The room was empty.

Hayden got Alpha's attention and used hand signals to point toward the slightly skewed doors to the laundry chute. Unsure if the space was large enough to hide Chepe and Hannah, the two proceeded with caution, shouldering their rifles and pulling their sidearms. Alpha raised his hand and counted down five fingers until he made a fist, indicating to Hayden that she should swing the doors open. He quickly moved in front of the cabinet and pointed his weapon into the void.

"Escape hatch?" He whispered his question.

Hayden glanced around the room one more time and dropped to a knee. She looked to the floor below them, allowing her headlamp to shine on the space where the laundry basket once stood. "I don't know, but it's the only way out of here."

Alpha quickly alerted X-Ray and Bravo team that Chepe had escaped with Hannah to the sixth floor. He darted through the kitchen door, keeping his rifle ready to shoot anything that threatened him.

Hayden chased after him, her eyes checking every doorway and dead body as they made their way to the stairwell. When they reached the sixth floor, they slowed their pace and quietened their step. They nodded to one another, and Alpha burst into the hallway, facing right, while Hayden took the left side.

They'd illuminated their infrared laser sights on their rifles as well as the tactical flashlights attached to the weapons' quad rails. The element of surprise was lost and now the two were hunting their frightened prey.

Room by room, they searched for Chepe, Hannah, and any anarchists who might attempt to ambush them. The sixth floor appeared to be empty. Then Hayden found the hallway leading to the fire escape. She cautiously approached the door and discovered the broken glass. She peeked outside and saw that there was blood on the steel landing and on the handrails.

"I think he escaped this way!" she shouted to Alpha.

He ran down the short hallway and took a look outside. Hayden moved in the opposite direction and entered the hallway.

"Hannah! Can you hear me? It's Hayden. Your parents sent us to get you."

Alpha joined in. "Hannah!"

Hayden walked slowly toward the utility room, where the door was left ajar. She'd cleared the room moments ago, but in her haste, she might've missed something.

Her flashlight lit up the room and she tried again, but in a softer tone of voice. "Hannah, baby, are you here? Your mom and dad miss you, and so does Handsome Dan. He's tired of playing with Prowler." Hayden managed a chuckle as she thought of the absurdity of those two wrestling with one another. It wouldn't be a fair fight.

"He doesn't like cats," a meek voice responded.

Hayden turned to her right and walked slowly toward the large washing machine that had been gutted for parts. She kept her rifle at low ready just in case.

Hannah's angelic face peered from around the washer, the gag resting just below her lower lip against her chin. Her hands were still tied behind her back, but she was able to move by squirming and wiggling against the wall and the washer.

Hayden shouldered her rifle and knelt down to help Hannah

extract herself from the hiding place. "Come on, honey. We've got you now. It's over."

Just as Hannah was pulled out and set on her feet, Alpha entered the room unannounced. Hayden drew her sidearm and swung around with the barrel pointed at her partner.

"Hey, careful, quick-draw," said Alpha with a chuckle. Relieved to see Hannah alive, he addressed her. "There are a lot of folks who're worried about you, young lady. Not to mention the fact that you abandoned your post on the drone squad."

"Um, I know, but the man came—"

Alpha laughed and walked up to Hannah. The burly man picked her up and gave her a bear hug. "Come here, Hannah. I'm just kidding you. We're so glad you're safe. Whadya say we get outta here and go see your parents. Okay?"

"Are they mad?" Tears streamed down her face.

"No, honey," replied Hayden. "Of course they're not mad. They've been very worried about you, and they'll hug you harder than this big guy, trust me."

Alpha turned toward the door and keyed his microphone. "X-Ray, this is Alpha team. Over."

"Go ahead, Alpha."

"We've got her. Over."

"Great news. I'll let him know. Out."

Alpha paused as they entered the hallway and turned to Hayden. "Did he say him?"

Hayden, who was carrying the fifty-pound girl down the hallway, replied, "Yeah."

Alpha thought for a moment. "Him who?"

CHAPTER 23

East Independence Expressway
Uptown Charlotte, North Carolina

Moments earlier, X-Ray and Delta had some action of their own. "I've got a light-colored pickup tearing out of the parking lot," X-Ray announced into the headset he used to communicate with the various teams used to rescue Hannah. He was directing the statement to Delta, who stood vigil on the hillside, monitoring the activity through his binoculars.

Delta immediately responded, "I saw it. Driver's in a hellfire emergency. At least he has wheels, unlike the rest of the vermin who scampered off on foot. Does Alpha still want us to stand down on the people escaping?"

"Hold on," X-Ray replied to him. "I need to replay the drone footage."

X-Ray then turned his attention to the monitor that displayed the drone footage for the east side of the Varnadore Building. Both drones had been in the air for quite some time and were due to be brought back down to their operators, as their batteries were drained.

X-Ray addressed Delta again. "The driver's a male. He appears to be hunched over, like he's cradling something. I don't know, it's hard to tell."

Delta immediately noticed the fleeing vehicle. "The truck's coming this way on the on-ramp, headed eastbound on the freeway."

"Wait." X-Ray paused for what seemed like an eternity. He rubbed his temples, trying to remember. "Delta, that might be Chepe's truck. The lead vehicle returning to the Varnadore after the attack was a white Chevy Avalanche."

"We've gotta be sure!" shouted Delta as he ran down the hillside and found his way to his Silverado. He fired up the powerful V-8 engine and spun the tires as he pulled off the wet grass mixed with gravel.

"I can't help you with the tail," X-Ray warned. "The drones are out of juice."

"No problem, I can see his taillights."

"Delta, also, you'll be out of radio range in just a few minutes."

"Roger. Let me know if conditions at the Varnadore change. I need to know if Hannah is in that truck!"

X-Ray's voice was excited. "You've got it. Go get them!"

Delta floored the gas pedal and the heavy truck raced ahead. He'd driven squad cars in the past during high-speed pursuits, but never anything as big and bulky as the Suburban. He wasn't sure how fast it would go, although the car salesman had bragged that it was capable of doing one hundred thirty miles per hour.

He was about to find out. There was no traffic on the expressway, only the occasional stalled vehicle that had pulled toward the side of the road. The white Avalanche that Delta pursued must not have noticed him because as he hit one hundred miles an hour, he closed rapidly on what he suspected was Chepe's truck.

Delta was within a quarter mile of the Avalanche when he glanced to his left and noticed the Rick Hendrick family of car dealerships. The irony didn't escape him as he closed within fifty feet of the Avalanche's tailgate. Hendrick, one of the most successful owners in NASCAR racing history, would be proud to see two Chevys duking it out for the win, with the loser destined to die.

X-Ray attempted to contact Delta, but the transmission was garbled.

"I … Alpha. Chepe escaped. But … Hannah …"

Frustrated, Delta keyed his mic. "Say again, X-Ray. You're breaking up."

Suddenly, the Avalanche lurched forward. Chepe, or whoever was driving, had discovered Delta on his tail and tried evasive maneuvers. He rapidly gained speed, forcing Delta to chase after him as the speedometer registered a hundred miles per hour. The rpms on the Silverado's engine reached a fever pitch as his speed climbed.

"Do you copy, Delta? Hannah is safe. Chepe has escaped."

"Good! I've got him in my sights!"

Delta's words were never heard by X-Ray, as he was now out of range and on his own. The man responsible for the raid on the Haven and, ultimately, the death of his son was now going to be brought to justice.

His sweaty palms gripped the wheel as he pulled behind Chepe's truck. They were now miles away from the Varnadore Building, but ironically, they'd just passed the new location of the Varnadore Company as the two sped toward the Charlotte suburb of Matthews.

Delta hearkened back to his training as a police officer when he'd learned pursuit techniques. One of the most effective ways to end a high-speed pursuit of a suspect was to execute a PIT maneuver. Sometimes referred to as a Precision Immobilization Technique, or also a Pursuit Intervention Technique, the result was the same—spin the suspect's vehicle from behind during a chase.

Although the PIT maneuver can be achieved in three easy steps, factors like traffic, road conditions, and vehicle speed complicate matters. Delta had performed the technique on several occasions in his career but never at speeds in excess of a hundred. Ordinarily, his superiors would tell him to back off at high speeds like this, opting instead to utilize air support to follow the subject vehicle.

On this early morning, Delta didn't have any backup, nor did he have any witnesses. If he successfully executed the PIT maneuver, it was unlikely that Chepe would survive the wreck, not that Delta cared. He didn't have anybody to answer to except the memory of his son.

Delta had successfully matched Chepe's speed and eased up on his right rear bumper. His goal was to gently nudge the right rear fender with his left front, causing Chepe to lose control. It was no different than what a NASCAR driver did on the short tracks of Richmond or Bristol. A gentle nudge forced the rear end of the lead vehicle to get out of sorts, allowing the race driver to make the pass.

Only this was different. Delta would upset the back of Chepe's truck, causing him to lose control, but then he'd accelerate to complete the PIT maneuver. At slower speeds, the suspect vehicle would spin sideways and eventually come to a halt. At a hundred-plus, anything could happen, including Delta losing control as well.

Delta had mastered the practice of left-foot braking that enabled him to match the suspect vehicle's speed precisely. He recalled the technique and gently steered toward Chepe's right fender. He had to be careful to make both the requisite contact and the subsequent steer-through as gentle as possible to avoid throwing them both into a fiery crash.

Delta nudged Chepe, but not hard enough. The Avalanche fishtailed slightly, but Chepe corrected it. Delta tried again, a little harder this time. He kept constant pressure on the throttle, and he steered into Chepe's truck.

Momentum took care of the rest.

Chepe lost control, overcorrected, and went sailing off the shoulder of the freeway down an embankment. His truck didn't appear to slow down as it rose up the other side of the ditch and sailed into the air, bounced once on the service road, and roared across until it drove head-on into a post office.

Immediately upon impact, the Avalanche was crushed by the brick and granite structure before bursting into a spectacular eruption of flames and debris.

Delta brought his truck to a screeching stop and then threw it into reverse, spinning his tires into a cloud of black smoke and burnt rubber. When he was in front of the point of impact, he leapt out of his truck and walked to the shoulder of the freeway to view the results of his efforts.

He defiantly raised his right hand and gave Chepe's burning truck the middle finger. "Go to hell. Return to sender!"

CHAPTER 24

The Varnadore Building
Uptown Charlotte, North Carolina

After Bravo team cleared the remainder of the building, they rendezvoused with Alpha team on the sixth floor. Leading the way, the ex-soldiers escorted Hannah to the ground floor, and rather than bother unlocking the door, Bravo found a cinder block and threw it through a plate-glass window, allowing a rush of fresh air to enter the building and the smoke generated by their stick grenades to billow out.

Hannah, who was now walking on her own, covered her face with the bandanna used by Hayden to lend the appearance she was one of the anarchists. As it turned out, the operation had moved so briskly that the anarchist-apparel subterfuge was unnecessary.

Alpha summoned X-Ray, who told him that Delta had chased after Chepe. He instructed X-Ray to rally the troops and meet in front of the Varnadore Building, as it appeared there were no remnants of Chepe's group remaining in the area except for the dead.

Within minutes, the group had assembled and were all congratulating each other. When Hannah revealed how she'd moved the laundry basket, causing Chepe to crash hard onto the floor, the group erupted in laughter and exchanged high fives.

Sirens could be heard in the distance, but X-Ray advised them that the police scanner revealed a high-rise fire in downtown Charlotte had occupied all available fire departments and police precincts. The group agreed that this shoot-out might not garner any type of law enforcement investigation.

The smoke coming out of the building began to dissipate as Delta pulled into the parking lot, with his Silverado only slightly damaged from the high-speed chase involving fender banging.

After exiting the truck, he immediately hugged Hannah and then pulled Alpha aside to explain what had happened. The taller Alpha slapped Delta on the shoulder several times as they spoke, and then the two men exchanged a bro-hug, indicating that any differences between them had been squashed.

"I think we're done here. What do you guys think?" asked Alpha as he and Delta joined the rest of the rescue team.

Hannah was the first to respond. "I think I'm ready to go home."

"I'll bet you're hungry," said Hayden as she knelt down next to the young girl. She reached into her pocket and pulled out a silver foil package and handed it to Hannah. "Your mom said you liked blueberry Pop-Tarts. Well, they just happen to be my favorite too."

"I love them!" exclaimed Hannah as she ripped open the package and pulled out one of the delicious pastry snacks.

"Well, you know, I'm a big believer in girl power, and I happen to know that some of the strongest women I've read about love blueberry Pop-Tarts. I think you've earned these."

Hayden pulled some debris out of Hannah's hair, and then something caught her attention. She quickly backed up and placed her hand on her pistol grip.

"What've we got?" asked Alpha.

"Looters," replied X-Ray. "Look at 'em."

The group hadn't noticed that a group of people, likely curiosity-seekers and residents of the neighborhood, were running through the broken window and carrying out anything that wasn't tied down.

Cans of food, cases of dry goods, bedding, and supplies were all exiting the Varnadore Building as fast as the locals' feet could carry them.

"Unbelievable," began Delta. "They're stepping over dead bodies in order to get in and out."

"That's desperation," added Alpha. "Well, it's not our problem. Let's get out of here before a cop wanders up or Chepe's people decide to come back."

The group gathered their gear and followed Delta and Alpha in the lead truck as they headed back to the Haven and Hannah's anxious parents.

CHAPTER 25

Haven House
The Haven

Every parent experiences an emotional moment on a scale they never thought possible in their lives when their children are born. From the exhilaration of hearing the heartbeat in the womb, to the first kick in the mother's belly, through the heart-bursting pride at their child's first steps. Even as they grow older, the stomach-wrenching worry of a teenager who is late coming home one night makes parents realize when it comes to their children, emotions are amplified.

The triumphant caravan was approaching the front gate when news began to spread throughout the Haven of their return, with Hannah safely in hand. Cort had been working the gate's security since the moment the teams had pulled out the night before. He hadn't slept, nor had Meredith, who'd hung out with him during the entire nerve-racking evening. Delta pulled the Silverado to a stop and allowed Hannah to jump out of the back seat to approach the gate.

When the vehicles approached, Meredith stopped her nervous pacing and ran to her husband's side. As the vehicles pulled into view, she became weak in the knees as emotions overcame her. She strained to look for Hannah, praying to God that she was in one of the cars, safe and unharmed.

At first, Meredith reached through the iron bars to greet her child, but then she remembered the side gate accessible through the gatehouse. Before the security guards could open the main gates, Meredith bolted around the wall and through the guardhouse, where she collided with Hannah in a tangled mess of motherly love.

Cort finally caught up with his family, at first standing there in shock as tears rolled down his cheeks. His mouth agape, words escaped him as the joy of seeing his only child safe and sound froze him in time.

Finally, Meredith rose to her feet, helped Hannah up, and the close-knit Cortland family held each other tight, vowing never to separate again. However, promises made during an emotional moment can't always be kept, but at the time, they feel good nonetheless.

Ryan was one of the first to arrive, followed by Blair. They allowed Cort and his family to enjoy their emotional reunion, opting instead to get a quick debrief from Alpha and his team.

"Everybody okay?" Ryan began with an obvious question. He and Blair were fully aware of the dangerous mission undertaken by everyone who had left to rescue Hannah. They all knew the risks, but Ryan needed to know that they had come home safely, too.

"Yeah, not a scratch," replied Alpha as he removed his utility belt containing his sidearm, extra magazines, and a few leftover smoke grenades. He handed off his gear to one of the guards standing nearby, who was eager to help. "Charlie inhaled too much smoke. She complained that her respirator kept fogging up, so she stopped wearing it."

"Was it defective?" asked Ryan.

"Nah, user error," replied Alpha with a chuckle. "I straightened her out on the way back. Listen, Chepe is dead. Delta took him out." Alpha turned to see Delta standing off to the side, holding his ex-wife and Skylar in a solemn hug. While the Haven's residents were thrilled to see Hannah's safe return, it was not lost on any of them that Ethan would be gone forever.

"Good," said Blair. "I hope it was painful."

Alpha smiled and twisted his back until an audible crack could be heard. "Let's just say he went out in a blaze of glory."

A sizable crowd began to form around the front gate as the Cortland family broke their embrace and accepted congratulations for Hannah's safe return. While kids and adults alike spoke with Hannah,

Cort and Meredith made the rounds, personally hugging and thanking every member of the rescue effort.

Even hardened, tough ex-soldier Alpha managed to get emotional as Meredith spoke about what her daughter's safe return meant to her. Alpha told them briefly about the rescue and then finished by relaying the way Delta had caused Chepe's death.

The Cortlands and Hightowers spoke to one another last, sharing the excitement and sorrow of the last forty-eight hours. Ryan wanted the conversation to continue, but he decided to move the welcome home party up the hill, closer to Haven House. One never knew when a straggler might pass by their entrance or approach the gate.

Apparently, Blair had the same idea and raised her voice to get the attention of the crowd. "Hey, everybody! I know that we're all grateful to Alpha and his team for rescuing Hannah. There are reasons to celebrate, both for Hannah's return and to honor the lives of those we've lost. May I suggest we all go up to the house and get away from the front gate? You know, for security reasons. I've got food and drinks ready to go. I'm sure we wanna hear the details of Hannah's rescue, and I want us all, as a group, to remember those we lost during the attack."

"Great idea, Blair," added Ryan. "Please, let's head up there now and allow security to put the vehicles away. Alpha, Delta, all of you, please join us. I'll have somebody return your gear to Haven Barn."

The murmur of voices could be heard as people finished up their conversations and started new ones. They began the trek up the gravel driveway toward the house, except for X-Ray, who stood meekly to the side. Blair noticed this and whispered to Ryan, "I need to speak with X-Ray."

"What do we do with him now?" he asked.

"I'm the toughest critic and judge here. That said, I think he's earned his way back in."

"Good, I agree."

"However, he's on probation. From now on, he reports directly to me. I wanna know what the little weasel is working on at all times."

Ryan laughed and gave his wife a playful shove. "You're tough.

Look at him. He's about to wet himself thinking he's getting banished."

Blair managed a devilish grin. "Oh, believe me, I'll make him think he is. Then I'll make him wish he was. Finally, he'll be thanking me for the second chance."

"That's the way you roll."

"Yup," she added as she walked with purpose over to X-Ray.

Ryan made sure the front gate security team had their marching orders and that the residents were on their way, and then he stopped to survey the scene. He'd envisioned the community coming together as a family through the common need for safety, and to overcome adversity when it presented itself.

The Haven had been tested early on. In some respects, they'd failed in their preparations despite their best efforts. The loss of three lives was a testament to that. On the other hand, the group had jelled when they had to.

Ryan smiled, quietly patting Blair and himself on the back for managing triumph out of tribulation. Once again, as they'd done so many times in their life together, the couple turned lemons into lemonade.

Winning.

CHAPTER 26

Haven House
The Haven

Slaphappy from exhaustion, the adults chatted away, partaking of a glass of Rosa Regale from Blair's private stash. The sparkling red wine came from a specific wine grape grown in northwest Italy. It was a light ruby red color, but most importantly for Blair's personal taste, it had a sweet flavor like a dessert wine. Coupled with the lack of sleep and the desire to lift their spirits, it only took two glasses to immediately cause the residents to become chatty.

Meanwhile, Hannah was holding court in the media room, away from the watchful eyes of the adults. With the other kids gathered around, and the four-legged babies sprawled out on the hardwood floor, Hannah gave the blow-by-blow details of her abduction and captivity.

Then, with the drama that only a master storyteller can manage, she explained her decision to pull the laundry basket away from Chepe's landing spot. She had the kids rolling in laughter as she described how he'd groaned in pain when his ankle snapped. She stood on one leg and hopped around, using animated gestures to imitate Chepe as he made his way out of the utility room.

Of course, Hannah never let on how utterly terrified she had been during the entire ordeal. And when the other kids left the room to get a snack, she asked Skylar to stay behind so that she could tell her how brave Ethan had been. He'd died a hero, she insisted, and Skylar should forever be proud of what her brother had done to protect Will.

After a couple of hours, fatigue took over and the wine began to cause some eyes to gloss over from exhaustion. The celebration began to break up, and eventually, the group dispersed, leaving only the Smarts, Sheltons, and Cortlands behind.

"Ladies," began Ryan as he reached for Cort's and Tom's arms, "may I borrow these gentlemen for a moment before everybody heads to their cabins for a mid-afternoon nap?"

Donna chuckled. "Of course. Meredith, Blair, this is the time when the roosters slip away to congratulate themselves on a job well done. They'll likely bust open a bottle of scotch, pour a few more rounds, and then we'll have to put them to bed, where they'll snore blissfully well into the night."

Tom began laughing. "Now, Mrs. Shelton, why would you want to taint these fine ladies' images of their husbands?"

Blair rolled her eyes. "Tainted? Pshaw. Ryan only waited for the others to leave so he wouldn't have to share the good stuff."

Ryan smiled, rolled his eyes, and shook his head. "My missus takes no prisoners, but I love her so. Actually, no drinks. Cort needs to get some rest, and Tom's on antibiotics. I had to promise Angela that he'd stick to no more than two glasses of bubbly."

"All right, go ahead, then," said Meredith with a smile. "I'm sure Hannah can wait another few minutes."

Ryan led the guys into the study and gently pushed the door partially closed. His face grew serious as he paced the floor. He looked through the sheer curtains and then turned to his two top advisors. "It's time to make an honest assessment here. Chepe is dead and I think we've established that he was one of the top thugs working for the Schwartz family. Here's what I need you to think about, and we can reconvene later to discuss it."

"I know what you're thinking," interjected Cort.

"Me too," added Tom. "The question is whether this is over. Chepe and his anarchist buddies were readily available to attack us and to get to Cort. Whoever gave him the orders, whether Schwartz or someone else, is still out there. It's possible they'll make another run at—"

Tom's sentence was cut off by a call to Ryan's two-way radio. "Front gate to Haven House. Over."

Ryan held his index finger in the air, stopping Tom from continuing his thought. "Go ahead, Front Gate."

"Um, sir. There are two men here for Mr. Shelton. Uh, they're wearing Air Force uniforms."

Tom's eyes grew wide as he stared at Ryan's radio. A puzzled look came over his face.

"Stand by," said Ryan into his radio before turning to Tom. "Who knows you're here?"

"Nobody," he replied. "I mean, oh god. The girls. Our kids know we're here. What if …" A look of shock overcame his face and he raced for the door.

"Tom! Tom!" shouted Ryan as he and Cort chased after him. "Don't assume anything."

Tom ignored Ryan and found Donna in the living room with the ladies and Hannah. They noticed the look of alarm on his face and stood to greet him. Then Tom caught himself.

"Um, sorry to interrupt," he began, intending to hide his concerns from Donna. "I've gotta run down to the front gate with Ryan and Cort for a moment. Donna, will you wait here for me?"

She took a step toward him, but he backpedaled. "Dear, of course. But what's wrong?"

"Oh, probably nothing. We've just got a visitor to deal with. We'll be back shortly."

Tom turned to the guys and guided them to the front door with his eyes. They picked up on the cue and led the way.

Once outside the house, Ryan reiterated to Tom that he shouldn't worry, but the older man remained unconvinced. He was the first to enter the Ranger and tapped his leg impatiently until Ryan had them heading to the front gate.

When they arrived, two Air Force officers stood solemnly in front of the gate, being held in place by the security guards' rifles. Ryan drew closer and Tom squinted in the bright sunlight to get a better a look.

"Oh, God, I know one of them. It's Major Hicks from Joint Base Charleston. His rank, um, he outranks my oldest daughter, who is a captain."

Tom was making reference to the fact that a death notification contingent generally requires one of the personnel to be at an equal or greater rank than the deceased soldier.

The Ranger had barely come to a stop when Tom flung open the door with his noninjured arm and dashed to the gate.

"Major Hicks? I don't understand. Is it my daughter?" Tom's voice was hopeful, but full of trepidation.

"No, Colonel. I've been asked to deliver a message to you. Eyes only, sir."

"What?" Tom was dumbfounded as the major extended his arm through the gate with an envelope enclosed. He took the letter and then studied the major. "Major, how—?"

"Sir, there's more," Major Hicks continued. "I've been instructed to tell you that a chopper is parked nearby and is available for your use, if you so choose. In addition, I've been asked to give you this." He nodded to the captain, who stood stoically by his side.

The man removed a satellite telephone from his jacket pocket and handed it to Tom. "It's encrypted, Colonel. There are preset phone numbers programmed for you. It's chargeable with any USB device, sir."

"Thank you, Captain," said Tom as he rolled the satellite phone. He addressed the major. "What's this all about?"

"Sir, the correspondence is self-explanatory," he replied. "I'm not authorized to add to it other than to say the chopper is at your disposal."

Tom turned and looked at Cort and Ryan, who'd inched closer to listen to the conversation once they heard it didn't have anything to do with Tom's family.

Tom opened the sealed envelope and read the short letter. He shook his head and looked to the ground. Then he took a deep breath and turned to Cort.

"It's your father-in-law. He's dying."

PART THREE

CHAPTER 27

George Trowbridge's Residence
Near Pine Orchard, Connecticut

Cort, Meredith, and Hannah were excited at first as they climbed aboard the Bell 525 Relentless helicopter, one of three owned by George Trowbridge. With its use of fully integrated avionics coupled with an advanced fly-by-wire controls system, it provided the highest safety rating of any personal helicopter. Capable of holding twenty passengers, the Bell 525 cruised at a hundred thirty knots as it flew toward the Trowbridge residence. The crew made a quick stop for fuel at Dover Air Force Base in Delaware and then hugged the Atlantic seaboard, allowing the Cortlands an unparalleled view of Atlantic City, New York City, and Long Island as it descended toward Meredith's familial home overlooking Long Island Sound.

Full of apprehension, the family hastily departed the helicopter ducking under the massive blades rotating above their heads. They were greeted by Harris who filled them in on Trowbridge's condition as they walked to the main house.

"Meredith, it has been some time since you've seen your father, so I want to prepare you," said Harris as he glanced at the estranged daughter and the granddaughter he hadn't seen in many years. "His health has steadily declined since he was diagnosed with kidney failure. You combine that with the other ailments that beset a man of his age, such as vascular disease, and, well …" His voice trailed off as he became filled with emotions.

Meredith stopped and reached for Harris's arm. "You've been very loyal to my father, and I can't thank you enough for being there for him on a personal level. As he grew older, he had the opportunity to change his life. Most people his age look for a quality of life that is far simpler. You know, reading the daily newspaper, watching their favorite programs in the easy chair, and solving ever-more-difficult sudoku puzzles."

Harris regained his composure and laughed. "Yes, my father was that way. Yours was not. He was a driven man. Um, still is, excuse me. He just never found a way to release the reins of power that he'd become accustomed to wielding. I think he's now aware that it's almost over. That's why I took the extraordinary measures to reach you."

Cort asked, "Does he know we're coming?"

"No, not really, although in his weakened state, he will still be aware that the chopper has arrived. He'll be asking questions, but I suspect once he sees you, he'll understand."

Hannah looked up at Harris. "Is my grandfather going to die?"

Harris didn't attempt to respond, looking instead at Cort and Meredith. Talking with children about death was above his pay grade.

"Honey, we don't know yet," replied Meredith. "Let's go see him and say hello, okay?" She'd already asked the question when she caught herself.

Cort turned to Harris and whispered, "Is there any reason Hannah can't see him?"

"No, it's fine. He's under the best of care. Now, there are lots of machines and medical personnel around. I hope that doesn't frighten her."

Cort chuckled. "Um, she's been through a lot. I don't think much will frighten her."

Harris nodded and continued toward the house. Within a minute, they were standing in the grand foyer.

"Excuse me for a moment while I check in with the doctor," said Harris as he ran up the stairs, taking two at a time.

Meredith showed Hannah around, explaining to her that this was where she grew up before she'd met Cort. Hannah had been very young and didn't remember the last visit to the estate. Cort had been there recently, but Meredith hadn't returned home in many years.

There were some new paintings adorning the walls and several photographs of her father with foreign dignitaries as well as Washington politicians. Cort pointed out some of the more notable people pictured, especially those whom Hannah might recognize.

After a few minutes, the medical team emerged from the master suite and descended the stairs to introduce themselves to the Cortlands. They made small talk and then the team explained Trowbridge's diminished condition.

Harris took Hannah on a tour of the home's main level, which included the piano room, the enclosed swimming pool and gym, and her grandfather's study. While they were away, the doctor brought the Cortlands up to speed.

Meredith listened intently as she was bombarded with a barrage of complex medical terms like uremia, hemodialysis, fistula, and shunt. She asked for explanations to help her understand the medical jargon. Ultimately, they provided her a history of her father and the blood-purifying machine that kept him alive. And then his primary physician brought them up to his current condition.

"The medical equipment that we've employed in his care is the best money can buy. Frankly, it's better than what most community hospitals have at their disposal. His treatment, however, is not a cure. It's a life-extending mechanism designed to prevent the toxic substances from building up within his body that would necessarily have resulted in his death some time ago."

"He was fully alert when I saw him on New Year's Eve," Cort interrupted.

"That happens sometimes before a patient's condition worsens," explained the doctor. "Over the past week or so, Mr. Trowbridge has complained of constantly being cold. His aches and pains have worsened. He is increasingly short of breath. And despite our constant monitoring of his condition and, frankly, due to his excessive need to converse with others …" The doctor's voice trailed off as he cast a glance in the direction that Harris had taken Hannah for a tour.

"What do you mean?" asked Meredith.

"He's developed mouth sores and has increased difficulty in swallowing, which has resulted in a loss of appetite. Elderly people in general have a tendency to cut back on their food intake in their later years. For Mr. Trowbridge, the lack of sustenance can hasten his death."

"I have to ask something," began Cort. "Does my father-in-law have a DNR order?"

A DNR, or do not resuscitate order, is a legally recognized document executed by a patient while he is still of sound mind and body. Also referred to as a living will, it details a person's desires on how they are treated medically in the event they are unable to communicate their wishes on their own. Oftentimes, the DNR orders health care professionals not to take extraordinary means to keep the patient alive. This includes withholding cardiopulmonary resuscitation, or CPR, as well as other forms of advanced cardiac life support in the event their heart stops working or their breathing fails.

"He does, as well as a durable power of attorney for health care," replied the doctor. Unlike the living will, which generally applies to a patient who has little or no hope of recovery, a durable power of attorney appoints someone, usually a trusted family member, to make health care decisions, as well as financial ones, in the event the patient becomes mentally incapacitated.

"Good," replied Cort. As a former attorney, he was thoroughly familiar with the legalities surrounding these two health-related documents, as well as the use of living trusts to avoid probate when settling an estate. He'd created similar documents for him and Meredith, which also provided for the care of Hannah should they die before she turned eighteen. "Well, I assumed that George would have something like that in place. I'm glad that Harris summoned us. With Meredith here, she can make the decisions—"

"Um, excuse me, Mr. Cortland," interrupted the doctor. "Actually, Mrs. Cortland is not the person named in the durable power of attorney. You are."

"Me? Why wouldn't he—" Meredith answered his question for him by catching herself. Then she continued. "Because his daughter was being a selfish brat at the time and he probably didn't trust me to do the right thing."

Cort tried to console his wife. "Honey, we don't know that."

"It doesn't matter, Cort. He was right. I trust you with those decisions, why wouldn't he?"

Cort was anxious to change the subject, especially since Hannah was returning. "Can we see him now?"

"Yes, he's unaware of your arrival, but he is awake and lucid," replied the doctor.

"Doctor, how much longer does he have?" asked Meredith.

"It's hard to say," said the doctor.

Meredith pressed him for an answer. "Hours? Days?"

"Well, I meant what I said. Mr. Trowbridge is a fighter and he could manage to live for weeks or a month. There are so many variables to consider. Might I suggest that you focus on today? When I took him under my care, we had an understanding. One day at a time."

Cort smiled and reached out to shake the doctor's hand. "I agree. Thank you so much for all you've done for him. One day at a time, starting with today."

CHAPTER 28

George Trowbridge's Residence
Near Pine Orchard, Connecticut

Tears flowed as Meredith and her father reunited. Apologies were exchanged and heartfelt words of love were spoken between the estranged daughter and father. Also, Hannah was reacquainted with her grandfather. Trowbridge perked up as she told him about her life and what her interests were. She talked about her school studies, her hobbies, and gave him a full briefing on the exploits of Handsome Dan.

Cort was proud of Hannah for not burdening Trowbridge with the story of her abduction and rescue. Cort planned on discussing Chepe and his ties to Schwartz when the opportunity presented itself. His father-in-law did not need to know how close Hannah had been to being killed.

With Trowbridge finding a newfound strength, Cort took the opportunity to slip into the hallway to speak with Harris alone. They gently pulled the master suite doors shut and spoke in hushed tones just outside the door so that they could be close by in the event of a problem.

"I need to bring you up to speed on something," Cort began as Harris provided him his undivided attention. "The Haven, which you're clearly aware of, was attacked a couple of days ago. Hannah was abducted and taken into Charlotte by a guy named Chepe."

"Chepe?" Harris's recognition of the name was instantaneous. "He's one of the top guys in Schwartz's anarchist army. What's he doin' in Charlotte?"

"I don't know for certain, and now that he's dead, we won't get it out of him."

Harris wandered away from Cort and thought for a moment. "Why would Chepe come after the Haven or kidnap Hannah?"

"He was after me," replied Cort matter-of-factly.

"You? I don't get it."

Cort offered his theory. "I understand that Schwartz and Jonathan have this rivalry thing going with George. They're like big political bulls in the arena, fighting one another for supremacy."

"The old man was arrested," interjected Harris. He thrust his hands in his pants pockets and stared out at the Bell helicopter and Long Island Sound beyond it. "Cort, we initiated the FBI raid that took him down in order to take advantage of the president's martial law declaration."

"Are you saying this is an act of revenge?" asked Cort before continuing. He gave his assessment. "Jonathan couldn't get through all of the security around here and decided to send his henchman to come after me and my family."

"Possibly," replied Harris.

Suddenly, the master suite doors opened, and Meredith emerged from her father's bedroom. "Guys, he's getting tired, and I need to get Hannah some lunch. Daddy asked that you two come inside for a moment."

Harris and Cort exchanged glances before walking into Trowbridge's inner sanctum. They didn't have an opportunity to finish their conversation, and as they approached Trowbridge's bedside, the tension showed on both of their faces.

"Gentlemen, I am dying, but I am not yet dead. Nor am I blind. But let me assure you, my patience is thin, and one of you had better start talking."

Cort nodded to Harris, indicating that he should shut the bedroom doors. He took the brief delay in responding as an opportunity to gather his thoughts. He wouldn't lie to Trowbridge, but some facts would be omitted.

"I'll get right to the point," began Cort, hoping the direct approach would prevent Trowbridge from questioning his account of the events. Even then, the man in his weakened condition could still discern fact from fiction.

"Please do," said Trowbridge as his eyes opened a little wider.

"The Haven was attacked by a group of anarchists led by a guy known as Chepe, real name Joseph Acuff."

"Schwartz's man," muttered Trowbridge. "Jonathan's retaliating against me."

"Harris and I were discussing this in the hallway, and we believe that to be the case," said Cort. "The attack was repelled, not without loss of life on our end, however. The group mounted a posse to hunt Chepe down, and he was killed when they found him."

Trowbridge nodded his acknowledgment, but he was still deep in thought. His tired eyes focused on Cort's, peering deep into the younger man's soul, searching for the truth. "There's more."

Cort continued. "Yes, sir. I have a question about the initials MM. Is that related to you?"

Trowbridge swallowed hard and his mouth suddenly became dry. He pointed to the glass of ice chips that was a constant fixture by his bedside. Harris quickly helped him moisten his mouth with the ice.

"There is lots to discuss, Cort, and the Minutemen are part of that conversation. My network of allies and operatives stretches around the globe. Within this country, the Minutemen are my version of the deep state—a clandestine government within the government. These are people who are loyal to me."

"Politicians for hire," added Cort.

"More than that," said Trowbridge. "Bureaucrats, military, media executives, and business owners are all Minutemen within my control. They are widespread throughout the country and offer services that have proven to be indispensable to what I believe needs to be done."

Cort was now hearing what he always assumed, that someone rich and powerful was behind the New Year's Eve attacks, not a foreign nation's operatives or terrorists. "I'm not here to judge or criticize methods. Truthfully, at least based on what I know, I think I can understand the logic behind your methods. The question I have is whether this is over, or do I need to worry about the safety of my family and our friends at the Haven?"

Trowbridge grimaced as he tried to raise himself higher in the bed. Harris rushed to his side and reminded him that the doctor forbade unnecessary stress or activity. Trowbridge brushed him off with a wave of his hand.

"Jonathan Schwartz may have taken his shot and missed, but he won't stop there. He'll simply try a different tack."

"Does Schwartz know about the Minutemen or have access to your contact list?"

Harris took that question. "No, not to my knowledge. The entire list is only available to Mr. Trowbridge, Hanson Briscoe, and myself."

The name struck a nerve with Cort. "Briscoe? The name is familiar. Bonesman, correct? But he rarely participated in the gatherings."

"That's right, son," said Trowbridge, who suddenly referred to Cort affectionately. "Did Briscoe reach out to you?"

"No, not me, but another person within the compound besides Tom Shelton. Well, two others. One is legal counsel to the president, Hayden Blount, who received a cryptic message early on. A warning of sorts."

"Most likely that was from Samuel," said Harris, who was referencing Supreme Court Justice Samuel Alito, Hayden's mentor and a fellow Bonesman. "He thinks very highly of her and has strongly urged us to advance her opportunities. For now, she does valuable work for the president."

"Who is the other?" said Trowbridge, who was growing short of breath.

Cort moved closer to Trowbridge and replied, "A computer hacker named O'Reilly. He goes by the nickname X-Ray. He claimed to have been told by his handler, someone within the Minutemen hierarchy, to inform them if I had been seen. It had to be somebody who knew that X-Ray would be going to the Haven."

"Not necessarily," countered Harris. "This directive was put out well before our arrival there. It was, um, sorry, sir, um, Mr.

Trowbridge's way of keeping up with your whereabouts."

Cort looked to his father-in-law, whose face was ridden with guilt. He closed his eyes and nodded, affirming Harris's statement.

Cort sighed. "Meredith must never know this. Any of it, agreed?"

"Yes," said Harris, who expressed Trowbridge's sentiments as well.

"Now," continued Cort. "X-Ray exchanged a series of text messages with his handler, one of the Minutemen. It indicated an attack upon the compound was imminent. Who would that be?"

"Briscoe," whispered Trowbridge. "He's aware of my deteriorating health, and that someday I'd yield what I've built to someone else. He's power hungry."

"Weren't you two close?" asked Cort.

"Yes, of course. Son, he was not family."

Cort stepped back. Meredith was his only family, at least by blood relation. Then it dawned on him. Trowbridge was establishing a connection between Briscoe and the attack upon the Haven, and it stemmed around the heir apparent to the Trowbridge power base.

"Are you talking about me? You want me to take over? I'm not sure this—"

Trowbridge spoke up. "Son, it is your destiny."

CHAPTER 29

George Trowbridge's Residence
Near Pine Orchard, Connecticut

"George, I have no problem with the way you've done business in Washington. Influence peddling is as old as the day the concept of government was first introduced five thousand years ago. Further, I can't argue that this nation needed some form of shock treatment. Something drastic had to be done or the great American experiment would've collapsed and later been replaced with something far different. I don't think I'm prepared to take over in the midst of an undeclared second civil war."

"You are, son, without a doubt in my mind. Briscoe saw the handwriting on the wall, and he sought to eliminate you as collateral damage."

"Wait, are you saying he knew I was on Delta 322?"

"I am, yes," replied Trowbridge. "Furthermore, it's likely he used my love and concern for my family by putting out an all-points bulletin to keep up with your whereabouts. Instead of providing you a ring of protection, it appears he shared the information with Schwartz."

"Sir, how would he do that? Briscoe should be hiding deep in the woods after—" Harris caught himself and attempted to deflect by offering Trowbridge more ice chips.

"After what, Harris?" Cort insisted upon a response. "If I'm to be involved, I need the total picture."

"I suspected his betrayal and ordered him killed," replied Trowbridge.

Cort rolled his head back and forth on his shoulders. He needed to release the tension that was building up inside him. The tension turned to anger. "I take it you missed."

"Yes, and he's gone missing," replied Harris.

"With all of your resources, you haven't been able to find him?" Cort was incredulous.

"Well, there were trust issues during this transition period and considering Mr. Trowbridge's health. We only have a limited number of people that we'd like to get involved at this point."

Cort wandered away from the bed and studied his surroundings. His father-in-law had become a prisoner in his bedroom, and now he was consumed in his final days by a vendetta against two men who were fighting back—using his family as pawns in the battle. He took a deep breath and exhaled.

Trowbridge tried to explain. "Son, the cancer within my ranks had to be eliminated. It was the right call."

"I don't disagree, but the job isn't finished. That's up to me now."

"What are you saying?" asked Harris.

"I will not let this family's legacy go down in history because of a traitor like Briscoe. I don't know how he's connected to Schwartz, but there is no other explanation as to how Chepe would know about the Haven."

"I agree," said Trowbridge. "What do you have in mind?"

"Schwartz needs to be killed. His death will be a message to his father, who will hopefully rot away in a federal prison, and it will gut the Schwartzes' political power. Those two have micromanaged the far left's anarchist ways for decades."

"Yes, go on," said Trowbridge, who was suddenly more engaged.

"Briscoe is a traitor to you, his fellow Bonesmen, and all who are trying to preserve our nation as envisioned by the Founding Fathers. He made this personal by trying to take advantage of your ill-health to shift power into his hands."

"They both need to go; we acknowledge that," said Harris. "We can't find them."

Cort was blunt. "It's no longer your concern." He faced his father-in-law. "You groomed me to take over, so let me prove that you've made the right decision."

"I have resources. Let me help."

"No, sir, but thank you. Your point regarding trust of others is well taken. At this time, you need plausible deniability, especially as it relates to our fellow Bonesmen and others within the Minutemen. They might not understand your attempt to assassinate Briscoe. In addition, it could taint my ability to lead them in the future."

"You don't have the ability—" began Harris before Cort stopped him.

"Harris, I admire you for your service to my father, and I look forward to working with you in the future. I will handle this."

Cort approached Trowbridge's bed and took the man's cold hand in his. The warmth emanating from Cort caused a smile to cross the old man's face. The physical touch was symbolic of the mutual love and respect the two had for one another.

Cort leaned down and whispered, "Trust me."

CHAPTER 30

George Trowbridge's Residence
Near Pine Orchard, Connecticut

Cort didn't want to waste any time searching for Briscoe and Schwartz. They might or might not be involved together, and if they were, they might be unaware that his family had fled for Connecticut. Not only did he owe it to the residents of the Haven, who'd risked their lives for his family, but he wanted to call on them to assist him in hunting down the men who were ultimately responsible. Plus, there was now more at stake than just revenge. America was on the brink.

Cort's conversation with Meredith, and then together with Hannah, was a difficult one. They both insisted upon returning with him to the Haven. They saw that as their home now, their family. Hannah loved her new friends, and Meredith had a sense of involvement that she'd never felt in Mobile.

He promised her that remaining at her father's home was necessary due to his health, and he reminded her of the continued threat to Hannah to help make his argument. He felt it was somewhat underhanded to play on Meredith's emotions that way, but it ended the discussion. The Cortland women would stay within the safer confines of the Trowbridge estate, and Cort would take the helicopter back to the Haven.

Cort chastised himself for continuing to lie to his wife and daughter. The conversation was partly truthful, but included was a whopper of a lie of omission that might haunt him for the rest of his life. He was hell-bent on revenge, and he needed his new friends to exact it with him. He trusted the Smarts, Alpha, and the others at the

Haven. Besides, he was still skeptical of how he had been discovered there, and by whom.

Harris, whom Cort wanted to consider beyond reproach, might have sought the same kind of power that Briscoe tried to take. Cort speculated in his mind that it was possible the two men were working in concert with one another. Briscoe's escape from one of Trowbridge's hit teams was more than fortuitous; it was as if the man's life was blessed by the Lord Almighty himself.

For that reason, Cort had to make his own arrangements. He had seasoned military people, an ex-LEO who knew how to think like a fugitive, an experienced hunter in Hayden, and X-Ray, who for all of his misdeeds, was a master at using computer technology to their advantage.

With an air of confidence, Cort strode into his father-in-law's suite before he left. Harris was taking notes, and the conversation between the two men abruptly stopped when Cort entered.

"Cort, Mr. Trowbridge and I were discussing—" began Harris when Trowbridge raised his hand and stopped him.

"Allow me. Cort, we have taken the time to make a list of trusted people to track down Schwartz and Briscoe. You do not have to put your new friends at risk."

"No," said Cort brusquely. "I stand by my earlier decision. I trust my people, and they're more than capable."

"Son, these are trained operatives. Highly trained by our CIA in covert tactics. One of them was on the SEAL team that attacked Bin Laden's compound."

"I understand that, and I don't want to argue with you. Please, you've got to trust my judgment or I'm the wrong man for the job. Not just the task of locating Briscoe and Schwartz, I mean the whole thing. All of it."

Trowbridge frowned, but nodded his acquiescence. "I will not interfere, but I will insist on something."

"Maybe," said Cort defiantly.

"Once you locate their whereabouts, I take it you will be pulling your best people out of the Haven. Correct?"

Cort quickly replied, "Yes, that is a possibility."

"Then allow me to fill the Bell with personnel and weaponry. Also, tactical gear that is military issue, which will help protect the compound as they go after these men. My people will stay on the perimeter, protecting the families, while you do what you have to do."

Cort couldn't argue with Trowbridge's offer. It would also help him sell the entire operation to Blair and Ryan, who would certainly balk at gutting the Haven's security team. Besides, all of the residents could use some peace of mind after what they'd been through.

"Okay. I agree. Thank you."

"Thank you, son. I want to help you, but I recognize that you need to find your own way."

"Excuse me, gentlemen, I'll need a few minutes to notify the men. They're prepared to travel on a moment's notice. Also, I'll fill the chopper with gear."

"Thank you," said Trowbridge before adding, "And, Harris, satellite telephones also. I want Cort and his people to be able to reach out to us if necessary."

"Yes, sir." Harris scurried into the hallway and down the stairs, leaving Trowbridge and Cort alone.

After Harris left, Cort closed the door and turned to speak. Trowbridge was reflective and motioned him closer. He reached under his covers, and when he pulled his arm out, he was holding a cell phone.

"This is yours now. It is encrypted with the highest available security. Only three people have one like it. One is Briscoe and the other is Harris."

Cort took the phone, which was the most recent iPhone device. It didn't look any different from the one he used to carry every day.

"Other than its enhanced security, is there anything else special about it?" asked Cort.

Trowbridge motioned for him to return it to him. Even in his diminished capacity, he was able to navigate the settings app on the phone. He found security and pressed several keys on the pop-up keyboard display. Without warning, he lifted the phone toward Cort's face and pressed a button.

"This can only be unlocked by you now," he said as he handed the phone back. "The contacts list is written in code. You'll find the key to the symbols and numbers in the notes, which are locked and require a passcode."

"What is it?"

"Eighteen thirty-two, Taft, three-two-two," he replied before explaining, "Eighteen thirty-two was the year of our founding. Alphonso Taft was one of the original founders of the Skull and Bones. Three-two-two represents the room number at the lodge, the holy place that you will soon enter when the time comes."

"This is how I contact the Minutemen?" asked Cort.

"All of them, son. The Minutemen, military personnel, foreign diplomats. If need be, the President of the United States."

"He knows about all of this?" asked Cort, waving the phone around as he spoke.

Trowbridge chuckled. "No, of course not. Plausible deniability."

"Those are my words," said Cort with a smile.

"Yes, but you're not the first to use them. Cort, there is much to be learned, and circumstances have cut your education short. I want you to know that Harris can be trusted. I suspect part of your reasoning in acting outside the confines of my network is his possible involvement."

"Yes, that's true."

"Son, if his goal was to assassinate you, then the chopper carrying my family would've never landed on the back lawn. You will lean heavily upon him at first. At some point, you will choose your own *consigliere*, your counselor. One who will continue what I began many years ago."

Trowbridge began to cough, and he frantically rubbed his throat as if he was choking. He motioned toward the stainless-steel medical table by his bed.

Cort hustled to the table and offered both water and ice chips. Trowbridge gulped water and then began to cough as if he was drowning. He winced in pain as the fit subsided.

"Are you okay? Do I need to get the nurse?"

Trowbridge slowly waved his hand in front of his chest and shook his head. "This happens more frequently. Son, I'm dying. I will hold on as long as I can. For the benefit of Meredith and my granddaughter, but also for you. You are my son. I've known it since my daughter proudly introduced you to this family. I have planned my life, and my death, around you."

"George, that's very nice of you—" started Cort before Trowbridge continued.

"You are more than the protector of my family. I'm looking to you to safeguard my legacy, which is to preserve this nation. I've started us down an uncertain path, but I wholly believe it is the only course of action to protect the nation. I can only be judged by God, and I suspect my day to account for my deeds will be coming soon."

Cort took Trowbridge's hands again. "You have the best care available and two strong women by your side now. I'll be back when the job is done, and now you can rest assured I will handle matters the best way I can."

Trowbridge squeezed Cort's hands and smiled. "I love you, son." Then his eyes closed, and his feeble hands let go.

CHAPTER 31

The Haven

The final leg of the ride from Connecticut to the Haven aboard the Bell helicopter was blessed with clear skies and a lack of turbulence. Cort attributed the smooth ride, which lacked the sudden sideways movements and occasional abrupt changes in altitude typical of flying in a helicopter, to the size of the Relentless 525 model. He'd flown in shuttle flights aboard choppers many times between DC and surrounding cities to follow Senator McNeill to meetings or speaking engagements. The senator seemed to enjoy the swooping motions common to helicopter flight; Cort did not. After his fateful ride on Delta 322, he liked flying even less.

He was grateful that he was scheduled to arrive back at the Haven before dark. Once, during a nighttime landing, he had trouble with his vision. His eyes had difficulty focusing on a point on the ground, and the spatial disorientation caused him to be consumed by motion sickness. Today, with so much at stake, he didn't need the added stress.

The normally deafening thumping sounds of the rotors weren't heard in the Bell. The noise-reduction measures built into the Bell's cabin, coupled with redesigned engines, served to reduce any intrusion into his thoughts.

He'd be asking a lot of the Smarts and the people he'd call upon to hunt down Schwartz and Briscoe. He had to convince them that the dangerous undertaking was about more than revenge.

Revenge was like a storm. It was easy to lose your way in a storm even though you weren't far from your destination.

After the attack and subsequent rescue of Hannah, he'd now be calling upon some of them to risk their lives. However, this time, it was for more than the Cortland family. It was for the sake of God and country.

As the pilot swooped across the Outer Banks along the Atlantic Ocean, Cort caught a glimpse of several fishing boats bringing in their catch. The abundance of fish off the North Carolina coast was a necessity as the food supply chains in America came to a screeching halt.

Corporate farming operations, which made up most of the grain production in America, had stopped due to excessive costs and fuel shortages. Fruits and vegetables, the majority of which were produced in California, never made their way to the eastern half of the U.S. In Mexico, Central, and South America, countries that ordinarily picked up production of fruits and vegetables when California's growing season ended, imports to the U.S. stopped in order to focus on feeding their own.

As a result, communities and geographic regions stepped up their own food production. States that bordered the oceans began to rely heavily upon their fishermen. Governors allocated fuel reserves to the fishermen to the detriment of other industries. State and federal coastal patrols were established to protect the fishermen, both while on the open sea from pirates, who'd begun to attack the boats at the end of the day's catch, and when they arrived in port, where crowd control was necessary to fight off hungry residents.

The seasoned pilot circled the Haven twice, banking at a sharp angle to view the area around Haven Barn, where Cort had instructed him to land. Cort saw members of the Haven security team scramble to get into position. He had worked with Alpha long enough to know that he wouldn't order his people to fire upon the chopper despite its intrusion into the Haven. Dropping a helicopter into the middle of the Haven's security would've been suicidal, and also, Alpha didn't have itchy trigger fingers.

The pilot expertly set the Bell down as grass, small rocks, and dirt began to swirl in the air, driven by the downward thrust of the fifteen-million-dollar aircraft. Any members of the Haven who'd ventured out from behind their protective cover immediately scampered back behind a tree or rushed to cover their faces from being pelted.

Amidst the deluge, the pilot began to shut off the engines. As the powerful rotor blades slowed, the residents of the Haven began to show themselves. Cort, as the only recognizable passenger, departed first. He told the security team to hold back until he'd taken a moment to explain.

With the assistance of the pilot, Cort emerged from the chopper and immediately waved at Alpha, Bravo, and Charlie, who'd taken up positions on the edge of the forest about twenty yards apart from each other.

"It's all good!" shouted Cort, waving his arms toward Alpha. "These guys are here to help."

Alpha emerged from the woods first, and then Ryan appeared unexpectedly from Cort's left. Several other members of the security team emerged from the barn to his right. By the time they entered the clearing, the rotors had stopped and Cort didn't have to shout.

"Ryan, Alpha, everybody," he began, "I've got lots to talk with you about. First, let me tell you that Meredith and Hannah have remained at her family's home in Connecticut." He turned to the chopper and waved at the operatives, who kept their weapons ready but stayed within the interior compartment. One by one they emerged, wearing khaki pants, long-sleeved black shirts, sunglasses, and dark caps—the uniform of the private contractor.

Alpha stepped toward them and sized up their appearance. He provided them an imperceptible nod, a tribute, as recognition swept over both groups. They might not have known each other personally, but they certainly knew who the other was, in their souls.

Alpha turned to Cort. "You brought the cavalry."

"Sort of," said Cort. "These guys will be at your disposal. If you'd like them to stay out of your way, they'll patrol your outside perimeter. If you want to use them on the inside, you can. Either way, they're staying to fulfill a role in support of the Haven."

"Why?" asked Ryan, who walked up to Alpha's side to study the newcomers.

"I'll explain," replied Cort. "But before we get into details, I want you to see some of the presents I brought from my father-in-law."

Cort approached Trowbridge's operatives and gave them instructions to unload the crates of weapons and military-grade gear designed to both enhance the security capabilities at the Haven and to be used in any mission that might materialize in support of Cort's targets.

Simultaneously, Alpha waved Bravo and Charlie forward as the ex-military personnel got acquainted with Trowbridge's people. There were laughs and high fives exchanged as the military hardware was unloaded.

Ryan joined Cort's side, who said, "I come bearing gifts." It was a reference to the Three Wise Men bringing gold, frankincense, and myrrh to Jesus upon his birth.

Ryan chuckled and watched intently as the group unpacked the crates and passed the weapons around. "Yeah, there's another old saying that goes something like *beware of Greeks bringing joyous bounty and endowments*."

Cort let out a hearty laugh, his first in a long time. "Does that chopper look like a Trojan Horse to you? If it was, the target, me, would've been dropped somewhere over the Atlantic and they would've gone back to George's place."

Alpha had wandered back to Cort and Ryan. "Very nice, Cort. Your people are on the ball."

"They're our people now," said Cort before adding, "to an extent."

Ryan continued to be skeptical. "I feel a *but* or some other some-somethin' comin'."

Cort looked both men in the eyes and patted them on the shoulders. "Fellas, we have another operation to undertake. As Jefferson said, the tree of liberty must be refreshed from time to time with the blood of patriots and tyrants. It's time to water the tree of liberty."

CHAPTER 32

Haven House
The Haven

While Bravo and Charlie worked with Trowbridge's security personnel to get unloaded, the rest of the group made their way to Haven House to listen to Cort's proposal. Tom and Donna Shelton were already there with Blair. Delta was called up from the front gate, and Hayden, who had taken a team outside the Haven to go hunting, was recalled to join them.

It was dark when Hayden arrived, and the rest of the group had made small talk over dinner while they waited. A roaring fire warmed the living room, and rather than sit formally around the dining table, Cort suggested everyone get comfortable while he took a seat on the massive stone hearth.

"I feel like daddy is about to tell us a story," said Hayden with a mouthful of venison stew. This drew a laugh from the crowd, and some playful teasing was thrown in Cort's direction. The group had always been close, but the attack and Hannah's rescue had brought them together as a family.

"Well, in a way, what I'm about to propose sounds like it comes straight out of a political suspense novel," began Cort. "Let me lay it out for you and confirm some of the things we already suspected."

"You mean as it relates to the New Year's attacks," interjected Donna.

"And afterwards," added Cort. "My father-in-law, using his right-hand man, Hanson Briscoe, was responsible for the attacks that occurred New Year's Eve. There are lots of reasons for his ill-conceived plan, but the bottom line is it set off a course of events that has escalated since."

"He tried to have you killed?" asked Hayden, who was still eating.

"No, that was Briscoe. You see, George is dying. In fact, his health has rapidly deteriorated since the first of the year. Even before that, however, Briscoe wanted to be the heir to the political machine that George had built. When it became obvious that George intended to turn over his power base to me, Briscoe had to take me out."

"Whoa!" exclaimed Hayden, who abruptly stopped chewing and swallowed her last bite. "Ladies and gentlemen, may I introduce you to King Cort, the second most powerful man in Washington behind my number one client."

"King Cort?" Blair asked with a chuckle. "Are you kidding?"

"No, Blair, not at all," replied Hayden. "George Trowbridge has his finger in every pie, thumb on every politician, and has the ability to direct virtually every decision that has a geopolitical impact on our nation. Cort is the new George Trowbridge."

"Not until he passes," interrupted Cort. "I want to downplay the magnitude of what Hayden has described. I want you guys to know that I never sought this job, nor am I fully prepared to take it. I assumed Briscoe or another one of the Bonesmen would be anointed the head of the Trowbridge political kingdom."

"These guys are Skull and Bones?" asked Tom.

"Yessir," replied Cort. "Another long story but suffice it to say that a feud that began thirty-five years ago has resulted in America being on the brink of a second civil war, and my father-in-law fired the first shot."

Alpha chimed in. "They were cannon blasts. But somebody decided to fight back."

"Yes. György Schwartz and his son, Jonathan," said Cort. "They control the myriad of so-called grassroots protest movements around the country. They fund these groups and therefore can dictate where they wreak havoc."

"How does this explain the involvement of Chepe in the attack upon the Haven?" asked Ryan.

Cort furrowed his brow, as he still was not one hundred percent sure of the answer. "Jonathan Schwartz, who took control of the anarchists because his father has been arrested, decided to sic the dogs on me as payback for George orchestrating his father's arrest. Or Briscoe and Schwartz are working together."

"They hate one another," said Hayden.

"Adversity makes strange bedfellows, counselor," joked Tom. "The question is what would prompt Briscoe to take the extraordinary step of drawing the Haven and Cort's family into his personal quest for power?"

"It's a vendetta," replied Cort. "George tried to assassinate Briscoe several days ago and failed. The man has fallen off the radar, and it's possible he has teamed up with Schwartz."

"That would be an odd coupling," said Hayden with a chuckle. "Cort, you obviously have something in mind. Am I correct?"

Cort nodded and stood in front of the group. "While I agree with my father-in-law with respect for the need to jolt our country back onto the right path, I wholly disagree with his methods. Too many innocent lives were lost. I believe there could have been a better way."

"Such as?" asked Ryan.

"Targeted assassinations of those responsible for sowing the seeds of discontent," he quickly replied as if he'd been thinking of the subject matter for some time. "Without creating martyrs, the most prominent voices of the opposition could've been silenced using several methods. But what's done is done. Now we have to stop the bloodshed and give the president the opportunity to bring the nation back together."

"Is he capable?" asked Delta.

"I think he is, but he has to do it in such a way that spans the political abyss. He has to look less divisive and more like a *reconcilliator*."

"*Reconcilliator*," Blair began to ask. "Is that even a word?"

"It sounds like a George W. Bush word," replied Ryan with a laugh.

"Yeah, yeah," said Cort, who enjoyed the ribbing. "You guys know what I mean and that's what matters. My point is this. If we want to put an end to this and make the president look good in the process, we need to mete out justice to the two people who are the heads of their respective snakes."

"Briscoe and Schwartz," said Ryan.

"Right," replied Cort. "If we can take them out before inauguration day, Wednesday the twentieth, which is fast approaching—"

"It is?" asked Donna. "I've lost all sense of time."

"Yeah, me too," said Blair. Then she directed her question to Hayden. "Okay, let me ask the president's attorney something. Hayden, you and Cort are inside-the-beltway types who understand Washington's way of thinking. Would the president be better off if these two were eliminated?"

Hayden thought for a moment and responded, "He'd be better off if he took advantage of a decline in hostilities rather than having to deploy the U.S. military on American soil in violation of posse comitatus. He'd be setting a dangerous precedent to do that."

"I agree," said Cort. "By removing Briscoe and Schwartz from the equation, the titular heads of the two warring sides of the aisle will no longer be able to direct their ground troops, so to speak. The Schwartz funds to the anarchist groups will be cut off. Briscoe's power over military and law enforcement resources will be taken away."

"Makes sense," said Ryan.

"Okay, where are they?" asked Alpha.

Cort grimaced. "Um, I have no idea. I need to use X-Ray to find them."

"Can you trust him?" asked Blair, who felt better about the young man but still had lingering doubts.

"I have to. With Briscoe alive and still pulling the strings of his operatives, I'm not sure who I can trust. Besides, I've already elevated his security access to make it easier. I also have new communications, satellite, and computer gear to help him."

"These new men," began Donna, "the ones you brought along, are they going to search for Briscoe and Schwartz?"

Cort shook his head. "No, I'd like to pick a team and do it ourselves. They'll remain here, under Ryan and Blair's direction, to protect the Haven while we're gone."

"Why don't you use the operators?" asked Blair. "They're better trained than our people."

"Maybe," replied Cort. "However, there is the matter of trust and loyalty. You see, they aren't aware that our targets include Briscoe. They think they're here to assist in the Haven's security. I need to keep our mission close to the vest."

Blair continued to play devil's advocate. "Schwartz and Briscoe have resources, too. What makes you think they haven't surrounded themselves with an army of operators like your new guys?"

"They're probably more cautious than I am at the moment. Both of them are on the run while I'm on the offensive. They just don't know it yet."

"It gives us an element of surprise," muttered Alpha. "If they're together, hiding out, they may have reached a false sense of security because of the passage of time."

"Exactly," said Cort. "Listen, one of the first conversations we had as a group when everyone arrived was the meaning of the letters *MM* in the cryptic texts some of us had received. It took an eight-year-old boy to point out the obvious. George Trowbridge envisioned a clandestine army of Minutemen who'd leap into action when the opportunity presented itself. He called on the Minutemen and, depending on how you look at it, they performed admirably."

Cort paused to study the faces of his new, extended family. He wanted to gauge their reaction before he asked them to take a big risk, not only for him, but for their country. He'd never considered himself an orator, but in the moment, he found himself channelling patriots from years past.

"I'll be taking control of the Minutemen as George's days on Earth dwindle. That said, for now, I need Minutemen of my own to correct the course he envisioned and start anew. I hope that you all will be with me."

CHAPTER 33

Schwartz Lodge
Near Kutztown, Pennsylvania

Over their days holed up together at Schwartz's Lodge in the hills outside Kutztown, Briscoe and his adversary had become friends. Naturally, they discussed politics, a topic that consumed their lives both before and after the New Year's attacks. They also discussed world affairs, finance, and America's world standing. Their discussions never became heated and oftentimes resulted in a point-counterpoint type of exchange in which the two men tallied their points and kept score.

The consensus, usually after an emptied bottle of brandy or two, was that both sides of the political spectrum wanted the same thing, they simply disagreed on the means of achieving their goal.

They were fully aware that chaos was rampant in the streets of midsize to large cities. Oddly, they observed, small hamlets like Kutztown remained largely unaffected by violence. Kutztown was, however, feeling the pinch of the collapse of the nation's economy. America's critical infrastructure such as utilities, albeit intact in the majority of the country, still couldn't help the crippling of the internet and the world's financial markets.

The inability to process payments for goods and services struck the U.S. especially hard. It was a society built on credit and the use of plastic to exchange money for products. Over the past two decades, the nation had become a cashless society more and more. It was not unusual for a McDonald's customer to whip out a debit card to pay for their kid's Happy Meal.

This followed on the heels of a century-long process in which cash replaced precious metals as a means of currency. Long before President Richard Nixon announced that the U.S. dollar would no longer be backed by gold in August of 1971, the use of gold and silver as a method of payment had disappeared.

After New Year's Eve, precious metals in the form of gold, silver, and even junk silver, a term used to describe U.S. coinage that was minted prior to 1965, became the currency of choice. In reality, older quarters were anything but junk, as they were made of ninety percent silver, compared to the newer quarters, which combined nickel and copper to create the twenty-five-cent coin.

A barter marketplace had been created in Kutztown, which predominantly accepted junk silver as payment for ordinary household products, and pure silver and gold for larger items of value.

Jonathan had a small quantity of precious metals and currency stored in a safe at his family's lodge. He and Briscoe were careful not to throw money around, hoping to avoid drawing unnecessary attention to themselves. On their shopping excursions, they didn't go to any shopping location twice in successive trips. They wore hunting gear to blend in and tried to avoid casual conversation.

With each trip, they stocked up on food and supplies, together with ample supplies of liquor. The two men found that the more inebriated they became, the more they managed to agree on political issues. Perhaps, Jonathan suggested, legalizing marijuana was the key to bringing the country back together. As he put it, maybe we could all adopt a *don't worry, be happy* approach to solving the nation's problems.

"I'm ready when you are," said Briscoe as he emerged from his bedroom. Wearing camouflage clothing and a hunting cap caused him to resemble Elmer Fudd from the Bugs Bunny cartoon.

Jonathan, for his part, resembled a noble gentleman ready to mount his horse and follow the hounds into battle. The two aristocrats might have thought they blended in with the locals, but in reality, they stood out because they didn't look the part of country boys who loved to hunt.

"Let's go," said Jonathan as he opened the front door to allow Briscoe to pass in front of him. They hadn't bothered to lock the door during their outings, and in their days together at the lodge, they hadn't been contacted by any unwanted visitors.

He drove a little faster than normal, as the two men had gotten a late start on their day. Their evenings were filled with conversation and, increasingly, the liberal consumption of liquor. As a result, it wasn't out of the ordinary for them to drink until the wee hours of the morning and awaken at noon or later.

"I know we've talked about this several times," began Briscoe as they drove along the bumpy driveway toward the two-lane road that bordered the front of the Schwartz property. "I still have no desire to reach out to any of my people, assuming, of course, I still have any people." He emphasized the last word in the sentence to make his point.

"You're a man without a country," quipped Jonathan as he swerved to dodge a pothole, one of several on the old country road. "And I'm a man who needs to leave this country."

Briscoe asked, "When do we make our move? Is it too early to look for a way out?"

Jonathan had contemplated these same questions often throughout the day. He'd determined it was best to do nothing for now. "I don't have a sense of urgency, Hanson. The feds haven't swooped down on the lodge, and I imagine they're busy elsewhere. As for you, assuming Trowbridge is still looking for you, he'd never suspect that you'd be with me, much less here."

"You're suggesting status quo," said Briscoe.

"I am. We've got money or, to be more precise, negotiable currency in the form of gold and silver. We have supplies that we supplement with our trips into town. And we still have weapons. It's not enough to equip an army, but we can most certainly defend ourselves against the run-of-the-mill burglar."

"Okay, I'm of the same mindset. Truthfully, this has been very relaxing for me." He paused and then laughed. "I've even grown to tolerate your company."

"Feeling's mutual, neocon," said Jonathan, referring to a label often used to describe men like Briscoe. The word was short for *neoconservative*, a political movement born in the sixties with liberal hawks who'd become estranged from the increasingly pacifist foreign policy of the Democratic Party.

Neocons were known to advocate the expansion of democratic ideals and American national interests into international affairs, much to the chagrin of those who espoused America-first policies. They tended to see military solutions to foreign-policy challenges.

Briscoe let out a hearty laugh. In times past, Jonathan's statement might throw Briscoe into a rage in which he argued the nuances of neoconservatism and the differences from President Ronald Reagan's concept of peace through strength. However, after becoming friends, the two found they could trade barbs without getting offended, something they felt like all of America needed in order to bridge the political divide.

The two men teased one another, and Jonathan playfully pretended to turn the wheel hard to the left in an effort to throw Briscoe out of the Kawasaki Mule. Briscoe quickly grabbed the handlebar and feigned falling by swinging his right leg outside the vehicle.

As he did, his cell phone gradually slipped out of his pocket and bounced onto the shoulder of the road, tumbling over and over into a farmer's driveway, where it sat baking in the unusually warm winter sun.

CHAPTER 34

Kutztown, Pennsylvania

Sofia Horst was walking her palomino pony along the fence row that surrounded the family's homestead on Krumsville Road, the route taken by Schwartz and Briscoe into town on a regular basis. Like her parents, she did her daily chores of tending to the horses and chickens, not paying attention to the strangers as they drove past. Folks in Kutztown had a tendency to stick to themselves, and the Horst family was no different. Berks County had been settled mainly by Germans, most of whom emigrated to the United States from their hometowns in southwest Germany along the Rhine River. They brought their love of farming and ability to raise livestock with them, finding the fertile lands around Kutztown to closely resemble their beloved Germany.

Sofia was speaking softly to her pony when her eyes wandered toward the driveway of their farmhouse where it met the road. She saw a cell phone lying faceup in the gravel. She tied off her horse and climbed over the split-rail fence to retrieve the phone. Her family didn't have a cell phone, so she knew it wasn't theirs. Not knowing what to do, she jumped on her horse and rode up to the house to alert her father.

"It wasn't there this morning," he said as he turned it over and over in his hands. The phone had been scratched, and the display had cracked as a result of bouncing off the jagged limestone rocks of the driveway.

His wife emerged from the kitchen, where she'd been making apple strudel, a German favorite that was a mainstay of the families living around Kutztown. "Turn it on and maybe you can determine who it belongs to."

"It won't have a name on it, I don't think," said her husband.

"That's true, Papa, but the phone contacts list might allow you to recognize the names. Maybe it belongs to one of our neighbors?"

Sofia's mother playfully twisted the young girl's earlobe. "How do you know of such things?"

"My friends in school all have cell phones," she replied.

"They do?" asked her father.

"Yes, Papa. It's actually normal."

He laughed and handed her the phone. "Well, it isn't normal for me. Go ahead, turn it on and look for a name."

Sally took the phone from her father and powered on the display. The iPhone's lock screen appeared. The display remained lit up for thirty seconds and then shut off.

"It has a passcode and face recognition," observed Sally.

"What?" asked her father.

"Never mind, Papa," she replied politely. "I can't make it work without a password."

"Maybe the person who lost it will try to call," offered her mother. "If it's turned on, will it ring? You can answer it and tell them where to pick it up."

Sofia shrugged and replied, "I don't know. Maybe? I have to remove the cabbages around the fence posts by the front gate and replace them with tulip bulbs. I'll keep turning the phone on. Maybe they'll call. If they don't, I'll set it on a post with a sign for them to find it."

"That's fine, dear," said her mother. "Be here at five to prepare dinner. No excuses, okay?"

"Yes, ma'am," replied Sofia, who hustled off to plant her flower garden. She religiously powered the phone on and off as she awaited a phone call that never came.

*****

The two faux hunters descended upon their favorite shopping stop—Weis Plaza. In addition to a grocery store, the Weis family operated a gas station, a liquor store, a bakery, and a small feed store complete with hardware supplies. It was one-stop shopping for Schwartz and Briscoe, and their trips made them known to the proprietors, who especially appreciated their method of payment.

While Jonathan negotiated a deal to purchase groceries in bulk in exchange for gold bullion, Briscoe filled their shopping cart with all of their favorite foods and drinks. He was waiting impatiently for Schwartz to finish his conversation, and unconsciously fiddled with his pants pocket.

That was when he noticed his cell phone was missing. Briscoe, who'd had nothing but the clothes on his back when he arrived at the Schwartzes' lodge, together with the murder weapon and his cell phone, kept both on his person whenever he ventured out. Despite his newfound friendship, Briscoe still felt the need to protect himself in the event Schwartz turned on him, or they were discovered by their pursuers.

Cold beads of sweat flowed down Briscoe's forehead as he searched frantically through his clothing. He looked through the groceries stored in his cart, to no avail. He even retraced his steps throughout the store, thinking the phone might have fallen out in one of the aisles. Finally, after inquiring with the single store clerk stationed at the register, he summoned Jonathan to tell him about the problem.

At first, Jonathan wasn't quite as panicked as Briscoe was. However, as the two searched the four-wheeler and the ground around it, Briscoe explained that someone with sufficient computer hacking skills could attempt to break the unlock code assigned to the phone. If it remained powered on for a long enough time, it could be discovered through triangulating Verizon's network.

Jonathan gained a sense of urgency, and the two quickly left town and headed back to the lodge. As they drove, they focused on searching the left side of the road, which was closest to where Briscoe had been seated on the trip into town.

It was 5:30 and almost dark when they came across the Horst family's farm. Jonathan began to laugh as he pointed to a fencepost with a cardboard sign nailed to it.

"It appears someone has done our job for us," he said as he nudged Briscoe with his elbow.

"Thank God," Briscoe mumbled before exhaling. Before the four-wheeler came to a stop, he jumped out and raced up to the post, where he found the battered iPhone. He looked around to see if anyone was watching. Relieved that they were not seen, he tore the sign off the post and threw it in the back of the Mule.

Jonathan said jokingly, as he paraphrased a Bible verse, "What was once lost is now found." He had no idea how profound his statement was.

CHAPTER 35

X-Ray's Cabin
The Haven

X-Ray reveled in his newfound position: hunting down the two men who appeared to be responsible for the collapse. He was also glad to be back in everyone's good graces. He'd gone from being a pariah and shackled to a post in a toolshed to the lead investigator in a digital manhunt.

Finding people who didn't want to be found was one of X-Ray's specialties. He was very capable of being successful in this search even without the additional tools and clearances provided by Cort, although they certainly helped him in his quest.

X-Ray had a mental checklist of digital tools at his disposal. Video footage, credit card transactions, cell phone triangulation, and the FBI files associated with the Schwartz arrest were just some of the avenues he traveled down. After Cort upped his clearance within the government spy agency computers and increased his computer capabilities by giving him access to multiple internet networks via satellite, X-Ray could conduct multiple database inquiries simultaneously and remain completely anonymous by using his VPN software.

He'd spoken to Cort prior to getting started in order to learn as much about the two men as he could. It was interesting for X-Ray to learn that he'd been in direct contact with Hanson Briscoe, the architect of the New Year's attacks. *Flattered* was the more appropriate word, but X-Ray didn't want Cort to know that. It was X-Ray's direct interaction with Briscoe that had almost gotten the Cortland family killed.

While the data was being processed, X-Ray studied the background of the two fugitives. He wanted to learn as much as he could about them from the various law enforcement databases at his disposal. There was voluminous information on Schwartz but precious little on Briscoe.

During his research, X-Ray learned of the murder of the caretaker and his wife at Monocacy Farm. Their car had also been stolen in the getaway.

X-Ray used this information as a lead, thinking that Briscoe might have been directly or indirectly involved. However, his ability to search the satellite video footage was hampered when several gaps appeared in the NSA's coverage of Pennsylvania and parts of Maryland. Scouring footage for a nondescript vehicle could take a team many weeks, and he was only one man.

X-Ray was busy scouring through credit card records and bank accounts when he suddenly got a hit from the Verizon server. Using the list of phone contacts that Cort provided him from his newly acquired cell phone from Trowbridge, a number assigned to Briscoe showed the location of the phone in the area of Kutztown, Pennsylvania.

The exact location couldn't be pinpointed unless the phone remained powered on and in use, but the ping displayed on his screen provided him a ten-square-mile area using a cell tower along Route 222 that ran through the small town.

X-Ray got to work researching the asset and real estate holdings of Briscoe, his family from years past, and then entities he was associated with, including those of George Trowbridge. X-Ray vowed to overturn every stone to find these men, cementing his position within the Haven.

He resisted the urge to release his cursory findings to Ryan or Cort at this time. This would simply bring undue pressure on him to provide further information that would take time to find. When he presented his report, he wanted it to be complete so that he could accept the appropriate level of *attaboys*.

It was nearly dawn when X-Ray's tired eyes decided to call it a day.

He was about to shut down his system for a few hours before resuming the search when he had an idea. In his briefing with Cort, the possibility that the two men were working together had been raised. X-Ray considered this and looked at the facts surrounding the attack on the Haven.

"Obvi!" he exclaimed, using the millennials' version of the word *obvious.* He changed his focus to searching the Schwartz family's holdings in the area of Kutztown. This was a monumental task, as the family's assets were held in layer upon layer of legal entities, both for profit and nonprofit.

And he'd have to go back many years. Schwartz had made billions dating back to the sixties. X-Ray would need to deploy all of his computer hardware to identify and cross-reference these legal entities to see if there was any connection to Pennsylvania and then, more narrowly, to the area west of Allentown and east of Harrisburg.

He decided to search county by county. He quickly worked his way through the property assessors' records in Lehigh, Schuylkill, and Lebanon counties, simply to rule them out. Then he focused his efforts on Berks County, a metropolitan area that included Reading and over four hundred thousand residents.

His eyes grew weary and several times he almost nodded off at his keyboard. He perused the records for the boroughs and townships of Berks County and consistently narrowed his search. Then he came upon the Schwartz Lodge, only it was owned by an obscure entity several decades old. What gave away its ownership was the size of the property, with several hundred acres being incorporated into the tract, and where the tax bills were sent.

He studied the property assessor's entry:

1730 Pennsylvania Avenue, Northwest
Washington, DC 20006

"Bingo!" X-Ray yelled inside the close confines of his cabin. "Let's see what companies are headquartered there and do another cross-reference."

With a newfound vigor, fueled by several Monster Energy drinks, X-Ray began to pound away at the keys and studied the tenant roster of the twelve-story office building situated in the central business district of Washington, mere steps from the White House.

He scrolled through the tenant list revealed on the Compstak website, an aggregator of property information, lease agreements, and other transactional details for commercial buildings around the world. He read the names aloud.

"EIG Global Energy. King & Spalding. Qualcomm. PRTM Management." Then he stopped. He shook his head as if he needed to clear his eyes from some sort of obstruction.

X-Ray jumped out of his chair and began to rapidly walk in circles. "Oh my god! Oh my god! I've gotcha! Yep, sure do."

He jumped back into his chair and scrolled through the list again and then clicked on the link to make sure he was certain that the name he recognized was not simply similar to the one he associated with the Schwartz family.

X-Ray pushed back his chair and ran to the kitchen, where his two-way radio was charging. He thought for a moment, as he wasn't sure who to contact first, Cort or Ryan. He decided to reach out to Ryan. *He runs the place.*

While he excitedly relayed his findings to Ryan, the monitor showed a series of slideshow images that were labeled *Taking Inclusion Seriously*, *Anticorruption*, *Governance & Accountability*, and others.

These were the pet projects of the Schwartz family, and they were displayed on the nonprofit entity's website known around the world as the *Open Society Foundation.* It was the Open Society Foundation that paid the taxes on their hunting lodge, and it was a mistake that would lead Cort and those who followed him right to the front door of Jonathan Schwartz and Hanson Briscoe.

Part Four

CHAPTER 36

The Haven

Ryan leaned into Blair and whispered, "I have to say that they're going into this much better prepared than the other day. X-Ray hasn't slept in thirty-six hours."

Blair nodded and replied, "Yeah, he's drunk his share of Red Bull and Monster Energy. He turned down coffee. Says it's bad for you."

"I never said he was perfect," replied Ryan as he laughed under his breath. The two developers of the Haven, visionaries who'd taken the former movie set of the *Hunger Games* and turned it into a preparedness community, continued to eavesdrop on the conversations between Alpha and the teams he'd picked to raid the hunting lodge owned by the Schwartz family.

Cort addressed the ex-military members of the team. "Guys, do we really need to do surveillance? It seems to me that we should take them by surprise. Our watching them might get discovered, and look how big this property is. They could scatter and we'd end up hunting them through the woods."

"Here's the thing, Cort," began Alpha. "First, we have to confirm that they're there. Second, we can't assume that they're alone. If Schwartz brought in his security team, we're up against something more formidable than those useful idiots at the Varnadore Building. We have to go in there with all the information available to us."

Ryan offered another thought. "Plus, wouldn't it be beneficial if you somehow caught them apart? You know, one guy goes out to get firewood or take a piss or something."

"Absolutely," replied Alpha. "I think the plan is fairly straightforward and requires patience to implement. We try to establish a pattern of activity and get a feel for the terrain, etcetera."

"May I add something?" asked Delta.

Alpha nodded and gestured for Delta to continue. "Yeah, man. Go ahead."

"At Philly SWAT, when we initiated fixed surveillance, the term used for a stakeout, we often formed into three-man teams. A lot of police units like the two-person approach, but we used three if the surveillance period was going to be lengthy. A fidgety cop had a greater potential for being discovered than one who was fresh. Also, if there was an unexpected entrant into the surveillance field, the third member of the unit could check it out without compromising the primary objective. If someone enters the perimeter of the location, the third officer could follow while keeping eyes on the subject's location. It was a variant of the ABC method. Officer A stays with the building, with officer B as his backup. Officer C follows the new entrant into the field of surveillance."

"That would help if these guys have perimeter security," added Bravo, who'd spent time with the DEA. "Ideally, we'd go in there with nine people, allowing for three teams."

"The blueprints show multiple entrances," offered X-Ray.

"True, but the north side of the structure doesn't have any exits, only second-floor windows. Three teams could cover the sides of the lodge with doors."

Before this conversation, Alpha had identified the personnel going on the raid. After some argument, Cort was confirmed as part of the team. He had no formal training with close-quarters combat, although he was more than proficient with the use of his weapons. In the end, he demanded to be included because he couldn't allow his new friends to fight this battle for him. He acknowledged that he shouldn't have been involved in rescuing Hannah because of his emotional connection. However, eliminating Schwartz and Briscoe was all business for him.

The participants in the raid would be X-Ray, who'd remain in his cabin and feed them information from the satellites if they were available. He'd also monitor Briscoe's cell phone use. Alpha was teamed up with Hayden. Bravo and Charlie would work together. Cort was partnered with Delta.

Alpha paced through the media room. X-Ray had mirrored his computer to the large video monitor and constantly scrolled through images he'd obtained of the blueprints and satellite flyovers. Finally, he made a decision.

"Okay, we have the benefit of this being winter and the foliage is off the trees. On the one hand, that helps our field of vision, but it also could expose us. Kudos to Ryan and Blair for purchasing snow camo in a variety of sizes. The combination of whites, grays, and hints of brown will help us blend in. With the night-vision binoculars provided by Cort, we can do things a normal surveillance team can't. I think we need to stick with our core six."

The group discussed logistics a little while longer and then realized it was getting late. They needed a good night's sleep and agreed that they could go over the details again during the flight north. Alpha would review the insertion point with the pilots in the morning and assign gear to the team before they departed. Just as the group was breaking up, Tom Shelton addressed them.

"Everyone, I've sent soldiers into battle before. It was part of my job, just as it was theirs to defend our country and preserve our freedoms. I never imagined that we'd be fighting a war on our own soil, much less against one another. Yet that's what our future holds. You have an opportunity to make a difference. Actually, to make history, although the only people who will know of your brave accomplishments are those of us in this room.

"History always gives the Monday-morning quarterback the opportunity to interpret, second-guess, and oftentimes revise the true account of what transpired. But I often wondered if war could've been averted more often if circumstances were different. I think Cort has made the case that hostilities between left and right in this country can be tamped down if two of the players responsible for sowing the seeds of discontent are taken off the playing field. For that reason, what you are doing will prove to be historic.

"Yet dangerous, too. You're prepared, but still, you're going in blind. I urge you to be patient. Get the total picture. Wait for the perfect opportunity to strike, and come home safe to your families, and us."

"You've got it, Commander!" shouted Alpha in a roaring baritone voice that shook the soundproof walls like an explosion in a war movie.

"Oorah!" Bravo and Charlie echoed his sentiments.

The group exchanged words of encouragement and then accepted hugs from Ryan and Blair. Tomorrow, they'd have their game faces on, and heartfelt sentiments or emotional goodbyes needed to take place now.

Finally, Donna stepped forward with a zippered canvas bag. "There's one more thing. Since the beginning of time, when soldiers went into battle, they carried a talisman, an object that brings good luck and protects them from harm. Blair and I have something for all of you."

She reached into the bag and handed out the lucky charms to the team. She provided each one a hand-carved arrowhead with a string wrapped around its notch. The triangular piece of stone, primarily consisting of flint or obsidian, had a serrated edge with accompanying bevels near the notch.

Blair explained, "These are arrowheads we found around the Haven when Ryan and I first bought the property. We took them to an archaeologist at the university in Hickory to confirm that they are authentic and not left over from the *Hunger Games* filming. These arrowheads were most likely used by Cherokee warriors and hunters long before North Carolina was settled by early colonists. The Cherokees believed that a hand-carved arrowhead, used as a talisman around your neck, was a symbol of protection, strength, and courage. They believed that the arrowhead protected them from illness and acted as a guard against evil. These arrowheads can deflect any negative energy, protect you from your enemies, and absorb their power so you can turn it back on them."

Donna began to hand them out to each of their warriors. The moving gesture resulted in more tears and hugs all around. Even the toughest among them, Alpha and Bravo, couldn't hide their appreciation and emotions.

With the talismans lovingly placed over their heads by Blair and snuggled against their chests for protection, the six were prepared to make history.

CHAPTER 37

Outside Kutztown, Pennsylvania

The Bell Relentless helicopter was one of the quietest in its class, but in a rural area in which activity had all but stopped, the sounds of its rotors could be heard for a mile. A northwesterly wind was blowing on the afternoon the team arrived outside Kutztown, resulting in the pilot picking their alternative landing area over two miles east of the Schwartz Lodge.

The plat map for the property indicated there was a primary driveway that led westward away from the lodge, but a secondary driveway also appeared on the east end of the property, leading to County Road 737, which was also known as Krumsville Road. Alpha felt most comfortable using the atmospheric conditions to their advantage and approaching the lodge from the east.

Despite an abundance of farmland in Berks County, the lodge was nestled in a remote, heavily wooded area bordered to the south by Pennsylvania State Game Lands Number 182. The hunting tract, which totaled two hundred seventy-three acres, was located about three miles northwest of Kutztown, along Saucony Creek.

X-Ray had provided the team topography maps of Game Lands 182 to give them a feel for the lay of the land surrounding the lodge. From rolling hills to narrow creek bottoms, the elevations ranged from six hundred feet to a low of three hundred sixty feet along the creek bottom. X-Ray had identified a hill that overlooked the lodge, assuming tree cover didn't obscure the view.

The chopper landed and the team quickly exited. Within a minute, their gear was quickly unloaded, and the chopper took off to refuel for the return trip home. It would return to extract the team when

Alpha contacted the pilots via the satellite telephones provided by Trowbridge's people.

After checking one another's chest rigs and donning the white camo attire, they set off on foot for a three-mile hike through the fields and woods of Berks County toward the lodge. Using his GPS, Alpha led the group, who moved in teams of two, spread apart by twenty yards, but making an effort to maintain visual contact with one another. They moved forward deliberately, taking precautions to avoid detection by the locals. The last thing Alpha needed was to be confronted by the local law enforcement. He'd have a hard time explaining the military hardware they possessed.

The group found its way through scrub plants and across agricultural fields to Saucony Creek, where they followed it on a westerly path until they were located due south of the lodge.

Alpha suddenly raised his fist, causing the group to pause and drop to a low crouch. He'd seen movement up ahead, and in the low light of early evening, he wanted to be cautious.

"Foxy, take the lead," he said, patting Hayden on the back, and she moved forward, walking softly along the edge of the creek. An experienced hunter, she was the lightest on her feet.

She held her AR-10 at low ready, her eyes searching for movement. She adjusted her vision to take advantage of the Bering Optics night-vision riflescope, one of the many useful toys provided by Trowbridge.

"I see you," she whispered to herself as she raised her rifle and studied the target through the scope. A white-tailed deer moseyed along the meandering creek bed, periodically pawing at the moist ground in search of her winter diet of twigs, dormant grasses, and red oak acorns, which remain viable and edible much longer than their white oak cousins. Hayden smiled as she inched forward. "If this were another day …" she added as her voice trailed off.

As she got closer, the deer, who was upwind, didn't notice her silent approach. Hayden decided to announce herself by tossing a rock in the animal's direction. She didn't want to startle the deer too much, which might create a ruckus in the woods.

With the deer hopping through the woods, Hayden gave Alpha the all-clear signal and waved the team forward. When they caught up with one another, Alpha studied the GPS. He was trying to locate the hill they'd identified in the chopper earlier. Once he located it, he plugged the coordinates into the GPS device, and each of the other members of the team did the same.

This hill would act as their primary rally point in the event they got separated, with the chopper's landing point for extraction to be determined based upon conditions on the ground. If the mission was successful, the extraction would be quick and take place on the Schwartz property. If there was trouble, the team would rally on the hill and then backtrack to the original insertion point to be picked up.

Over the next thirty minutes, they made their way through the woods, a job made difficult by a dark, cloudy night. Alpha used a combination of hiking trails and areas of standing pines that had little vegetation underneath, allowing them to speed up their progress. Everyone was careful to avoid snapping twigs or rolling ankles on the uneven terrain.

"Here we are," announced Alpha as he dropped into a crouch. He raised his field glasses to get a better look at the lodge. The two-story structure featured cedar-shake siding and roof shingles. On the southern end, a tall stone fireplace divided several plate-glass windows that overlooked a lawn reaching toward the woods. A faint, flickering light could be seen through the glass, most likely coming from the flames in the fireplace.

The members of the team fanned out across the hilltop and retrieved their binoculars to take a look. The surroundings were assessed, and points of surveillance were determined. After the group conducted a radio check of their two-way units, Alpha got them into position, one team at a time.

Now they watched and waited for their opportunity to pounce.

CHAPTER 38

Schwartz Lodge
Kutztown, Pennsylvania

Of the six members of the team, Delta was the only one who'd engaged in multiple stakeouts. He'd practiced a variety of surveillance procedures and had learned to deal with adverse conditions, as well as boredom. On this night, the team was fortunate that the weather was favorable. After the cold spell that had engulfed the Eastern United States the week after New Year's Eve, unusually mild temperatures had become more prevalent. Without the benefit of AccuWeather to plan by, the team had to be prepared for anything.

Delta provided them the benefit of his experience as he guided them into place. First and foremost, he told them, was to get into position unnoticed. If either Briscoe or Schwartz caught a glimpse of movement outside, they might hunker down, flee, or, if they had a security team on the property, initiate a firefight.

He also reiterated a word that Alpha and Tom had used during their briefing the night before—*patience.* Stakeout work could be long and arduous, especially when the ultimate goal of the team was to assassinate their targets. Sitting in an unmarked car full of coffee and snacks was one thing. Observing their targets for purposes of assessing their defenses with the ultimate goal to kill them was much more difficult. One hasty pull of a trigger, or even a mistake in judgment that revealed their location, could imperil the entire operation.

With the teams in place, they periodically checked in with one another without becoming chatty on their comms. Delta and Alpha spoke the most, constantly checking in as they became more comfortable that their two targets were alone.

Delta and Cort had positioned themselves nearest the lodge in order to see inside the large plate-glass windows that flanked the stone fireplace. Even in the dim light, Cort, who had seen both men at various political functions over the years, could accurately identify them and confirm their presence.

More importantly, Delta and Cort were able to determine that the two targets were alone inside the spacious lodge. For hours, until well after midnight, they hadn't seen any other human activity, whether inside or outside the lodge. Occasionally, a gray squirrel scampered across the grounds around the home, drawing the attention of several rifle barrels as it hopped from tree to tree.

"I've got movement," announced Bravo, who was teamed up with Charlie. The two were assigned the east end of the lodge, which contained a large wooden deck on the lower level. A combination of Adirondack chairs and patio furniture dotted the spacious area overlooking a small pond.

"Roger," said Alpha quietly into his radio. "Go ahead."

"One male. Maybe six three. Dark hair. Smoking a cigarette. Check that. Smoking a cigar."

Cort, who allowed Delta to communicate with the team, had an earpiece that allowed him to listen into the exchange. "That's Jonathan Schwartz. He's a cigar connoisseur."

"Is he alone?" asked Alpha.

"Roger," Bravo quickly replied. "I can take the shot. Easily."

Alpha was quick with his response. "Negative, Bravo. Stand down, but eyes on the prize." Naturally, he'd like to catch the two men separately, but it needed to be done quietly so they didn't alert the other one.

For several minutes, Jonathan casually walked along the deck, periodically stopping to take a deep draw on his cigar, illuminating the cherry on the end, and then exhaling a puff of smoke, which floated into the air.

All teams waited, hoping that Briscoe would suddenly appear on the deck. With the two men alone and probably unarmed, Bravo team could end this mission with a few well-placed rounds.

*****

Jonathan took in the night air and the stillness provided by the surrounding woods. The lodge was enveloped in trees except for the hundred yards of grassy lawn that surrounded the building. During the winter, the Kentucky bluegrass that was predominant in that part of Pennsylvania lay dormant but provided sufficient cover from the heavy snows the region was accustomed to.

He had no qualms about smoking the cigar inside the lodge, although he was respectful of the fact that Briscoe was a nonsmoker. Typically, he'd position himself near the hearth, allowing the heat of the flames to carry the cigar's smoke up the chimney.

However, he needed a break from the conversations with Briscoe to be alone with his thoughts. He missed his father, who was much more than that. György Schwartz was his mentor, partner, and best friend. Father and son shared a special relationship with common interests ranging from matters of international finance, advancement of their political ideologies, to sharing a fine cigar.

Oddly, Jonathan had never smoked a cigarette. There were several reasons that a cigar was more relaxing to Jonathan. Partly because of the social aspect, but also because of the time it took to smoke.

A cigarette could be smoked in just a few minutes. To Jonathan, smoking a cigarette was more about getting a nicotine fix than it was taking a moment alone with one's thoughts. Smoking a cigar required an investment. Depending on the size, a cigar took anywhere from thirty minutes to two hours to enjoy. It gave him the opportunity to take time away from the demands of his complicated life. It provided him an outlet, as an excuse, to enjoy a glass of brandy, sit in a comfortable chair, and relax.

Medically speaking, a cigar supplied his body with nicotine, lots of it. In fact, the average cigar contains more than ten times the nicotine of a cigarette. This served up a healthy dose of relaxant to a man who lived in a pressurized world of high-stakes financial games and political machinations.

Above all, for Jonathan, he simply liked the taste. His favorite smokes provided a variety of flavors, each subtle in their differences, much like coffees and fine wines.

He casually paced the deck, drawing on his Fuente Fuente OpusX. The lengthy double corona provided him a smooth boldness with a sweet lingering taste.

Alone with his thoughts, the nicotine began to take effect, relaxing his body and allowing his mind to clear itself of clutter. He forgot about hiding from the FBI. He put Briscoe out of his mind for the moment, a man who should be his mortal enemy, but because of circumstances had become his ally.

Jonathan took a deep breath, chasing the previous draw of his cigar with a healthy dose of fresh air. His mind was devoid of thought, until it wasn't.

A chill overcame Jonathan's body, causing him to pull his sweater a little tighter across his chest despite the warmish temperatures. He lifted his cigar and studied the thin trail of smoke, which rose a few feet into the air before floating away.

Genetically speaking, he'd inherited many traits from his father, including an unparalleled intuitiveness. Some might refer to the gift as being clairvoyant or as possessing a sixth sense beyond the widely recognized human senses of sight, hearing, touch, taste, and smell.

Jonathan's ability to perceive beyond the five senses was one of his best attributes and a tool that he'd used on many occasions when dealing with others, whether in a boardroom or when testifying before Congress.

He considered another draw on his cigar, hoping to shake the uneasy feeling that had overcome him. Then he decided against it. His mind screamed warning bells. His body's adrenal glands responded as a fight-or-flight response took hold.

I have to remain calm. Am I being paranoid? Or watched?

Jonathan calmly rubbed the cigar out on a deck rail and defiantly flicked it toward the woods, unknowingly in the direction of his watchers.

CHAPTER 39

Schwartz Lodge
Kutztown, Pennsylvania

Jonathan calmly walked inside the lodge, closing the door behind him. Briscoe sat quietly in the semidarkness, sipping his brandy and watching the flames dance in the open fireplace. The shadows created by the stone surround, coupled with a protruding, rustic mantel, mesmerized Briscoe as the brandy numbed his senses. Progressively each day, Briscoe consumed more of the sweet-tasting spirit. Jonathan assumed it was the only way that Briscoe could cope with the situation he was in. Drinking to dull the senses and escape from his troubles was a weakness in Briscoe that Schwartz tolerated simply because he enjoyed the man's company. After this, they'd no longer be *besties*, as the younger generation would say.

Jonathan paused at the door, facing Briscoe. He moved his right hand behind his back and turned the bolt lock on the patio door, causing a loud click that caught Briscoe's attention.

"Expecting the boogeyman?" Briscoe said with a snicker.

"Briscoe, I want you to listen to me and be calm as I speak," began Schwartz. "Do you understand?"

Telling a sober person *don't look* almost always results in the person looking anyway.

Briscoe's reaction, fueled by alcohol, was much different. He shot up out of his chair in alarm. "What? Is there somebody out there?"

Jonathan rolled his eyes and immediately moved to calm Briscoe down. He took him by the arm and walked him over to the bar. He spoke softly as they walked through the living area. "I don't know for certain. It's just a feeling."

"Something has you spooked," began Briscoe, who'd suddenly moved from a state of half-drunkenness to stone-cold sober. The candlelight from the lanterns on the bar top illuminated Jonathan's face. "I can see it in your eyes."

Jonathan reached for the brandy and poured himself a glass. Then he topped off Briscoe's. The two men raised their glasses and offered one another a toast, as had become their custom.

"I was finishing my cigar and a sudden sense of dread came over me. Maybe it was the brandy. I don't know, but something caused me to change my mood."

Briscoe raised his glass to his lips but didn't take a sip. His voice was serious. "It's the same feeling I had at Monocacy Farm the other day. It wasn't paranoia. Rather, it was more like a heightened sense of awareness. Something in my gut was screaming—*run!* So I did."

"My gut is telling me that we're being watched," said Jonathan. "We need to make a decision."

"Like what? Run? To where?"

Jonathan took his brandy and calmly walked to the center of the room, avoiding the windows and doors and using the massive support posts as something to lean on. Subconsciously, he was using them as cover. "It could be nothing, Briscoe. We could take our rifles and confront them."

"That's suicide if they're Trowbridge's people. Or even if it's the FBI. Trowbridge is pulling their strings, too."

Schwartz walked toward the fireplace and sat on the hearth, intending to keep his profile low. "Under the circumstances, it could be someone who wants to break in. You know, burglars. If they saw me on the deck, it might have changed their mind. I just think there's something more to it."

"What do you suggest?"

Schwartz rubbed his temples. He was more interested in protecting himself than his newfound friend, who'd outworn his usefulness at this point.

"We can catch them by surprise if we take off," he began, skewing his plan to benefit himself. "I'll go in one direction; you go in another. If we split up, it will be harder for them to pursue us. If I'm wrong, and hopefully I am, then we can always come back and finish our brandy."

Briscoe seemed conflicted. He set his glass down and began to walk toward the patio doors before catching himself. He turned to Jonathan. "I'm an old man and not capable of outrunning trained killers, if that's what we're facing. I successfully escaped the mansion because of the tunnels. I won't fare so well in the woods."

Jonathan thought for a moment. An opportunity had presented itself, one that would lead the assassins, if any, after Briscoe. "You take the four-wheeler, Hanson," he said sincerely, using Briscoe's first name for effect. "I was outside on the deck long enough to know that whoever might be watching us didn't approach the lodge in a vehicle. It was too quiet. By taking the four-wheeler, you can easily get away and then, if necessary, make your way back later and retrieve your vehicle from the barn."

Briscoe nodded and his mood lightened. "This may be much ado about nothing, anyway. However, I do appreciate your offer, one that makes sense. What about you?"

"I know these woods," replied Jonathan. "I've come here off and on most of my life. I'm familiar with the trails, the terrain, and the places to hide. Like you, I'll make my way back to the barn when it's safe. And, like you said, it may be nothing but paranoia getting the best of me."

Jonathan didn't really believe that last statement. He had convinced himself that there was a threat surrounding the house, and he patted himself on the back for convincing Briscoe to become the proverbial rabbit in the chase.

"Well, then," started Briscoe, "I guess this may be the time we part ways. Jonathan, I never imagined that you and I would meet, much less share lively conversation and a bottle of brandy. I don't know what the future brings for us both, but I hope that we can evade our pursuers and meet up again someday for a drink."

After Briscoe's heartfelt statement, it would've been easy for Jonathan to make a better effort to protect the older man from harm.

In the end, his survival instincts ruled his decision-making.

"I agree, my friend. I hope that I'm wrong and, afterwards, we can reconvene our brandy tasting. But for now, let's talk about how we're gonna pull this off."

*****

"All teams. I've got headlights. East drive, near the road."

Alpha whispered his observations into the microphone attached to his chest rig. He'd been constantly surveying their surroundings in addition to remaining focused on the lodge. The last thing he wanted was company.

Delta came on the radio. "Roger that. They appear to be stationary at the entrance. Maybe there's a gate?"

Alpha thought for a moment. If Schwartz had seen them, or if his security personnel were patrolling the property's east and north boundary, which consisted of local roads, they might be returning. The time was right for the teams to make their move, but he needed to cut off this vehicle, too.

He exhaled and gave his orders. "Delta team, secure the east entrance. Do not allow that vehicle to approach. Bravo team, hit the east deck. We'll cover the west entryway."

"Alpha, this is Delta. Roger. Out." Delta and Cort backed away from the house and made their way to the washed-out gravel driveway that led from the lodge to Krumsville Road.

"Roger, Alpha. Bravo team advancing now. We'll move in on your go."

Hayden, who'd remained in a prone position for the last hour with her rifle trained on the front door, rose into a low crouch to join Alpha. She shook off the stiffness and adjusted her hair under the camouflaged Duke Blue Devils ball cap.

"I'm ready," she told Alpha with a nod.

"All right, we'll follow Delta's advice on how his SWAT teams would hit a subject's location."

On the helicopter flight, Delta had discussed how SWAT teams conducted raids. Naturally, law enforcement used more than two teams of two, but the principles were the same. Each team was to form a single-file line known as a *snake*. This minimized the number of team members who became a vulnerable target to the subject.

Alpha and Bravo would run point for their respective teams. It was their job to breach the entry first and neutralize any subjects they encountered. These two men had the most experience in close-quarters combat. The point man in a raid such as this was the person most often required to make a split-second decision. He had to assess whether the subject was armed, hostile, or perhaps simply a hostage or innocent bystander. The results of this instantaneous analysis were matters of life and death for all involved.

All four of the team members had practiced clearing buildings and rooms during their time at the Haven. Each member was assigned an area of responsibility when entering a room. Both Alpha and Bravo were ambidextrous, allowing them to be accurate using their weapons both left and right handed. Hayden and Charlie were more comfortable clearing the left side of a room.

Alpha had the forethought to bring some of the smoke grenades left over from the raid on the Varnadore Building. The smoke, coupled with his bellowing voice in the darkness, would serve to disorient Briscoe and Schwartz as they entered the lodge. All it took was a distraction of a few seconds for the two teams to take defensive positions and identify their targets, being careful to avoid friendly fire.

Delta told them that ninety percent of all SWAT call-outs ended without a shot being fired, and the subject was surrounded without injury. He also warned all of them to be aware of the enormous number of variables they might encounter. All successful raids were dependent upon proper training, quick decision-making, and avoiding shooting other members of the team.

Alpha gave the order.

"Go." A simple two-letter word with deadly ramifications.

Both teams slowly approached their assigned entrances, opting to disregard the garage doors that were built into the basement of the lodge. Moving quickly from point to point, the teams used landscape features and trees to mask their approach. They used the bounding overwatch approach, which was successfully utilized by law enforcement and military, until they reached the final stretch of open ground to the doorways. Then, single file, the two teams raced across the lawn with their weapons drawn and their bodies hunched over to maintain a low profile.

Alpha arrived at the stone entryway first and pressed his back against the wall so he couldn't be seen through the windows flanking the front door. Hayden was hot on his heels, quietly making her way to the other side of the door.

Alpha keyed his mic. "Alpha team in position."

"Roger. Bravo ready."

Alpha knelt down and reached across the glass panes until he had a firm grip on the door latch. He pressed down with his thumb to determine if it was locked.

It was.

He thought for a moment. He'd have to break through the glass to unlock the bolt lock from the inside. He'd need a distraction, which meant he'd have to send Bravo team in a few seconds ahead of him.

"Bravo team. Over."

"Go ahead, Alpha."

"On my go, you'll enter first. I need three seconds of cover."

"Roger. On your go."

Alpha made eye contact with Hayden, who nodded her understanding. He turned his rifle around and prepared to smash the glass panes with the buttstock. Then he keyed his mic.

"Go, Bravo!"

The sound of breaking glass could be heard on the other end of the lodge, and Alpha responded by crashing through the entry door side windows. He reached a gloved hand through the shards of glass that stuck out of the frame, and flicked the lock open.

Hayden moved swiftly to open the door and then kicked it with a hard crash against the interior wall. She dropped to a knee and immediately began to scan the left side of the open living area with her rifle.

Seconds later, smoke began to billow into the rafters of the vaulted ceiling near the fireplace as Bravo team ignited their smoke grenades.

Alpha followed suit, and the big man deftly got into position to scan the right side of the room. Then he bellowed, the words coming out of his chest like an angry gorilla warning the world of his might, "Give it up! Briscoe, Schwartz, you don't have to die tonight!"

Just as he shouted the words, the sound of the four-wheeler racing out of the garage caught all of their attention.

"Dammit!" shouted Alpha. He debated whether to back out of the room and give chase. He sent Bravo and Charlie instead.

"Bravo, run them down!"

"Roger!" The sound of shuffling feet could be heard through the smoke as Bravo team exited the lodge and ran onto the deck. Then Alpha spoke into the comms. "A single four-wheeler headed east away from the building. Comin' at ya, Delta."

Delta calmly responded, "Roger. I see headlights."

"Bravo team, assist Delta team and chase down that four-wheeler. Foxy and I will clear the building."

"Roger."

Alpha whispered to Hayden, "It's you and me."

"Isn't it always?" she said with a determined look.

CHAPTER 40

Schwartz Lodge
Kutztown, Pennsylvania

Briscoe was panicked and drove the Kawasaki four-wheeler as fast as it would go. He silently cursed himself for not studying Jonathan's operation of the side-by-side vehicle in the past. It was somewhat top heavy due to the roof over the cab, but its longer wheelbase seemed more stable than what he imagined. Nonetheless, in his haste and somewhat inebriated state, he was unsuccessful in avoiding potholes or uneven parts of the driveway, which was nothing more than two ruts divided by a weed-covered hill of gravel.

Several times as he raced down the driveway, a route he'd taken a half dozen times since his arrival at the Schwartz lodge, Briscoe had to retrieve his rifle lying on the seat next to him, which threatened to bounce out. Each time he took his eyes off the road to grab the weapon, he lost control of the steering, causing him to careen from one side of the driveway to the other.

He finally corrected and got comfortable with his speed. He focused on the roadway that was only a few hundred yards away. That was when he saw the lights. At first, he couldn't make out if they were headlights or flashlights. Either way, he jammed on the brakes and slid to a stop in the loose gravel.

He turned around, considering a retreat to the main driveway that led to the west. He was unfamiliar with where that led, but it might provide him an opportunity to get away. He searched the cab of the Mule to find the gearshift. In his panicked state, with the complications of darkness, he couldn't find the lever, which was next to his right leg.

Briscoe's eyes grew wide as he saw two flashlights approaching from the house, the light bouncing from ground to sky as his pursuers ran toward him. He turned and slammed the palm of his hand around the dashboard until the headlights of the Mule were turned off. The dark surroundings relieved him, and he decided to race forward, using the lights on the country road as his guide.

He pushed the gas pedal to the floor. The Mule bolted forward after spinning its tires slightly. Briscoe held the steering wheel with a death grip in his left hand as he raised the hunting rifle with his right. He was prepared to shoot his way out.

He got close to the road and opened fire, shooting wildly and out of control toward the headlights of the vehicle in front of him. His shots missed the mark, but the vehicle suddenly spun its tires on the asphalt and raced away from him.

Now Briscoe was truly confused. He assumed the vehicle was part of a team sent to capture him. He wondered if he was wrong about being pursued by people with flashlights behind him. He slowed the Mule, turned to look back, and saw that he was still being chased.

He turned his headlights back on and headed toward the road once again. He was almost there when two men appeared in the road in front of him. Briscoe didn't hesitate. Using his knees to hold the steering wheel steady, he raised the rifle and took aim. Just as he squeezed the trigger, the Mule jerked to the right, knocking his rifle against the roof support and sending the bullet flying into the sky, well over the head of his target.

Two weapons opened fire upon the Mule, raking the front end of the vehicle with bullets. Briscoe dropped the rifle and regained control of the four-wheeler. He reached into his jacket pocket and fumbled for his pistol.

The four-wheeler hit a pothole, and the left side suddenly dropped down before careening upward. This last jolt caused Briscoe to lose control of the gun, and his ride.

The Mule sped forward, but then took a hard left turn down an embankment, where it crashed into a fallen tree. Briscoe was thrown forward, over the steering wheel and headfirst into a pine tree. The softer wood did nothing to suppress the impact the pine had on Briscoe's scalp, which was now laid open, exposing the raw nerves and blood vessels surrounding his skull.

Briscoe lay on a bed of pine needles, staring skyward, his twitching body numb from the contact with the tree. Warm blood oozed down his face, blocking his vision. He wanted to slip into unconsciousness. He wanted to die. He wanted this to be over.

It was not his time, yet.

*****

"Is he still alive?"

Two fingers pressed against Briscoe's neck. Then the person wiped them off on her shirt.

"Amazingly, yes." A female voice. Maybe she'd have mercy.

Briscoe tried to discern if he was dreaming, semiconscious, or having an out-of-body experience. Somehow, his brain was functioning at a very high level of awareness, but he was unable to see or move his body on his own.

Maybe it was for the best, he thought. If he played dead, like an opossum, they'd leave him be. Those little critters get stressed and go into shock. They look comatose for hours. You leave them lying there and suddenly, voila, they wake up and mosey off to look for something to eat. No harm. No foul.

That sounded like a plan, Briscoe's borderline delusional brain told itself. His ability to reason and comprehend had been replaced with irrational thoughts brought on by the intense pain he was feeling.

That's the ticket. Play opossum. Take a little break. They'll go away, and then I can just gather my strength later and go home. Back to Monocacy Farm. A place where I have always been comfortable.

Except for the ghosts of the caretaker and his wife, who surely would be waiting for him.

Briscoe waited and listened as the voices became muffled. They faded in and out as his consciousness came and went.

Come on, people! Go away!

He was screaming internally, trying not to move as he played the opossum game.

His pleas were not heard and, therefore, were ignored.

"Let's drag him up to the house and see what Alpha wants to do." A male voice gave the orders. "Everybody grab an arm or a leg."

What? No! I'm dead, see?

"On three. One. Two. Three!"

With a jerk, Briscoe was hoisted into the air, and it wasn't to be taken by the angels to meet God. He was, however, destined for Judgment Day.

CHAPTER 41

Schwartz Lodge
Kutztown, Pennsylvania

Alpha worked with his recollection of the lodge's floor plan obtained by X-Ray during his search of building department records connected to the FBI's massive data-collection program. In today's world there was very little information stored electronically that hadn't been backed up by federal law enforcement. If it was stored at the state or local level of government, then the federal government had a mirror image of the data at their disposal as well.

He and Hayden meticulously moved through the house, not taking any risks in their search for Jonathan Schwartz. Alpha was relieved that the two men appeared to be alone. The human factor was the single biggest cause of a raid going bad, Delta had cautioned.

After clearing the lower level, they moved up the sweeping wooden staircase that led to a landing overlooking the living area below. The smoke from the grenades had begun to dissipate, mostly being sucked up through the chimney as the fire began to burn out due to lack of attention.

Every once in a while, Alpha would call out for the men, not knowing whether they'd both escaped via the four-wheeler, or possibly left one behind in the house. Thus far, their search had been fruitless; then they reached a game room upstairs that featured a full-size snooker table and several gaming tables, including blackjack and poker.

Hayden motioned toward two sets of patio doors leading to a large balcony on the north side of the residence. One of the doors was left slightly open, just enough to allow fresh air to enter the space.

Alpha and Hayden approached the doors simultaneously, once again moving slowly in a crouched position. They scanned the glass doors in search of movement, prepared to unleash a barrage of gunfire if either Briscoe or Schwartz showed themselves.

They reached the door and Alpha took the lead, moving out on the deck and dropping to a knee in a defensive position. Just as they had cleared the rooms inside the lodge, Hayden took the left side of the deck while Alpha moved right. The massive deck structure spanned the entire width of the lodge and included a spiral staircase made of wrought iron at the end.

Once they realized they were alone and that one of the men might have escaped using the staircase, Alpha relaxed and then slammed his fist on the deck railing.

"Are you kidding me?" he complained, clearly aggravated that they hadn't taken into account the rear exit.

Hayden picked up on his aggravation and offered an excuse. "Listen, this deck wasn't supposed to be here. Heck, the plans didn't even show those patio doors." She pointed over her shoulder with her thumb.

Alpha strutted along the railing, looking over the side as if one of his targets might suddenly appear to wave hello. He shook his head out of frustration and aggravation.

Hayden joined his side. "Whadya wanna do? We can track—"

Hayden's sentence was cut off by the sound of gunfire coming from the east end of the property. Radio chatter erupted between Bravo and Delta as more shots rang out.

The two rushed to the end of the deck closest to the action and held their breath, focusing their senses on the gun battle. A few more shots rang out and then they suddenly stopped.

Alpha hesitated, and then after sixty seconds, he reached out to the two teams on the radio. "Sitrep."

Bravo quickly responded, "One tango down. Stand by."

Alpha looked to Hayden and smiled. They exchanged fist bumps.

"Bravo to Alpha. Over."

"Go ahead, Bravo."

"We've got Briscoe. ID confirmed. He's alive but banged up."

"Copy that," Alpha replied. "Bring him back to the lodge. We've got one on the run. Foxy and I'll hunt him down. Over."

Alpha adjusted his gear and motioned toward the spiral staircase. "Let's track this SOB down."

"Lead the way," Hayden said, patting the much larger Alpha on his shoulder. The two had grown closer as they'd worked together at the Haven, in the rescue of Hannah, and now. They knew how to anticipate each other's movements and had confidence in one another's abilities to have their back.

Alpha jogged to the stairwell and sailed to the bottom. A trail was clearly visible, and he followed it, racing through the woods in order to make up for lost time. He assumed that under the intense pressure, Schwartz would've relied upon familiar trails to get away from the house as quickly as possible.

They continued along the path for another fifteen minutes, following what they hoped was Schwartz's trail. Neither spoke, which served them well, as they didn't want to give away their position. Despite his large build, Alpha had learned to track an adversary by moving lightly on his feet. Hayden, who'd hunted all her life, possessed the skill of movement that only a seasoned hunter had—a deerlike gait.

They reached a fallen pine tree and paused to examine it. The top bark had been kicked off, revealing the white underside of the bare wood. On the other side, in the wet bed of pine needles and loose dirt, were the indentations of knees and hands.

"He tripped here," said Hayden, who then pointed a few feet beyond the tree that blocked the trail. "He landed there, and look at how he dug his feet into the wet ground to gain traction."

"Panicked," muttered Alpha.

"Yes."

Alpha led the way. In the darkness, the woods became a two-dimensional world. A canvas that he'd been trained to divide into thirds. His eyes constantly scanned left to right, right to left, and then forward as he pressed the pursuit. If he detected any movement, he raised his fist and the duo quickly stopped, adopted a defensive position, and used their senses to identify a possible target.

After ten more minutes of searching, Alpha became concerned. "This is taking too long. Under the tree cover, we have no ambient light, and he has the advantage of knowing the trail. Let's go to flashlights."

"Won't that give us away?" asked Hayden.

"Sure, but it might also force him into making a mistake. This guy's scared out of his mind. His hasty retreat caused him to trip over that log back there. If he sees us coming, he might fall again and hurt himself this time."

Hayden powered on the SureFire tactical flashlight attached to the rails on her AR-10. Alpha did the same and they took off again, the beams from their flashlights illuminating a narrow path through the thick underbrush that became more prevalent the farther away they got from the lodge.

The woods became denser as the duo trudged up the path, needle-covered branches reaching out to grab them along the way. Up ahead, the chatter of raccoons followed the screech of an owl. The woods came alive as the wildlife detected the hunters' approach.

Alpha ignored the cacophony of sounds, remaining completely in tune with his surroundings. Periodically, he'd stop to examine a broken branch. Hayden would point out a possible trail that veered off the main path. They'd take a moment to examine the ground for tracks and then continue on their west-southwest course away from the lodge.

Alpha recalled the plat map of the property and its proximity to the adjacent state game lands preserve. It was likely they were no longer on the Schwartz property, as they'd traveled at least a mile from the house.

They ran up a hill, and when they reached the top, they had a fairly clear view of their surroundings. Alpha stopped their progress and retrieved his binoculars from a pouch attached to his tactical vest. He scanned his surroundings, making a three-hundred-and-sixty-degree turn. He'd almost completely circled the landscape when he abruptly stopped.

"Foxy, I need another set of eyes," he barked to his partner.

Hayden pulled out her field glasses and joined his side. Alpha pointed ahead toward a one-lane road that could barely be seen. A beam of light danced across an open field, periodically shooting into the sky.

"That's gotta be him," said Hayden. "I've got a bead on his location. If I remember correctly from studying the maps, there's a place just west of here called Crystal Cave. It's a local attraction full of underground rock formations and caverns. He's headed that way."

Alpha didn't hesitate as he tucked his binoculars away and began to run down the hill. He wasn't in the shape he was years ago, but a soldier never rested.

Hayden, on the other hand, was a runner and could easily outpace Alpha. She rushed past him and took the lead. She had her bearings, and running through the woods reminded her of her childhood years when she spent so much time at her family farm in Upper East Tennessee.

She also recalled the days she'd spent spelunking, exploring the many limestone rock formations and caves that were prevalent in the Smoky Mountains. That was, of course, before she went into a cave one day and got stuck. She'd learned to deal with the claustrophobia that plagued her into adulthood, until it reared its ugly head on New Year's Eve when she was momentarily stuck on the elevator in her office building.

She tried to put the thought of searching for Schwartz in a darkened cave out of her mind as she enjoyed the cool air entering her lungs. Invigorated and enjoying the thrill of the hunt, she began to leave Alpha behind, who was struggling to keep her pace. To his credit, he didn't slow her down, allowing her to catch Schwartz on her own if necessary.

Hayden resembled a thoroughbred horse as she skillfully raced along the trail toward the open field beyond. She kept her eyes trained on where the dancing light had appeared earlier. When the woods opened up into the field, she smiled as the appearance of the broken stems of the tall grasses provided evidence that Schwartz had recently been there.

"We're coming for ya," she whispered through her deep breaths, not bothering to notice that Alpha had fallen well behind her.

CHAPTER 42

Crystal Cave
Near Kutztown, Pennsylvania

Jonathan Schwartz stumbled ahead, occasionally glancing over his shoulder in search of the people chasing him. His hands were bleeding, not from the fall that had occurred early on during his escape, but from pushing tree branches and sticker bushes out of the way as he rumbled through the woods in a state of panic.

When he left the house, he'd planned on finding his way to the barn to uncover one of the stolen vehicles and make his way to the highway. After running for fifteen minutes, he realized that he'd missed the trail that led to the barn closest to the northern boundary of the property, and his fear prevented him from doubling back to locate it.

As an alternative, he recalled a place that he'd discovered when he first came to the lodge with his father. With a final check on his pursuers, he crossed the one-lane country road and approached a steep hill that overlooked the east end of Kutztown. At the bottom of the hill was the entrance to a local geological attraction known as Crystal Cave.

The historic site—which was now surrounded by hiking trails, a picnic park, and even an eighteen-hole miniature golf course—was a favorite weekend destination of travelers, who enjoyed ice cream, geological souvenirs like collectible minerals, and exploring caves.

During Jonathan's first visit to Crystal Cave, his governess took him through the attraction the same way other families were accustomed to doing. But Jonathan was an explorer and he had his father's penchant for finding alternative means to doing things. He'd roamed the state preserve adjacent to the Schwartz property and eventually expanded his day trips to the land surrounding Crystal Cave. Tonight, with his life depending on it, Jonathan would find out if his memory of those childhood days served him well.

It did.

He located the narrow dark hole that entered the side of the steep hill overlooking the miniature golf course. The first time he found it, curiosity had led him inside. It was his courage, however, that allowed him to ignore the total darkness and the fear of the unknown and venture farther. He was rewarded with the discovery of a new void, a space large enough for a dozen people, that contained a small underground pond created by rain runoff.

This became his special place. A cavern in which he could come to be alone with his thoughts, without the pressure of his father trying to teach him the ways of the world or an overbearing governess beating him over the head about his manners.

Unlike his first adventure in the cave, when he had nothing more than a pack of matches to create light, he had a flashlight this time. He pointed the light into the hole and smiled as the familiarity of his hiding spot appeared to be unchanged. With a quick glance over his shoulder, he dropped onto his butt and slid through the grass until he was able to slowly drop himself into the cave.

The natural void in the ground, formed by the weathering of rock and the water runoff from the hillside, was no longer undisturbed, as he'd found it many years ago. Although it had not been incorporated into the Crystal Cave attraction, it had been discovered by local kids.

The inside was littered with cigarette butts, beer cans, and girlie magazines. Articles of clothing, empty wallets, and trash were strewn about. The once beautiful natural formation had not only been desecrated with graffiti on the cavern walls, but it smelled and looked like a partially emptied dumpster.

Jonathan shook his head in disgust as the fond memories of a place he'd learned to love as a kid were now ruined. However, it still could serve its original purpose—a hiding spot from those who wanted to control him or, in this case, kill him.

He caught his breath and then used his flashlight to get reacquainted with the interior of the cave. Appearing throughout the cavern were a variety of stalagmites, drapery formations, and calcite crystals, all geologic wonders that he'd learned about as he became more fascinated with caves in general.

He made his way deeper into the cave and found a canopy-like formation that he'd often used as a bed to sleep. He shook his head in disgust as he found an old mattress on the rock slab underneath the canopy. Using two fingers, he grabbed the mattress by the cording and dragged it out into the middle of the room.

Jonathan was ready to get settled in, comforted in knowing that they'd never find him. He felt for his handgun in his pocket and pulled it out. Then he stretched out on the rocky floor under the canopy and placed the weapon on his belly, allowing his breathing to cause the gun to rise and fall in a rhythmic motion.

Jonathan was ready to think about his future and how he was prepared to take a chance and reach out to his security team now. He had no other place to go since the lodge had been discovered by whoever was pursuing him. Once this imminent threat had passed, and his pursuers moved on, he'd reach out to his team and order them to take him to safety.

He was tired of running and hiding. Besides, that was his father's way, not his. However, Schwartz couldn't shake the feeling that someone was nearby—stalking, searching.

Hunting.

*****

Hayden slowed her pace as she reached the road. The path Schwartz left in the tall grasses of the field continued directly to that point and appeared to pick up on the other side. But she needed to wait for Alpha, who was a couple of hundred yards behind her.

She turned to flash the light toward him, and he waved his back and forth to acknowledge her signal. While she waited, she moved across the street with her rifle at low ready in case Schwartz planned to ambush them. Until now, she and Alpha had chased after the man without considering the fact that he could have easily stopped, found effective cover, and fired upon them at an opportune moment. After a quick glance around, she returned to the field to wait for Alpha.

Alpha finally caught up and did his best to avoid looking winded. Hayden knew better and gave the big man an opportunity to recover.

"He crossed here," she whispered before she led him across the road. A stand of arborvitae trees lined the road, partially blocking the view of the steep hill beyond. Boulders, glossy from the nighttime moisture, and knee-high grasses speckled the landscape on the hillside until a dramatic drop-off appeared just as the flashlight's reach ended. Hayden added, "Then the tracks suddenly stop."

"Do you think he jumped off the cliff?" asked Alpha as he fully recovered from the pursuit.

"Well, he certainly headed straight for it," she whispered back.

Alpha shouldered his rifle and Hayden did as well. He raked his light between the trees and then followed the broken grasses down the steep slope. Once he cleared the other side, he swept his light over the ground. He stepped forward for a closer look, then pointed at the knocked-down grasses.

"Footprints," she said, dropping to a knee next to them. "The grass around them is still popping up. It hasn't been long."

She rose and unholstered her sidearm. They were close and her senses told her that they might have Schwartz cornered, if he hadn't opted for suicide by cliff-diving.

Hayden moved ahead, careful to keep her footing. Alpha covered her with his rifle, but she kept her handgun at the ready just in case. The tracks continued down the hill and she shined her light forward to gauge her distance from the cliff that was looming ahead. Step by ginger step, she inched closer to the ledge, and then the footsteps ended.

Hayden stopped and flashed her light all around them, panning the grass, looking for the telltale signs of Schwartz heading in a different direction. Puzzled, she shrugged and continued on, a few inches at a time, until the grasses flattened out. The footstep-sized path suddenly became a couple of feet wide.

She mimicked the action, sitting down and sliding forward using her heels as brakes to avoid slipping downward. That was when she saw the opening. A small, man-sized space where the smashed-down grasses ended. She secured her position and turned to Alpha.

Using hand signals, she indicated he should be quiet, and then she pointed at her eyes and down to the ground several feet ahead of where she sat.

Alpha leaned forward and saw the dark void in the grass. He nodded his acknowledgment. Schwartz had gone underground—literally and figuratively.

Hayden started to inch back up the hill, but she began to slide. The wet grass was causing her difficulty and she began to lose her footing. Alpha quickly reached forward and grabbed the back of her tactical vest. Using the biceps that enabled him to do sixty-pound dumbbell curls in the gym with ease, he tugged her backwards until she was safely by his side.

She mouthed the words *thank you* and then motioned for them to step several yards back up the hill, where they could talk.

"I wonder if we could roll one of those boulders down the hill and plug up the hole," said Alpha, laughing under his breath.

"Nice thought, but it won't work," said Hayden. "He obviously knew about this place. There's no evidence that he had to search. He came straight for the cave's entrance, dropped to the ground, and slid in."

"So let's go get him," said Alpha, who stood a little taller and readied his rifle.

"Not a good idea," said Hayden. "I have experience with caves, and not all of them good. First of all, he knows what's down there, and we don't. If he's armed, we could be facing a gun barrel the moment we step foot at the bottom."

"I'll take my chances," said Alpha, showing his typical machismo.

"No, Alpha. Listen to me. There could also be a way out. It's not unusual for these types of openings to be created from water runoff. I think we're on top of Crystal Cave, the local geologic-formation-turned-amusement-park. He might have run out the lower entrance."

"Let's chase him down, then," insisted Alpha, who was anxious to catch the elusive Mr. Schwartz.

"If he knows his way around, it's most likely he's escaped already. We no longer have a way to track him."

"What do you suggest?" asked Alpha.

"Let's flush him out," she replied. "Between us, we've got six smoke grenades. We'll drop them in, one at a time, until he can't breathe or freaks out. Whichever comes first is fine with me."

Alpha stifled a hearty laugh. "I like it, Foxy. That's hard-core."

She slapped his chest rig and turned back toward the cavern's entrance. She ignited the first of her three smoke grenades, made sure that it was billowing gray smoke, and tossed it down the hole.

Then they waited.

At first, the sound was barely detectable. Hayden strained to listen, thinking she heard an indiscernible cough.

She ignited another grenade and let it sail downward. The stick-shaped smoke bomb bounced off the rock walls and tumbled downward until a thud could be heard.

Smoke was not coming out of the hole, which began to concern Hayden. There might be another entrance to the cave, and the slight winds could be carrying the smoke out well below their field of vision.

Again she listened.

There! She heard it that time. A hacking sound. Schwartz was down there, and he wasn't able to hide his inability to breathe.

She turned to Alpha and provided him a devious grin. She cracked open her last smoke grenade and tossed it down the hole with more strength, hoping that it would find its way deeper into the cave.

Hayden was tired of fooling with this guy. Like a relay runner holding her outstretched hand behind her back for a baton, she waited as Alpha placed another smoke grenade in it. This time she issued a warning to Schwartz.

"All right, Schwartz!" she shouted into the hole. "There's plenty more of that headed your way. Why don't you just come on out and we'll work this out?"

"Screw you!" he shouted at Hayden.

She shook her head and mumbled, "Well, that was rude." She snapped the smoke grenade and tossed it down. This time, she used a lobbing motion so the grenade fell down the shaft without touching the walls. She was trying to vary her techniques to fill the entire cavern with smoke.

Schwartz no longer tried to cover up his inability to breathe. The coughing sounds grew louder.

Hayden turned around. "I think he's coming up."

Alpha readied his rifle and took up a shooting stance. He waited for Schwartz to emerge from the hole. However, it wasn't his head that appeared first.

Schwartz fired several bullets through the opening. Hayden instinctively fell backwards as the whizzing sound of the rounds flew past her head.

Schwartz's attempt to fire wildly in their direction angered Alpha, who let out a guttural growl and pointed his rifle barrel downward, unleashing a barrage of automatic gunfire into the cave.

When he released the trigger, the sounds of bullets ricocheting off the rock walls could still be heard as smoke began to billow out of the hole.

"No more! Please, no more!"

Hayden stood and retreated from the cave's entrance a few paces. "Well, it's about time."

Alpha shouted into the cave, "Come on out, jerk-off. Put the gun in your pocket. I don't want some kid to stumble across it."

Thirty seconds later, their target emerged from the cave, one empty hand at a time. A ricochet had grazed his cheek, opening a gash that gushed blood onto his jacket.

"Don't shoot! I did as you asked. The gun's in my right jacket pocket."

Schwartz climbed out of the hole, and Alpha grabbed his right arm and pulled Schwartz up the hill and away from the hole. Hayden quickly searched his pockets and found the gun, which she removed before tucking it into her cargo pants' pocket.

"Stand up!" ordered Alpha.

Schwartz managed to get to his feet and began to turn around when Alpha shoved him in the back.

"Turn around and walk up the hill! Don't run, or you'll die!"

Schwartz tried to bargain. "Listen, I have a lot of money. Whatever they pay you, I'll double it. No, I'll triple—"

"Shut up!" shouted Hayden. "We don't want your dirty money. Keep walking or I'll shoot you just for the hell of it!"

Schwartz stumbled up the hill, regained his footing, and then walked again, his shoulders slumped in defeat.

CHAPTER 43

Schwartz Lodge
Kutztown, Pennsylvania

Cort stoked the fire, which was now putting out a tremendous amount of heat. The bright flames lit up the room, casting eerie shadows on the post and beam construction. Two Queen Anne chairs had been placed on either side of the hearth, separated by a table that held a couple of bottles of brandy, two filled glasses of the spirit, and a .357 Magnum handgun. Sitting in the chairs were Briscoe, whose lacerated scalp was laid open, and Schwartz, whose cut face only emitted a trickle of blood, which added to that which had dried on his cheek. Both men were cuffed at their feet and ankles with zip-tie restraints.

"What are you gonna do with us?" asked Schwartz, the only one of the two who was sufficiently coherent to speak. Briscoe, although alert and apparently comprehending what was going on, was unable to speak for some reason, likely from the blow to his head.

Not that it matters.

Alpha and the rest of the team stood near the bar, their arms resting on their weapons slung in front of them. Delta broke away from the group to stand near the doors leading toward the deck. He'd already expressed concern to the group that the gunfire would be noticed by the locals, and county deputies were probably being dispatched.

Nonetheless, the group stood by silently. This was Cort's show and they were prepared to let him play it out.

Cort looked into the faces of the men and women who'd loyally followed him into the Pennsylvania woods in search of the people who'd ordered the attack on the Haven. The last person he approached was Alpha, who spoke from the heart.

"I know what you're about to do. Cort, listen to me. You'll never forget what's about to happen. The looks in their eyes, the last words spoken, the feeling in your gut."

Cort raised his hand. "I get it."

"No, seriously. When I say forever, I mean forever. Every one of us has killed before, including Foxy, who ran over that guy in Richmond. Death is death, whether by gunshot or SUV or whatever else you might have in mind. You will live with this for the rest of your life. Are you ready for that?"

Cort patted Alpha on the shoulder and smiled. "This has to end. Now it's up to me."

"Guys, I hear sirens way off in the distance," interrupted Delta. "They might be responding to something else, but I doubt it."

Cort turned to address his captives, speaking to Jonathan first. "This is the beginning of the end of the civil war that has been brewing for decades," began Cort. "You and your father have been instrumental in funding the tools of discontent, from the media to the anarchists who have infiltrated America. Your father will die in prison, and you will die right here and now."

Schwartz was defiant as he challenged Cort. "By who? You? You're the one who's gonna kill me? Who the hell are you anyway?"

Cort was a changed man. The attack on the Haven and the subsequent kidnapping of Hannah, ordered by one of these men, or both, was not going to go unpunished.

"There is no justice except frontier justice," began Cort. "You two wanted a civil war, just like the eighteen hundreds, right? Well, this is how justice was administered back in the day."

Cort moved forward and picked up a glass of brandy. He swirled the spirit around in the glass and took a swig. Then he picked up the handgun, the heavy weight surprising him.

"Wait a minute," said Schwartz, who was trying every angle to live through the day or buy time. "I know you. You're Cortland, Trowbridge's son-in-law. You're no killer."

Cort allowed a devious, smug laugh. "True, on both counts."

"Well, your daddy-in-law, mister Southern boy, is no different than me or the vegetable over there," said Jonathan as he nodded in Briscoe's direction. "This whole plan was his idea, I'm told. So you gonna go kill him next?"

"He has to make his own peace," Cort shot back. "You're here to pay for what you did to my daughter and my friends. There'll be no judge and jury for you, Schwartz. Only justice."

"You don't have the balls to shoot me, Cortland. You don't get your hands dirty, just like Trowbridge."

"Just like you, Schwartz, I command an army. But unlike you, my army believes in the Constitution and America and everything our nation stands for. I aim to restore the freedoms and ideals upon which our nation was founded."

"You're delusional!"

"No, I'm right. This war of cultures and supposed social justice and rewriting of the Constitution will end. It starts with taking away the people who pour their money into organizations that stifle freedom of speech, freedom of religion, and suppress the history that made America what it is. This will be a long process, but it has to start somewhere. I say it starts with you!"

Schwartz used his feet to push himself away from Cort. Fear overcame him as he studied Cort's wild eyes. "You're not a killer, Cortland. You can't do it."

"I command an army, Schwartz. Briscoe, here, is still under my command. He'll do it."

"What? How?"

Those were Schwartz's last words. Cort lifted Briscoe's right hand, wrapped it around the .357 Magnum, and pointed the gun at Schwartz's head. Cort slowly assisted Briscoe in squeezing the trigger.

The loud report reverberated off the walls of the lodge as the heavy-grain bullet exploded into Schwartz's skull and blasted out the other side.

Cort kept Briscoe's hand on the weapon. Trowbridge's longtime friend and associate was still unable to comprehend what was happening, so Cort dispensed with the lengthy admonition for the man's misdeeds.

He turned the gun to face Briscoe's temple and whispered in the man's ear, "You betrayed your country. You betrayed your fellow Bonesmen. You took your shot at me and missed. Let's see if your aim is better this time."

Cort squeezed the trigger, ending the traitor's life.

CHAPTER 44

George Trowbridge's Residence
Near Pine Orchard, Connecticut

The report of the powerful handgun was still ringing in Cort's ears when Delta raised his voice to get everyone's attention.

"We've got to go. Now!" he implored.

Alpha motioned for everyone to follow him through the patio doors, and the group quickly responded except for Cort. He paused to look at the two dead men, whose skulls had exploded from the force of the bullets striking them so close.

He snatched the two bottles of brandy off the table and doused both men with the highly flammable spirits. Cort poured a trail of the brandy from the two dead comrades into the fire. As a final act, he broke the two bottles against the stone hearth, causing the residue in each of the bottles to instantly ignite into flames. Within seconds, both bodies were engulfed in fire, as were the bearskin rugs nearby.

"Cort! Now!" bellowed Alpha, bringing Cort back to the present. With a slight smile, Cort turned and bolted out the doors and followed the rest of the team down a short flight of steps into the wet grass.

"This way!" shouted Hayden, who remembered the path. The sky was beginning to lighten as the first sunlight of the day began to reveal itself. Visibility increased and so did the sounds of the sirens' approach.

The group was all business now, not speaking to one another and moving as quickly as they could through the dense woods toward the west. Cort, who'd become emotional after the speech and the subsequent killings, turned the satellite phone over to Alpha, who made the call to the pilots.

He ordered the extraction from the field near the cave in which Jonathan had been hiding. Alpha advised them to drop down, but keep the rotors moving, as they wouldn't take long to load up. He also told them to fly northward away from the pickup zone to avoid flying over the responding law enforcement officers at the lodge.

The pilot's response was puzzling. He said that their flight plan had changed. Alpha shook it off, not understanding the meaning at the moment, but instead focused on leading his team to safety.

Five minutes later, the group emerged from the woods just as the chopper was setting down on a flat part of the ground. It was after six that morning, and visibility was clear. Over the sound of the massive blades, they could hear sirens, as fire engines were now being dispatched to respond to the structure fire.

Alpha paused before entering the helicopter, glancing around the landing zone to see if they'd been followed or observed. Satisfied that they were clear, he piled in and pulled the door closed. Seconds later, the Bell Relentless was racing northward toward the Poconos.

The pilot banked hard to the right before he flew near the Wilkes-Barre area and then continued eastward toward the Atlantic Coast.

Alpha addressed the pilot through his headset. "What's your heading?"

"Sir, just before your request, we received a call from Mr. Harris," the pilot began to reply. He took a moment to explain the reasons to Alpha, who then turned around to the group.

Cort, who wasn't wearing a communications headset, had his eyes closed with his head leaned back against the padded headrest, exhausted and deep in thought. His head rolled back and forth as turbulence shook the helicopter.

He was recalling every second of the deaths of Briscoe and Schwartz, just as Alpha said he would. He had no regrets and was glad he'd added the final touch of burning the bodies. If a forensic team were to be dispatched to the location, it would look like a murder-suicide, fueled by alcohol.

Cort continued to consider the ramifications of what he'd done.

Further investigation would reveal that the two men hated each other. Both men were on the run. Schwartz, wanted by the FBI for financial crimes and conspiracy, and as Cort had learned from X-Ray, Briscoe was wanted for questioning in the double murder of his caretaker and the man's wife.

Cort had seen this before. Setting aside the fact that all county law enforcement personnel were overworked due to the collapse, as far as investigators would be concerned, the deaths of Briscoe and Schwartz were well deserved and allowed them to push several files off their desks.

His mind continued to wander from the lodge and then to his family, who were still at the Trowbridge estate. He considered sleeping until he was interrupted.

Alpha had leaned forward and patted Cort on the leg. "Cort, you awake?"

"Yeah," Cort replied, forcing himself to become more alert. "Yeah, Alpha. What is it?"

"They've routed us to your father-in-law's place. It was requested by someone named Harris."

"Yeah, okay. Um, did they say why?"

"He said to tell you *it's time.*"

Cort closed his eyes again and gently beat the back of his head against the seat. He took a deep breath and exhaled. Then he spoke under his breath.

"Well, here we go."

PART FIVE

CHAPTER 45

George Trowbridge's Residence
Near Pine Orchard, Connecticut

Alpha and the team hung back as Cort exited the helicopter and raced across the back lawn of George Trowbridge's estate to greet Meredith and Hannah. There was a misty chill in the air as a breeze brought moisture off Long Island Sound, but that didn't dampen the reunion of the Cortland family. Cort, who'd spent the majority of the flight from Pennsylvania recalling the events of the past twenty-four hours, didn't think about his appearance. As he approached his girls, he was puzzled as to why they suddenly stopped short.

"Cort, are you hurt?" asked Meredith as she looked him up and down. Cort's predominantly white coat had blood splatter on it, and there was some of Briscoe's flesh embedded in his hair. "Is that your blood?"

"No, honey. I'm so sorry. There, um …" Cort stammered as he struggled to find a plausible answer that was far from the truth. "There was an injury and I didn't have time to clean up when the call came through about your father. It's nothing, really."

Hannah didn't care about the blood. She rushed into her father's arms and held him tight, as only a loving child can do.

"Hi, Hannah-bear. I've missed you."

"I missed you, too, Daddy," she responded before pulling away. "You're sticky. Let's get you out of these nasty clothes, mister."

Hannah's parents began to laugh because her tone of voice was so *motherly*.

"Yeah, mister," teased Meredith. "You need to get more presentable, Cort. Dad's been asking for you, and the doctor has urged me …" Her voice trailed off as she glanced down at Hannah.

His young daughter, who'd matured exponentially in just a few weeks, finished her mother's sentence. She grabbed Cort by the hand and began to pull him toward the mansion. "Daddy, Grandpa isn't doin' so well. I was in there when he got sicker, and the nurses came rushing into his room and made me leave. I tried to tell them that I've seen people dying, but they still made me leave."

Tears streamed out of Meredith's eyes as Hannah spoke. Her child had experienced the worst of humanity in a short period of time and, rather than being traumatized, she began to grow up.

"Well, let's go see," said Cort as he allowed Hannah to pull him forward. Meredith caught up to them and hooked her arm through Cort's. Her tears subsided and a smile came over her face as the comfort of being by her husband's side took hold.

With the help of the estate's staff, fresh clothes that fit Cort were procured from the members of the security team. He quickly showered and gave Meredith an update on the Haven, even though he'd spent very little time there over the last forty-eight hours.

She told Cort that her father could die at any time, and whatever conversation he had with him could likely be his last. Cort quickly dressed and led Meredith across the marble-inlay landing that separated the guest bedrooms from the master bedroom suite—a prison cell of sorts that had restrained Trowbridge for many months.

Cort took a deep breath and pushed the doors open, revealing a flurry of activity around his father-in-law. Harris stood to the side with his smartphone in hand, intently watching his boss of many years in case he spoke. The doctor and the nursing team scampered about, checking Trowbridge's vitals, monitoring the equipment that was providing him life-sustaining assistance, and generally trying to keep the dying man comfortable in his final moments.

"Hi, Doctor," Cort said, announcing his presence. "I'm glad you reached out to me."

The doctor's response reflected his surly mood. "Young man, you really shouldn't have left. He's been in and out of consciousness. When he was coherent, he asked for you repeatedly."

Cort took a deep breath as guilt washed over him. He really thought he had more time. Time to *take care of business.*

"Yes, and I do regret that. Please give me his status."

"I'll keep it simple," the doctor began with a huff. "He's dying now. I mean right now. Everything we're doing is to keep him comfortable so that he can pass away in peace without experiencing a fit or seizure in his final moments."

"Is he sedated?" asked Meredith.

"No. He insisted against it," the doctor replied and then paused his activity as he stood to face Cort. "He wanted one final opportunity to speak with Mr. Cortland."

The doctor stepped back from Trowbridge, and he nodded his head at the medical team to do the same. They retreated to a round table in the corner of the room, where they could sit and rest while still being able to keep an eye on the medical devices hooked up to their patient.

While Meredith flanked her father on one side of the bed, gently squeezing his wrinkled, bony hand, Cort took the side where Harris was standing. The dutiful assistant seemed shocked at the prospect of Trowbridge passing away. He'd been the old man's constant companion and trusted aide for many years. Reality seemed to be setting in.

"Harris, I don't know how to thank you for not only being by George's side in his final days, but for being his devoted friend and ally. I know that he leaned heavily on you, and I can only imagine the sacrifices you made on his behalf."

Harris managed a smile and nodded, keeping his eyes on Trowbridge's face, ready to lean forward to listen to any words he might utter. "Thank you, Cort. He's a great man. Often misunderstood and unpredictable, but that's what kept his adversaries off balance, a true key to his success."

Cort studied his father-in-law's face and whispered to Harris, "He probably was unaware of my admiration for his accomplishments. Our conversations were always very businesslike. When he and, well, you know." Cort was about to make reference to the falling-out between Trowbridge and Meredith but stopped short, as he didn't want her to hear it.

"He admired you, as well, Cort. His plans for you are greater than you can imagine. There are just a few loose ends to deal with and then—"

"Two of them are eliminated," said Cort matter-of-factly, without averting his eyes from Trowbridge.

"Say again? Are you referring to—?"

"Yes, Harris. Both of them. No longer part of the equation."

Harris's face lit up and he squeezed his phone as he looked down at the display. "I'll be right back. I've got to make the call."

"Call?" said Cort with a bewildered look on his face. "The call to whom?"

Harris didn't respond and bolted toward the doors. He held his phone high over his head as he scurried out.

"What was that all about?" asked Meredith.

Cort looked at her and shrugged. He joined her side and the only family members of George Trowbridge stood vigil, a death watch, as they hoped for one final opportunity to speak with him before he passed on.

CHAPTER 46

George Trowbridge's Residence
Near Pine Orchard, Connecticut

For the next few hours, Meredith and Cort remained by Trowbridge's side. Meredith would leave at times to check on Hannah, who remained in her room reading. Harris wandered into the room for only a brief moment before the harried aide would leave again to attend to some important matter or another. Cort, however, never left. His guilt began to overwhelm him as he thought of the words he'd say to George if he woke up.

The doctor dismissed the nurses and approached Cort. His tone of voice was far different than earlier. "Young man, I want to apologize to you. My statements earlier were out of line and based solely upon my personal emotions, something that should never be interjected into my medical responsibilities to the patient, or his family."

Cort smiled and patted the doctor on the arm. "You're much more than that, Doctor. You've been a devoted physician who has taken a personal interest in George's care. We couldn't possibly ask for more. Besides, you were right. I deserved every word of what you said, and the way you said it."

"Well, young man, I'm truly sorry, both for my attitude and Mr. Trowbridge's condition. He and I have had many conversations about you. He thinks of you as his son, but more than that, he believes you're destined for greatness. I've known George for a long time. Since our days at Yale together, he's never been one to idly pass along compliments."

"Wait. Are you a—?" Cort's question was completed by the doctor.

"Bonesman? Yes, young man, I am. George and I have had a relationship spanning several decades. In fact, he was instrumental in my getting a fellowship at Johns Hopkins. My career, and any success I've enjoyed as a physician, can be traced back to George's unselfishness and our kinship as fellow Bonesmen."

Cort shook his head and looked down at his father-in-law. "Well, I had no idea."

"This will not be the last of the surprises you'll experience," began the doctor, who abruptly stopped. He pushed past Cort. "Excuse me."

The doctor pulled out his penlight and flashed it across Trowbridge's eyes. The patient's lids fluttered.

"Kenneth, I'm not dead. Get that light out of my eyes, please."

The doctor began to laugh, and the spontaneous eruption of emotion was contagious. Cort joined in, and soon even Trowbridge seemed to allow the corners of his mouth to turn upward.

"I'm here, George. I'm sorry I've been away."

"I know, son. I've been listening to you both for a minute."

"Eavesdropping?" asked the doctor with a chuckle.

"Yes, Kenneth. My old friend, will you find my daughter and that darling child? I need to see them, but give us a moment alone first."

The doctor nodded and squeezed his patient's hand. A look of recognition came over his face. He appeared to fight back tears as he leaned over and kissed Trowbridge on the cheek. He'd comforted patients like his old friend many times.

"Yes, of course," he whispered into Trowbridge's ear. "I will miss you, old friend."

"As will I. Godspeed, Kenneth."

Trowbridge raised his hand to touch the doctor's arm before he left. Then he motioned for Cort to come closer so he didn't have to raise his voice.

"There isn't much time, son. There is so much to say, so I will as long as I can."

"You're gonna be fine," interrupted Cort, trying to give hollow words of encouragement. He could see death beginning to overtake Trowbridge.

"No, my days are almost over, mercifully," Trowbridge said. His voice grew weaker, but he could still whisper. "I wish we had more time together. There is so much to teach you. Relationships needed to be built."

"I know," said Cort, fighting back the tears.

"You left to deal with—" Trowbridge's sentence was cut off by a wince of pain.

Cort stood upright and looked toward the door. The room was empty, and he considered chasing after the doctor. "What can I do to help?"

Trowbridge shook his head. "Just listen. Is it done?"

Cort leaned in to whisper, "Briscoe and Schwartz are dead. I did it myself."

"A rite of passage," whispered Trowbridge. "I have been there myself. There are no obstacles for you now. Son, you must lead with confidence and vigor. You must never exude any form of weakness."

"I'm not ready."

"Yes, you are. You must be. Too much is at stake."

Cort could hear footsteps outside the doorway and he glanced over his shoulder before speaking. "Meredith and Hannah are coming. What am I supposed to do?"

"Trust the plan," the dying man whispered.

"Plan? I don't know what it is."

Trowbridge wagged his finger for Cort to come closer. He whispered instructions as the bedroom doors were opening.

Cort's voice rose. "What? But how?"

Trowbridge mumbled the words, "Remember what I said about destiny. Godspeed, son."

"Honey, is everything okay?" Meredith's question was fraught with concern. She and Hannah rushed to the other side of Trowbridge's bed.

He gave Cort one last look and a slight smile. Then he leaned over to accept tear-filled kisses and hugs from his daughter. Hannah held it together for as long as a child could when watching a grandparent die; then she burst out in tears. She begged her grandfather to hold on. There was so much to talk about.

Trowbridge's eyes darted from Cort to Meredith to Hannah. He squeezed Meredith's hand with the last of his strength and then he spoke to Hannah first and then to his daughter.

"Hannah, darling child, I will miss your precious smile. My sweet daughter, I have always loved you. Do not cry for me. Just know that you're the most precious gift God has given me. I will protect you and your family from above. It's time for me to be with your mother."

Then George Trowbridge closed his eyes as he left to meet his Maker.

CHAPTER 47

George Trowbridge's Residence
Near Pine Orchard, Connecticut

Cort held his wife and daughter for several minutes. None of them spoke a word as they wept. Meredith sobbed as she lamented her father's death and chastised herself for being petty during the years prior. Hannah didn't understand the complications of adult relationships, she just focused on the fact that her grandfather appeared to be resting peacefully, never to be awake again.

Cort felt genuine sadness and remorse. His mind raced as he recalled the memories of his interactions with Trowbridge. In hindsight, and with his newfound perspective, he began to see the signs. The fatherly advice. The gentle nudge to make decisions that were in his best interest. The assistance as Cort rapidly climbed the political ladders available to only a few Washington insiders.

Cort was more than his daughter's husband. He was, for all practical purposes, *George Trowbridge Jr.*, kept at arm's length distance because of the strained relationship between father and daughter.

Cort had been reluctantly thrust into a position of immense power and influence, yet he could look back during this emotional moment to realize that this was Trowbridge's plan.

Either you control destiny, or it controls you.

Cort's destiny, as determined by the man who'd controlled him for years. That was what his words meant on New Year's Eve.

Trust the plan.

The plan was what was happening in this moment. *The plan* had been triggered on New Year's Eve and was meant to come to fruition upon Trowbridge's death. *But would it? And how?*

Trowbridge's final, dying wish reverberated in Cort's head.

This isn't over—not by a long shot.

A gentle tapping on the door caused the family to pull apart from their embrace, although Cort's mind had detached itself already. The solid wood door opened with a heavy sigh, as if it were also saying goodbye to its master.

Harris slowly entered the room. "Mr. and Mrs. Cortland, Hannah, I am so very sorry for your loss. George Trowbridge was a great man. An unsung hero who loved you all dearly."

"Thank you, Harris," said Cort as he approached the longtime aide to offer a hug.

The two men embraced, and as they did, Harris whispered in his ear, "Sir, they're waiting for you."

Cort pulled back and asked, "Who? Who's waiting?"

Harris ignored the question and motioned towards Meredith. "Mrs. Cortland, members of the staff are awaiting you and Hannah in the guest suite. They'll have hot tea, or a sedative, if you choose. I understand that your family is of the Southern Baptist faith. May I contact Pastor Coburn from Trinity in East Haven to come speak with you?"

Meredith, who was still emotional, became confused and stammered as she answered, "But we'd like to, um, I suppose I need to speak with Cort first."

Harris politely pressed her. "Yes, ma'am, soon you and your family will have the time to grieve. Would you like me to contact the pastor?"

Cort and Meredith exchanged glances before she replied, "Yes, of course."

Meredith put her arm around Hannah. She led her through the door onto the landing that overlooked the open foyer below. Cort was behind her with Harris by his side. As the family crossed the marble landing at the top of the stairs, they stopped and looked into the foyer.

Dozens of people dressed in various shades of black clothing, ostensibly in mourning for Trowbridge's death, stared at the

Cortlands as they emerged from the bedroom.

Meredith turned to Cort. "Honey?"

Harris looked past her and raised his arm, waving his fingers toward a member of the residence's staff to escort Meredith and Hannah to the guest suite.

"It's okay, darling. I'll be there shortly," replied Cort, having no idea whether that was true or not.

His eyes were fixated on the men and women who continued to file into the foyer from the parlors adjacent to the entry. He searched for a familiar face, hoping that the connection might make sense of it all.

There were none. All strangers, perhaps here to pay their respects to Trowbridge. Even Alpha and his team were nowhere in sight. He turned to Harris, but before he could speak, the loyal, faithful aide whispered to him, "It's up to you now, sir. They're waiting."

Cort was suddenly nervous. He could feel his palms become sweaty, and beads of sweat began to form just below his hairline on his forehead. He glanced back toward the master suite, looking for guidance from his mentor, who was no longer able to impart any words of advice.

Waiting for what? Am I supposed to thank them for coming? Make a speech? What?

Trowbridge's words bounced around Cort's head.

Trust the plan.

They wanted reassurance. They wanted guidance. They were looking for him to lead.

Cort began the most important speech of his life to that point. He rubbed his hands together and subconsciously placed them into the Merkel-Raute position.

Often referred to as the Triangle of Power, it was a hand gesture known by many as one intended to emit confidence and power. Cort rested his hands in front of his stomach so that his fingertips met, with his thumbs and index fingers forming a quadrangle shape. Many conspiracy theorists had suggested the gesture was symbolic of the Illuminati, the secret society dating back to 1776.

"Ladies and gentlemen, I want to thank you for joining us on this sad day. George Trowbridge, my wife Meredith's father, and a loving grandfather to our daughter, Hannah, has passed away quietly and peacefully.

"Now is a time for mourning and not for eloquent graveside eulogies. Arrangements will be made to announce his sorrowful death, and a date will be set for his burial.

"I will say this, however. George Trowbridge dedicated his adult life to the preservation of our great nation's ideals. He believed in the Constitution and the principles of the Founding Father's as enunciated therein.

"He and I have been very close since I came to Washington, communicating frequently on all matters concerning the best interests of our country. You know him well, as do I. I am now fully aware of his vision and my place as it relates to *the plan*."

Cort paused as a murmur came over the group standing below him. All of them were keenly focused on every word he spoke. Cort took a deep breath, his confidence rising.

"There will be much to discuss between us, and I must learn a lot from you. For now, I want to allow all of you to pay your respects to this great man."

Cort gestured for the group to come upstairs so they could enter the master suite and say their goodbyes to Trowbridge. He stood back against the plate-glass window, allowing the group plenty of room to walk past him. The sun began to peek through the clouds, radiating a variety of grays and white shades from the sun into Long Island Sound.

One by one, the men and women who were closest to George Trowbridge, fellow Bonesmen, approached. They'd moved heaven and earth to arrive at the estate. It was immediately apparent, however, that they were there for two reasons, the least important of which was to say goodbye to Trowbridge. They were there for Cort.

They stopped to shake his hand. Several of them bowed slightly to kiss the top of his hand. Cort was uncomfortable with the gesture at first, and then he naturally embraced it.

Few words were spoken other than offers of sympathy. Several Bonesmen uttered words of congratulations. Others simply smiled and stared into Cort's eyes, either trying to read him or to convey a message without speaking the words.

At one point, an older gentleman broke the trend of solemn greetings for Cort. He locked eyes with Cort and whispered, "Where do we go from here?"

The unexpected question caused a small group to pause around Cort, anxious to hear his response. Cort thought for a moment, during which time he glanced to his right. Meredith and Hannah had reemerged from the bedroom and were watching the processional as the Bonesmen passed by Cort.

Cort swallowed hard and responded to the man, "We finish what we started."

Those who heard his response began to smile, and the sound of chatter filled the cavernous space. Those who were waiting in line along the stairwell passed on his response. Those who'd already entered to pay their respects to Trowbridge heard the news. The atmosphere in the home turned electric, apparently a positive response to Cort's intentions.

Harris appeared out of nowhere and whispered to Cort, "I'm sorry that your family exited their room. I've admonished the staff."

Cort smiled and continued to shake the hands of the visitors, who now picked up the pace. He supposed they'd received what they came for.

He leaned into Harris and whispered, "Thank you. Now I need you to get the president on the phone."

Cort looked up and smiled as a group of several women preferred to hug him rather than shake hands. "God bless you, Michael," whispered one of them into his ear. He hadn't been called Michael in a long time. It caught him off guard.

Michael Cortland. Am I still Cort?

Harris whispered into Cort's ear again, "Sir, our customary means of communication is through his chief of staff. I'll get him—"

Cort cut him off. "Not this time, Harris. What I have to say to the president will be for his ears only, understand?"

"Yes, sir. Absolutely."

Harris scurried down the stairs and Cort's eyes followed him. Then he glanced back to his right, searching for Meredith and Hannah.

They were gone.

PART SIX

Three months later …

CHAPTER 48

Haven House
The Haven

"Seems like old times," Ryan commented as he adjusted his seat on the sofa. Invariably, when he took his seat on the couch, Chubby quickly climbed onto him as if he was her designated lap. For whatever reason, The Roo, who only weighed a couple of pounds less, but was somehow much lighter on her feet, opted for her mommy's lap. Either way, Haven House was dedicated to the comfort of the two lap pups who'd taken up their preferred positions and settled in for a nap.

"It does," Blair replied as she took another swig of water from her *bkr*, pronounced *beaker*, the neoprene-wrapped water bottle that had been her signature method of staying hydrated before America nearly fell apart. "I have to say, I kinda missed television. I know we complained about it all the time, but now we can see what's happening, and I feel pretty good about the recovery efforts."

"Yeah, me too. This is gonna be a big day."

Bret Baier, the Fox News announcer, could be overheard in the background as they waited for the president to appear at the podium in the Rose Garden. Several hundred chairs were filled with dignitaries, politicians, and the media for the event.

"By all accounts, the president is being given credit for his statesmanship in the presence of a constitutional crisis not seen in the country since the 1860s. With a flurry of executive orders that shifted members of our military who were deployed overseas into National Guard positions, the president gave state governors the manpower they needed to gain control.

"At first, some states, like New York, Illinois, California, and Oregon,

resisted the thought of our nation's military, albeit wearing the uniform of National Guardsmen, entering their states to gain control of the societal unrest. However, as the southern states quickly and efficiently tamped down the looting and violence, and with the District of Columbia regaining a sense of normalcy, other states elected to follow the president's plan of recovery."

Ryan laughed. "I bet they aren't giving the president kudos on CNN or anywhere else, for that matter."

"Now, Ryan, the president has asked us all to put aside our differences so that we don't find ourselves in the same mess that we were in several months ago."

"I just think that's easier said than done, darling. It'll take years for Americans to forget how violence exploded in the streets. Politicians still blame each other for what happened, although nobody has come forward to claim responsibility and, fortunately, no evidence has emerged to say definitively *whodunit*."

Blair allowed Ryan to complain and make his point. She was of the mindset to start over, as the president requested. She wanted to forget the political animus and hostilities that she'd seen escalate on social media. The nation was embarking on a fresh start and she wanted to embrace it.

She changed the subject as the news broadcast continued. "Did the Rankins get off okay? It was kinda sad, as they were the last of our core group to leave."

"Yeah, I think I'm gonna miss J.C. the most. That was one smart kid. Funny, too."

Blair nodded as The Roo squirmed in her lap, in search of a more comfortable spot before returning to the one she had. She licked her chops and closed her eyes again.

"They were hesitant to go back to Richmond, as the entire downtown area had practically been destroyed. As it turns out, their delay opened up the opportunity of her dreams. Hilton Head is a beautiful place, and I know they're excited to get back there."

"Well, I know Donna was thrilled, too," added Ryan. "Hilton Head is not that far from Charleston, and although Angela isn't an oncologist, she was a tremendous source of comfort for Donna when she feared her cancer was coming back. As she works through it, she'll have Angela as a sounding board."

"Donna began to look at Angela as a third daughter," said Blair. "I'm glad the two will live near each other, considering what's going on with Tom."

Ryan's cell phone rang. It startled them both and he shoved Chubby around to retrieve it from his pocket. He earned a series of disgruntled groans in the process. As he searched, he commented, "I'm still getting used to the phones working. I'm honestly not sure how I feel about it."

"Who is it?" asked Blair.

"Delta, I mean Will," replied Ryan before answering, "Hey, Will."

Ryan listened for a moment, periodically saying *okay* and *sounds good* before disconnecting the call. He leaned forward with a grunt and placed the phone on the table where he could reach it if need be.

"Anything going on?" asked Blair.

"Nah, he's gonna call it a day and turn the front gate over to the night shift," he replied.

"Is all of that still necessary?"

"Do you mean the patrols and gate security?" asked Ryan. "Yeah, for a little while, anyway. Once the grocery store shelves are full and folks get back to work, I'll be happy with simply guarding the entrance. Besides, we have Will in charge of the grounds and X-Ray handling drone surveillance. Why not use them?"

Blair shrugged. "I suppose. I'm glad the Hightowers decided to make the Haven their home. Their personal overhead is certainly low."

"Yeah, as in nothing," added Ryan.

"But wouldn't you think there would be a lot of bad memories here following Ethan's death?"

"He and I talked about that," replied Ryan. "As bad as Ethan's death made them feel, they look at the Haven as the reason their family came back together. I told him to stay as long as he wanted."

"*Ladies and gentlemen, the President of the United States!*" announced an aide to the president, who'd stepped up to the Blue Goose, the nickname given the large blue podium that the president speaks from.

The cameras panned wide, providing a view of the president, his wife, and his son as they took their positions by his side. Emerging from another angle was the president's chief of staff and the White House legal counsel.

"Look!" exclaimed Blair. "It's Hayden. Wow, that's really cool."

Ryan agreed. "You know, we didn't have a lot of time to discuss her representation of the president in that Supreme Court case. By the time she got here, the crap had hit the fan. Then, out of nowhere, she had to leave to get back to Washington."

"No kidding. We had so many helicopters flying in and out of here that I felt like we needed to build the Haven Heliport."

Ryan chuckled, causing Chubby's flubber to shake as he did. "Except now they're all gone. I was kinda hopin' that they'd forget about at least one of them. That would've been a nice addition to the fleet."

"Shhh," admonished Blair as she pointed to the screen. She turned up the volume. "He's speaking."

"*As you're undoubtedly aware, the fine justices of the United States Supreme Court have heard all of the arguments, and yesterday they issued their ruling in my favor. I commend them for not allowing politics to sway their decision and especially for recognizing that it's time for our great nation to heal.*

"*Although I had already been sworn in as the Constitution required, out of an abundance of caution, the chief justice came to the White House yesterday evening for a private ceremony in which I proudly placed my hand on the Bible and swore to faithfully execute my duties.*

"*Today, I have to my right, my White House counsel, Pat Cipollone, and the member of his team who shepherded this case through the courts, Miss Hayden Blount. I owe them a debt of gratitude for their perseverance and tenacity. Thank you both.*"

The president paused as the audience gave a rousing ovation to Cipollone and Hayden.

"Man, can you believe we know somebody that famous?" asked Ryan.

Blair responded, "It's funny how life can change. One minute, you're fighting for your lives. The next minute ..." Her voice trailed off as the president continued.

"*With the legal battles and formalities out of the way, it's time to get back to the business of governing. During these trying times, I have relied heavily upon my advisors and those within in the military as we executed a plan of recovery.*

"*By all accounts, we've successfully put down a modern insurrection, one that was born out of hatred and designed to undermine our government. To be sure, there is still work to do, and I'm prepared to admit that I cannot do it alone.*

"*After last night's duplicated swearing-in ceremony, I officially rounded out my cabinet. Those members of my cabinet who were temporarily appointed in the aftermath of the November bloodletting, as these people like to refer to it, are now permanent members of the cabinet, subject to a few confirmations.*"

The president then gestured at the media. Despite his calls for reconciliation, they continued to question his every decision, including the one that prompted today's Rose Garden ceremony. After smug laughter erupted among the attendees, except from the White House Press Corps, of course, the president continued.

"*Now, I have lots to say, but today is not just about me.*" The attendees chuckled at his statement. The president, who was in a good mood, accepted the subtle commentary. "*I know, I know. That's a surprise, am I right?*"

After further laughter, he raised his hands and became serious. "*Without further ado, I am pleased to announce that I have chosen Michael Cortland as my new vice president. Cort, come on up here.*"

The cameras swung to the right to show Cort walking up on stage, followed by Meredith and Hannah. All three had huge smiles on their faces, and Cort had an extra bounce in his step as he greeted the president. The two men heartily shook hands and then the president leaned back into the microphone.

"*I know how to pick 'em, don't I? Look how tall this guy is!*"

Bret Baier's voice cut in, using his low-key, soft-toned, golf-announcer approach. "*At six feet five, Michael Cortland is, in fact, the tallest vice president in American history, beating out Lyndon B. Johnson by an inch.*"

Baier's co-anchor, Brit Hume, added a comment. "*If Cortland were so inclined, and if he develops the gravitas and exhibits the presidential timber to seek the highest office in the land, he could surpass Abraham Lincoln as the tallest president.*"

Baier added, "*That would be ironic, would it not, Brit? Here's this relative newcomer to politics, charged with the responsibility of keeping a nation together, and he's being compared to Lincoln, who faced similar challenges.*"

"*History does repeat itself, Bret.*"

Cort thanked the president and stepped up to the podium, graciously accepting the raucous applause of those seated in the Rose Garden.

As the applause rose to a crescendo, Bret Baier continued. "*Cortland hails from Mobile, Alabama, although most of his career has been spent in Washington. A graduate of Yale, where he also played basketball, he's known as being levelheaded and a political outsider. He has never held office, and those who know him have stated that it was never something he intended to consider. Yet now he's one heartbeat away from being the leader of the free world.*"

Cort hugged Meredith and Hannah before gesturing for them to stand to his right. The president patted Cort on the back and continued to lead the applause for his nominee.

Ryan pointed at the television monitor. "Look, there's Tom. He's seated just to the left of Hayden. He's gonna make a fantastic chief of staff for Cort."

"Hey, do you see Alpha standing off to the side?" exclaimed Blair. "Wow, didn't he clean up well!" Alpha was wearing a dark blue suit with a Secret Service lapel pin attached to his jacket. He casually pressed his finger to his earpiece and appeared to mutter a few words as his eyes scanned the grounds.

"I've got chills," said Ryan. "This moment is nothing short of incredible."

"I'm really proud of them," added Blair.

Both Smarts sat a little taller on the sofa in anticipation of Cort speaking as the newly designated Vice President of the United States.

"*Thank you. Thank you. Good morning, everyone. Thank you.*" Cort patiently tried to calm down the exuberant crowd. He turned to the president and nodded his appreciation.

"*I must first thank the president for the trust and faith he has placed in me. And, on behalf of the American people, I want to thank him for saving our great nation from months, or even years, of strife, sadness, and death.*" Cort stopped and led applause for the president, who generously accepted it. It took a minute for the display of appreciation to die down before Cort could speak again.

"*The president has tasked me with the responsibility of finishing the job of bringing this nation together. Since day one of his presidency, he's called upon his business acumen to make America great again. Now he's ready to continue keeping America great!*"

The attendees gave Cort's statement a standing ovation that lasted for another minute.

Ryan commented on the tone of his statement. "This sounds like a campaign speech."

"Well, why not?" asked Blair. "Isn't it logical that Cort would be the heir apparent if the remainder of the president's term is as successful as the last four years?"

"I sure hope so. We'll be personal friends with the president. Can you imagine?"

"Don't expect an invitation to the White House, Mr. Smart," replied Blair as she gave Ryan a playful kick with her foot.

Cort continued. "*While the president attends to our nation's affairs, both overseas and here in America, I will be setting up a task force designed to deal with the terrorist attacks of New Year's Eve and the aftermath.*"

Cort leaned into the podium and his face turned serious. "*Let me be perfectly clear. Our nation has faced adversity in the past. We were blindsided on 9/11. We were dragged into a world war at Pearl Harbor. We've had foreign nations engage in war on our soil in the past.*

"*One thing that we cannot allow is Americans fighting Americans, as they did during the first Civil War. To be sure, I am angered by the terrorists who initiated the attacks against us on New Year's Eve. But I'm infuriated by the opportunists, the anarchists, who took advantage of our great nation in her moment of weakness to terrorize their fellow Americans.*

"*My promise to the president, and now to you, the American people, is this. I will dismantle the organizations that spew hate across this nation. I will expose who is behind the anarchist movement that destroyed lives and cities in the weeks following the terrorist attacks.*

"*And I will put safeguards in place that will stop these types of hate-filled organizations from taking advantage of the freedoms our Founding Fathers put into place in order to bully their fellow Americans.*"

Everyone on the stage stood to applaud Cort's statement, and the gallery responded as well. It was the loudest demonstration of support since the ceremony began, and Cort's voice could barely be heard over the noise.

He raised his hands over his head and shouted, "*Fare thee well and Godspeed, patriots!*"

The applause grew louder, and Blair became overcome with emotions. "Unbelievable."

Ryan, who'd been holding his breath throughout Cort's statement, finally exhaled and wiped the tears off his face. He muttered to himself.

"Choose freedom, and Godspeed, patriot."

THANK YOU FOR READING THE DOOMSDAY SERIES!

If you enjoyed it, I'd be grateful if you'd take a moment to write a short review for each of the books in the series (just a few words are needed) and post it on Amazon. Amazon uses complicated algorithms to determine what books are recommended to readers. Sales are, of course, a factor, but so are the quantities of reviews my books get. By taking a few seconds to leave a review, you help me out and also help new readers learn about my work.

And before you go …

SIGN UP for Bobby Akart's mailing list to receive special offers, bonus content, and you'll be the first to receive news about new releases in the Doomsday series. Visit: www.BobbyAkart.com

VISIT Amazon.com/BobbyAkart for more information on the Doomsday series, the Yellowstone series, the Lone Star series, the Pandemic series, the Blackout series, the Boston Brahmin series and the Prepping for Tomorrow series, totaling thirty-plus novels, including over twenty Amazon #1 Bestsellers in forty-plus fiction and nonfiction genres. Visit Bobby Akart's website for informative blog entries on preparedness, writing, and a behind-the-scenes look into his novels.